PRAISE FOR STAI

"Electric, unflinching characters grip the reader from page one and refuse to let go, hurtling headfirst into a story shot through with unmatched worldbuilding and a murder mystery for the (space) ages."

—Zoe Hana Mikuta, author of *Gearbreakers*

"With lush worldbuilding, high stakes, and a page-turning mystery, *Stars, Hide Your Fires* is impossible to put down. Brilliantly crafted and delightfully fast-paced."

—Rachael Lippincott, #1 *New York Times* best-selling coauthor of *She Gets the Girl*

"A delightfully mischievous adventure full of intrigue, betrayal, and a touch of romance. Get ready to join your new favorite rebel crew."

—Dahlia Adler, author of *Cool for the Summer*

"An edge-of-your-seat genre-bender with a ton of heart!"

—Alechia Dow, author of *The Sound of Stars*

"The sapphic murder mystery in space of my dreams!"

—Rosiee Thor, author of *Tarnished Are the Stars*

"A gripping space mystery with twists and more twists. I thoroughly enjoyed this fun romp of a read!"

—Vanessa Len, author of *Only a Monster*

"Jessica Mary Best doesn't hide her fire in this engaging novel."
—Miel Moreland, author of *It Goes Like This* and *Something Like Possible*

"Equal parts sci-fi, murder mystery, and fast-paced thriller. A sweet, gently played romance and a widely utilized, intersectionally diverse cast add nuance to Best's tantalizing debut."
—*Publishers Weekly*, starred review

"Descriptive world-building, inventive and gender-inclusive slang and symbolism, a vividly drawn cast, and fast-paced banter are joined by nonstop action and twisty revelations. . . . A high-stakes murder-mystery science-fiction thrill ride; great fun."
—*Kirkus Reviews*

"A clever, lighthearted tone and the banter-filled attraction between Cass and Amaris balance off-the-page violence and dark intentions. . . . Satisfying and inspiring."
—*Booklist*

"If a queer sci-fi romp where you have no idea who to trust but you do know whose faces you want to smush together and scream 'Kiss!!!!' sounds like your jam, this is definitely the new release for you."
—*Smart Bitches, Trashy Books*

STARS, HIDE YOUR FIRES

YOUR FIRES

JESSICA MARY BEST

QUIRK BOOKS

PHILADELPHIA

First paperback edition, Quirk Books 2024
Originally published by Quirk Books in 2023

The Library of Congress has cataloged the hardcover edition as follows:
Names: Best, Jessica Mary, author.
Title: Stars, hide your fires / by Jessica Mary Best.
Description: Philadelphia : Quirk Books, [2023] | Audience: Ages 14 and up. | Audience: Grades 10–12. | Summary: After traveling from her home planet to Ouris and sneaking into the imperial ball to steal from the galactic elite, expert thief Cass is framed for the unexpected death of the emperor, and must work together with a mysterious rebel to uncover the true plot and clear her name.
Identifiers: LCCN 2022041133 (print) | LCCN 2022041134 (ebook) | ISBN 9781683693512 (hardcover) | ISBN 9781683693529 (ebook)
Subjects: CYAC: Robbers and outlaws—Fiction. | Science fiction. | Mystery and detective stories. | LCGFT: Science fiction. | Thrillers (Fiction) | Novels.
Classification: LCC PZ7.1.B473 St 2023 (print) | LCC PZ7.1.B473 (ebook) | DDC [Fic]—dc23
LC record available at https://lccn.loc.gov/2022041133
LC ebook record available at https://lccn.loc.gov/2022041134

ISBN: 978-1-68369-434-2

Printed in China

Typeset in Adobe Garamond, Boucherie Sans, and Leo Sans

Designed by Elissa Flanigan
Cover illustration by Christina Chung
Production management by John J. McGurk

Quirk Books
215 Church Street
Philadelphia, PA 19106
quirkbooks.com

10 9 8 7 6 5 4 3 2 1

TO MY FAMILY,
WHO ARE ALSO MY FRIENDS,
AND TO MY FRIENDS,
WHO ARE ALSO MY FAMILY

1

I'm halfway through lifting a watch off an extremely drunk tourist from some fancy planet called Leithe when I first hear about the ball.

The scam is an old one. Jax calls it Bad Mook, Good Mook. It works like this: We wait at the port until someone with fancy clothes and a mound of luggage touches down. Jax plays the villainous urchin, darting in to swipe at a bag or a purse. It's the perfect role because you can't miss Jax—with their bright-red hair and home-brewed tattoos snaking up their arms, they stick out like a rusty screw set in high-polish titanium. I play the part of the virtuous local, running Jax off and offering to help carry all those bags in exchange for a story about the traveler's point of origin.

"I've lived on Sarn my whole life," I confide, wide-eyed. I can almost see Jax from the corner of my eye, mouthing along at a safe distance: "I only get to leave it in my dreams, but I know there's better worlds out there."

The story is key. You need to keep your target talking for this to work. It helps that Sarn, with its rolling dust clouds and general lack of greenery, is the kind of place that would make anyone misty-eyed for wherever they came from, and that's before you get into the fact that we're only a minor moon and tidally locked with our host planet, Danae, which means we get half a year of blazing sunshine, no night, and half a year of unrelenting darkness, no light. Either the mark takes pity on me and takes it upon themselves to expand my tragically limited horizons, or they're so disgusted by their experience that they can't hold back from bragging about how much better they have it back on their homeworld.

You can pretty much tell why they're here by looking at them. The ones not dressed for the elements—expensive fabrics that don't breathe, impractical shoes, the latest trend in body mods—have come for the Astera Oasis, the one remaining slice of Sarn's fertile soil, nestled at the bottom of a canyon the locals call the Big Split. The resort down there offers an "exotic" vacation for the wealthy, and work for the rest of us, provided you can bury your dignity deep enough to treat any paying customer like a demigod. My friend Pav's boyfriend Babbit busks there during the sunny season, and he says the tips can be good, but I've done the math and never found that kind of grind to be worth it.

The rest of our visitors—tight posture, clipped hair, boots made to last—are here to oversee one of the mines, strictly military ops since the peace talks failed and the war kicked into overdrive. Jax and I are careful to leave those folks alone. Even a standard-issue railgun is nothing you want to truck with. I've taken those things apart for scraps more times than I can count—they have these tiny screws that go for a few drocks each. If you know what you're doing, you can extract them by tapping the back panel in the right sequence, but sometimes a junkpicker will start working on a railgun not realizing it's still got the electromagnetic charge and end up losing a finger or a hand. You don't want one pointed at you, under any circumstances.

Every so often, a mark will try to drag Jax off to port security unarmed, but that never goes anywhere. The closest magistrate has a backlog of petty crimes so long, it'd make any law-abiding citizen weep. Once or twice, some determined swell tried to have Jax imprisoned on a ship and we had to scrap the whole con, but it turns out I can kick like a twister when I need to, and we've always managed to limp away.

When I'm lucky, our mark is happy enough to wax poetic about the lush green hills of Planet Wherever-the-Void on the way to the Opuntia, the one nice hotel in spitting distance of the port, where tourists recover from their trip before booking a ride down into the Big Split. Meanwhile, I fall behind a bit, mouth along with their curiously round mainworld vowels, and dip my thieving fingers into that luggage. A savvy traveler will think to count the bags when we're through; almost nobody stops to search them. You can't take enough to alter the weight, but plenty of little treasures have found their way into my rucksack.

At the end of our journey together, just outside the hotel, I clasp our dear target's hand, run through the usual litany of thank-yous, and if I'm *very* lucky, I'm back with the throngs at the port before anyone realizes they're light a bracelet or a ring. Nobody wears their best stuff traveling this far from the major moons or planets— there's nobody to impress but us—but a piece of mediocre jewelry will get you closer to a hot meal than a full day of scrap hauling.

When no more incoming ships are slated for the morning, we pawn whatever we've earned, and I split my take with Jax fifty-fifty. I spend the afternoon junkpicking, or when the port is busy, I can beg some odd jobs off the old women who run the market stalls. At the end of the day, if I've done good, that's something other than bare protein slurry for Dad and me come dinner time. If it's a bad haul, Dad and I make do with off-brand Pink Dream, which always tastes worryingly rancid but keeps you full enough to sleep if you can afford to mix it with a little milk.

"There's worse things, Cassie," Dad tells me on those nights, using whatever trick he has at his disposal to sneak me a bigger share than his.

"But there's a whole lot better, too," I say, using every trick he's ever taught me to sneak it back. It's gotten easier since his hands started shaking too bad for anything but junkpicking.

Today's first mark is promising, if a little tipsier than I'd like. Drunk people tend to get sloppy, which is a plus in our line of work, but they can be unpredictable. Jax has to all but yank the purse from the tourist's hands before earning any kind of response. My first thought, when Jax has been safely run off and the stranger starts in on a ramble about the places she's been, working as the personal assistant for some duchess, is that she can't be that well-traveled, or she'd know not to drink like this on Sarn. The atmosphere is too thin. No offworlder can hold their liquor here worth a dry, jagged shit.

My next thought is that this Ascension Ball she's rattling on about sounds only slightly better than the howling Void. Seems like the old emperor is announcing his successor in style, and to an incredibly exclusive group of guests.

"—dressed, of course, in the very finest finery in all of Ouris, and, between you and me, that is *very* fine," she manages, eyes locked on her own stumbling feet. As I sift through her heavy bag, I note her inflection on the word *me*. It's recognizably fourth-condition, marking her as female, but the way she forms it sounds much less like we say it here and much more like an announcer on the short-wave, with a bit of an accent on top. *Me, me, me,* I mouth along to get the trick of it as I determine that her watch is the only thing with resale value and idly wonder how much food I could buy after a day's work at the ball.

Then I wonder the same thing, with a little less idleness.

In a single motion, I scoop the woman's watch into my rucksack and refasten the clasp on the bag.

"What sort of finery, madam?" I ask in my talking-to-rich-people voice. Something halfway between how they tend to speak and the way I usually form my words—refined enough to sound trustworthy, not so fancy as to give the impression of a girl acting above her station.

The woman turns unsteadily to face me. "Why, my dear!" she cries. "Every sort. Rubies, sapphires, emeralds, Dionysian silks, gold, jadeites, lab-grown fur worth more than your own life—it's a feast for the eyes. The court on Leithe knows a thing or two about putting on a show, of course, but the Ascension Ball on Ouris will be something else entirely."

The kind of take you could pull from one night at a dance like that . . . it wouldn't be jerky-and-tinned-fruit money. It would be change-your-life-forever money. Never-worry-about-eating-again money.

"Where on Ouris, did you say, madam?" I murmur.

"Why, are you planning on procuring an invitation?" says the woman with a loud, braying laugh. "Good luck! *I* can't even get one, and I've been the duchess's right hand for a decade. The invites are handcrafted silver filigree and embedded with the emperor's personal encryption seal. Her Grace says the black markets are salivating at the thought of getting their hands on a few, but nobody on the list would ever part with one."

I duck my head. "Just trying to paint a mental picture, madam. It sounds fascinating."

"It's more than simply fascinating," she says. "One hundred of Ouris's most honored citizens descending on the city of Amphor, like flocks and flocks of exotic birds in the sunshine."

Amphor. There are cargo transport lines that run from ports on Sarn to Amphor. That's where they first started shipping away our topsoil, for the private gardens in the city center. Only the best would do, and back then, Sarn had the finest soil in the galaxy. These days, we don't even have much of that. *Dirt-poor*, as the joke goes.

I know better than to ask for a date and time. "How long does Her Grace have to prepare?" I ask.

She names a day, roughly a month from now. After that, I barely hear her over the wheels turning in my mind.

You could say Jax is displeased.

"One measly watch for all my troubles? Do you have any idea the mortal peril I put myself in, all so that you could report back with this clunker?"

They keep a running, foul-mouthed commentary under their

breath as we wait in the shadow of the port for our next victim. Other planets have city-wide climate control, leafy trees for shade, and artificial clouds piped in on demand. Here on Sarn, this dark, cool stretch of sand is precious real estate.

"It's an Agata," I counter in a whisper. "When we scrap it, the display screen alone will amount to a day's take, easy."

Jax makes a derisive noise and twists the single blue-painted washer hanging on a cheap chain around their neck. Modern custom is to indicate that you're neither male or female with a single circular bauble worn as a pendant, but Jax knows too much about thieving to ever go around flaunting anything worth more than a drock or two, and I think they've become fond of the washer. They've had it almost since they started going by the second-condition *I* when they were around thirteen.

"An Agata? Get the shit out of your eyes. It's a fake, you spume, a perfect piece of rotting *shrapnel*. No merchant on Sarn worth their sweat will take it once you crack that sucker open." They throw their arms up, and even their tattoos seem to writhe in frustration.

I frown. For all their bluster, Jax has a good eye, better than anyone else I know.

They sigh. "It's not a bad fake. I can see why you'd think it was the real deal. But the crystal's acrylic, the movement is just quartz, and I doubt the chip could power a can opener. No holos, no auto shifts for going warp, no nothing."

"It's got the right heft," I offer.

Jax just rolls their eyes. "You know how easy it is to make something *heavy*?"

"We sell it in one piece," I tell them, "to that awful newbie vendor who's trying to crowd out Dezmer and Mita."

"Theron," Jax says. "He's told you his name maybe six times."

This could well be true. "Fancy name for out here."

"You've heard his accent, right? He's a mainworlder for sure. He might even be from Ouris. On the run from something, that's my guess. Likely scammed some old gasser. You can't trust him, Cass."

"I know. But even if Theron thinks he's cheating us, we'll fetch more than the parts are worth."

Jax nods reluctantly. "Tell you what, friend, you better know what the Void you're doing."

A slow port day means the market is more or less dead, except for the black flies darting from one perch to another. Dezmer and Mita's stall is empty. They must be on break. But sure enough, a little too close to their spot is the interloper vendor and his display of shoddy goods and stolen luxuries. He does a decent business, either because it's a front for something else or because tourists have terrible taste.

"Got something for you, Theron," I call.

"Hope it's a date for tonight," says Theron, picking his artificially white teeth with an air needle. "The lovely Cassandra Zervas here to grace us with her presence, it's my lucky day!"

I bite the inside of my lip to keep from snorting. Nothing worse than some shithead who's convinced he's charming. To my left, Jax rolls their eyes so hard I can almost hear it.

"A genuine Agata," I tell him, pulling the forgery from my bag. Theron pretends to give it a careful once-over, although he knows less than me about watches, so it doesn't take long.

"Why aren't you selling to your usual pair of crones?" he asks.

"They can't give me the kind of price I need," I say.

"How much do you want, pretty lady?"

Even though I've always used the fourth-condition *I*, even though I have a cheap square bead hanging from my neck for all the world to see I'm female, something about the way Theron calls me a *lady* makes me want to scrub myself down with sand.

"Sixty drocks."

Theron laughs, disbelieving. "I was gonna say thirty at most."

"Then it's a good thing I'm here to say that what we want is sixty even."

Jax paces as we barter, uneasy with the whole process. They would've taken the thirty, especially knowing the watch is worthless, but the first step to selling a con is to believe it a little, and no way would I let a real Agata go for anything less than forty-five without a fight. Eventually, we settle on fifty, "or fifty-five for the watch and a smile," says Theron, winking.

"Fifty," I agree.

Once the handoff is done, we head back to our shade, Jax complaining mightily, me barely listening.

Jax snaps their fingers in my face. "You're looking half logged out."

"Call together all the usuals for dinner," I say. "I have a plan."

2

Dad's facing away from the door when I come in, humming something slow. He's patching a crack in the wall, which is maybe half mud and half reinforced with debris he's reclaimed and repurposed from ships that get scrapped here. A chunk of an old hull makes up most of our living space, but it's always letting in the dust from outside.

I can tell by the slump of his shoulders he's had a poor day of junkpicking. "Hey Dad," I say. "Jax says hi. And a lot of other words, naturally."

He turns, already perking up. I've never met anyone who holds on to a bad mood as loosely as my dad. We've got the same grayish-brown eyes, brown hair with just enough of a curl to always look a little unruly (although his is streaked with silvery strands already), calloused hands, and freckled skin that tans instead of burning under the Sarn sun, but the family resemblance ends there. Our temperaments are nothing alike.

"Naturally," he says, chuckling.

His laughter sets off a coughing fit. After I fetch him a tin of water, I plop down into what was probably once a captain's chair. It's lost most of its glamour and all of its cushioning, but if you really put your knees into it, you can still get it to swivel with a bit of protest.

"Had a decent haul at the port today," I tell him. "How do you feel about guests tonight?"

"Always happy to feed guests, Cassie," he says, "assuming we've got something to feed them."

"I bought stew on my way home."

Another cough, and this one rattles. "Enough for everyone?"

"With potato flakes," I add. "Which I also bought."

"A decent haul indeed," says Dad. "Tell me you kept safe?"

Dad doesn't exactly approve of Bad Mook, Good Mook or any of its related schemes, but he does approve of a living that doesn't require me to spend all day rooting through trash and facing off against the other scraphaulers. It's complicated.

I nod. "The lady was so drunk, there's no way she could identify us later. And I only took a watch."

"What kind?" Dad asks, leaning forward. His interest in all things mechanical lights up his face. I know from his stories that before he and Mom were together, he used to fix up the long-hauler she piloted. He was studying to get certified as a mechanic when his health took a turn. Now, he says the smell of engine grease makes him queasy.

"Dreck. A knock-off Agata. I sold it to Theron."

Dad frowns. "Theron?"

"The new guy at the market who thinks he's better than the rest of us."

"His name . . . he's not from around here," he says.

"Jax thinks he fled a mainworld."

"Be careful around him, Cassie," says Dad. He doesn't need to add that anyone from someplace like Ouris wouldn't relocate here unless something was wildly wrong. If Theron ripped off someone important, like Jax reckons, that's kind of the best case.

"He'll just think I was too ignorant to know the Agata was a copy," I assure him. "He's that type."

"Well, watch yourself."

"I will."

"Now," says Dad, rubbing his hands together. "What was this about stew?"

Our biggest pot is boiling away merrily on our thruster turned stove when Jax shows up with a bottle of grunk, which is a thick, chunky wine made from the canned fruit from a Standard Ration Shipment. Even in a tin, fruit costs so much that most people on Sarn only buy it for grunk. Pav unloads crates from freighters most of the day, and every so often, a can of something sweet will happen to fall into our hands. Jax's cousins handle the ferment. It's a community affair.

"You all take a seat. I'll get the cups," Dad calls, a note of pride in his voice. Ever since he figured out how to kludge together an opener that unzips the top of a can without leaving a sharp edge, everyone in the area drinks out of spent tins.

Jax sniffs the contents of the pot and grins. "Shit, is that two whole cans in there?"

"Three." I make myself comfortable on the floor. Jax joins me.

"Plus starch. We eat like proper upper-class mainworlders to-night."

"What's the occasion?"

"You'll see," I tell them. "Is Pav coming?"

"He's helping Dezmer and Mita close up shop," Jax says as Dad returns, bearing an armload of newly recycled cups. "Should be by any second."

"None for me, Dad."

"Snooty 'Mainworld' Bliggins over here," says Jax.

"I don't like feeling like I'm not in control," I counter. "Plus, it tastes like a bunch of sugar fell down a hole and puked its guts out. No offense."

"Sorry we're late," Pav calls from the door, where he's got Dezmer and Mita on each arm. He's almost bent double to accommodate their stooped frames. With his lanky build, tight dark curls, and angular jaw, he could be Dezmer's son, but as far as I know, Dezmer and Mita never had kids of their own. "Mita had her work cut out for her today."

"Making something fun?" asks Dad.

"Nah," says Mita. "Adjustments. Some tailor fit a tourist's jacket like a rotting riddle and I've gotta fix the thing."

Dezmer and Mita sell a little of everything, but what's kept the stall going for the eons they've been together is Mita's handi-work: sturdy rucksacks and handbags, beautifully embroidered scarves to shield your neck from burning in the sunlight, pouches to hold twin ceremonial bak daggers, which are by far the most common souvenir wealthy travelers take from Sarn. Mita's stuff is made to last. It's nothing like the purses Theron sells, which un-ravel under a stern look.

"This one kept talking slow and loud like there's something wrong with our coretongue," Dezmer adds. "It's enough to drive anyone to the bottle."

"Speaking of which," says Jax, who has uncorked the grunk.

As Dad ladles out our stew, thickened almost solid by the potato flakes, I lay out my plan to infiltrate the dance.

"The Ascension Ball, yeah," Pav breaks in. "I heard the soldiers talking about it, the crowning of a new emperor. Apparently, nobody knows who it will be, since Emperor Hyperion's got no living children and the wife's a noble, not a royal. They're nervous it might be Mynos."

"Who?" Jax slurs through a mouthful of stew.

"Emperor's little brother," says Mita. "Reading between the lines, he's a bully with a fool's streak wide as a world. Absolute power's the last thing he needs."

"Nobody *needs* power like that, absolute or not," I put in.

"Deep," Pav says. "Watch out. You're talking like a real revolutionary."

"The Voyria would never last on Sarn," I say. "It's too blazing hot here to try to overthrow anything."

Pav blows on his stew. "Heard from Rorsey that the Voyria intercepted an arms shipment, minutes from the front. Says they're arming up for a prison break."

"Rorsey's such a liar," says Jax. "Funny as it'd be to watch the Helian skyforce start just chucking whatever they could at the Zarinels—"

"Rotten fruit, tongue scrapers, toilet innards—" says Mita, eyes sparkling.

"There's no way. Every grunt in the skyforce would go down

with the ship before the empire parted with their precious toys," Dezmer says heavily. "What's the crown for, if not getting into stupid dustups with the Zarinel Federation over every unclaimed scrap of forsaken space?"

Dad is fidgeting with the ladle. A glop of stew drops on the ground. He's never liked talking about the war.

I set down my bowl. "Can we get back to this ball? Imagine the *marks*, people. A room full of the richest imperial suckers in the universe, all in their finest jewels, with their guards down and no competition. You take your pick, and you come back with a fortune to retire on."

"If you don't get caught," says Dad, frowning. "And if you can get to Ouris, and if you can get into the ball. If, if, if, Cassie."

"I have a feeling that's why we're here," Dezmer says calmly between bites.

"Dad's not wrong," I say. "There are three main problems, right? Getting to Ouris, blending in, and figuring out a way into the ball itself."

"You'll need a dress," says Mita thoughtfully.

"I can steal any old dress. What I need is a dress that actually fits me and looks the part." I turn beseeching eyes on Mita. "Which means I need to steal something a couple sizes too big, and then find someone who can tailor it to my measurements. Floor length."

"So the dress you lift off a rich offworlder," says Dezmer. "And you'll wear whatever jewelry you palm during Bad Mook, Good Mook?"

"Only enough to blend in. As simple as possible."

"Any mainworlder with working eyes is gonna know in a second whether your jewels are real or fakes," says Jax. "And most mucks don't take their best to Sarn."

"Well, that's why I'll need *your* working eyes," I tell them.

Pav knocks back a slug of grunk. "Are you suggesting we steal a ticket to Ouris, too?"

"Depends," I say. "You unpack from haulers all day. What's security like around the freight?"

Pav boggles at me. "You're gonna stow away inside a crate. How's that crate meant to get on the ship?"

"Easy," I say. "You're gonna put it there."

"What?" says Pav.

"With Jax as a distraction."

Jax swallows down the last of their grunk. "*Shit yeah* with me as a distraction!"

Pav shakes his head. "Go back to the part where—"

"You pack me into a ship bound straight for Ouris. It's only seven hours if the ship has warp speed, and anything headed to Ouris is gonna have warp. If I play my cards right, I could get out before anyone in the crew sees me."

"Okay, Cass," says Dezmer as Pav drops his head in his hands. "Let's say you make it to Ouris in a crate, maybe with a demagnetizer so you can break yourself out. Now you just need to sneak into the biggest imperial event of our lifetimes."

"That's the easy part," I say. "These imperial types like things the old-fashioned way. No bot servers or food dispensers. They're gonna have flesh-and-blood humans to hand them their snacks and scrape off their bunions or whatever. All I have to do is enter through the back with the other servants, find some discreet spot to change, and, from there, blend in with the rest of the guests."

"Sorry, Cassie, it just seems like such a risk," says Dad. "What if you get caught?"

Good thing I saw this coming.

"Pav," I say gravely. "I took the jackknife out of your pocket when you sat down."

"What?" Pav blinks at me as I flash a little folding knife and hold it out to him.

Mita snickers behind her hand. Dezmer gives me a slow, considering look and takes Mita's other hand, squeezing it fondly, their weathered tan and dark brown fingers interlocking.

"I can do this," I insist. "We split the take evenly amongst ourselves. A whole fortune, six ways. We could get off this rock. Go somewhere better. Some planet or moon where everything good hasn't already been dug up and sold to the highest bidder."

Pav slips the knife back into his pocket. "You'll have to be careful as surgery out there, Cass. Understood? We polish every part of your plan 'til it shines."

I grin at Pav. "So, yes?"

"Yes," says Pav with a sigh. I look around at the others.

"I'm up for the challenge," Mita announces. "Been a while since I put some time into making something for someone I actually like." Dezmer leans over, smacking a kiss on Mita's cheek, and that's all I need to know that she's on board as well.

I swallow. "Dad?"

It's Dad's turn to sigh. "When you set your jaw like that, you look just like her."

He doesn't need to say who. Mom's cargo ship was shot out of the sky when I was too young to remember her, but I know Dad carries her ghost with him everywhere, and that means I carry some piece of it, too. A haunting at one remove.

"It's my fault, you know," he says. "All those stories. I raised you to dream. To try."

"Then what are we waiting around for?" says Jax. "Let's try like nobody's ever tried before."

"I'll drink to that," I say, hope taking root in me like a weed.

Dezmer whoops, filling the unclaimed tin and sliding it over to me. I take a sip and immediately spit it back out into my cup. Jubilation or no, grunk is *foul*.

It's a good night. We make plans. Dezmer agrees to teach me all the dances she knows, both leading and following, and Jax gives me pointers on spotting fakes. A few hours in, Dad stands and yawns.

"I'm heading to bed, but the rest of you, feel free to stay. There's still food left. Don't let Cass send you home without some."

"Goodnight," I call after him.

We move outside after that, a little ways from our place. Sarn in the sunny season means it's blazing bright out still. We pick over the remains of the stew, and Dezmer and Mita fill us in on the latest market gossip.

After another hour or so, Dezmer and Mita head out. Pav and Jax linger, Pav helping me scour the pot with sand, Jax not even pretending to be useful.

"Thanks," I tell Pav. "Not you," I say to Jax, who makes a rude gesture back.

"It's not that late, you know," says Pav.

"I know."

Pav winces. "Your dad's been sleeping more."

"Yeah."

"Coughing more, too."

"Little wonder, the shit we breathe," I say.

"You know that's not it," says Pav, and I hear what he doesn't say, too: *You know he's not well.*

I turn in the direction of the port. I let my eyes focus and unfocus on the smears of glowing green in the distance, ships touching down and leaving every day and every night. They take off as soon as they can. Sarn isn't a place you stay.

"Been bad for a while," I admit.

"Yeah," says Pav, "but it's gotten worse. Like Babbit's eyes. Last time he made it out here, he said he was only seeing shadows. Life's a luxury. One we can't all afford for long."

There isn't much I can say to that. "Nothing that a shipload of money wouldn't fix."

I think about it all night and decide I don't stand a chance lifting a dress the way I usually skim jewelry, from the top of a suitcase. I finally settle on picking out a mark with a few garment bags and swiping one during the handoff to the hotel porter.

The next day, I come prepared with my mom's old rucksack, a deep and roomy thing with a few intriguing hidden pockets (all empty; I check). When I do finally score a long black gown off a nastily bickering couple, the thing doesn't fit. Can't even stretch over my hips.

"Sorry," says Mita, "letting out the seams only goes so far."

We're at her and Dezmer's place, which is sweltering, all the windows blocked by heavy cloth. We can't afford for anyone to see this stage of the plan. It'd raise too many questions.

Mita sighs, wiping sweat from her forehead. Dezmer reaches for a fan folded from an old recruitment poster, a blandly handsome soldier blurring as she stirs the thick air. The code strip at the bottom of the poster has long since faded into smudges of gray, but when she stills, you can make out the words, the climax of the Helian anthem: *May our reach yet expand as our visions are grand!*

"It's not a complete waste," says Mita. "If you steal another dress, I can slice this one up for panels and combine them. Something gold colored if you can. It would really suit your eyes."

I head out an hour later, covered in sweat, the imperial anthem stuck in my head. I hum it on my way past the mines extracting Sarn's last traces of silica to be used in the skyforce heat shields, past the port, and all the way back to our salvaged, dusty home.

All this time prioritizing dresses over riches means my take suffers. Dad and I eat a lot of Pink Dream, those first few weeks.

"It's not so bad," says Dad one night. "At least there's not much of it." He gives me a wan smile, ruined almost immediately by more coughing. I thump him on the back and remind myself why I'm doing this. It's not an adventure—it's the only way I'll be able to move him someplace where people might know how to fix what's wrong with him.

It's two weeks until the ball and we're starting to run out of time to fix me a dress when I spot a tourist wrapped in a rose-colored scarf, with several garment bags folded over one arm, awkwardly steering two suitcases that hover just above the ground—not quite high enough to avoid picking up a coat of Sarn's finest grime. I signal to Jax, who jumps into action, grabbing the woman's purse and making a run for it. Jax must be feeling the adrenaline because I have to practically sprint to catch them.

"Careful," Jax mutters when I'm in earshot, "saw her chatting with a skyforce muck at the port. I know she doesn't look it, but she's military."

I frown. We're about to break one of our only rules: you don't meddle with Hyperion's forces. It's the first thing you teach a kid on Sarn, once they're old enough to toddle. You let the people with the shiny boots and the short haircuts go about their business, and you keep your head down. But the Ascension Ball is right around the corner, and if we're going ahead with the plan, we have no choice.

I grab back the "stolen" purse and slap Jax open-handed across the face. "Fates will have you, thief!" I yell for good measure.

The tourist sighs in annoyance as I present her purse.

"You're just letting the thief get away?" says Rose Scarf, and I realize Jax is probably right—her clothes are colorful for a member of the skyforce but her posture is so absurdly straight, my spine aches just looking at her. Either she's military, or she's a dancer.

"Who, Spanner?" I say, inventing an alias for Jax. "Yeah, they're a menace. Unfortunately, they're also, uh." I bite my lip and glance toward the ground. "Maybe I shouldn't say."

"What?"

"It's very unseemly," I warn her, head still down. A classic hook. Never once in my life have I seen someone respond to such a warning with "Oh, well, if it's scandalous, never mind."

"Tell me." In her mouth, it's not a question.

"Spanner is—well, you know, people gossip out here, and the story goes that they're the illegitimate child of the magistrate."

That seems to throw her for a loop. "Really?"

"We cart Spanner in for one crime or another every week," I say. "But you know, you turn around and they're out again, causing a ruckus."

This earns a curt nod from Rose Scarf.

I smile as disarmingly as I can. "Would you like help carrying your bags, madam?"

Mita approves of the red dress I manage to walk away with. The next two weeks pass in a frantic blur of dress fittings, dance lessons, escaping-from-a-crate lessons, copying the mainworld accent every chance I get, and running Bad Mook, Good Mook until I'm lifting valuables from suitcases even in my dreams.

"Can we give it a rest?" Jax groans. For once, the sky has mustered a couple of clouds, and seemingly all the locals on Sarn are enjoying the chance to be out without immediately frying in the sun. We're cross-legged on the rough, sandy concrete, waiting for another ship to come in.

I shake my head. "I still need a formal square pendant. This one'll stick out."

"We've been at this for stinking *hours*," says Jax. "I've been running all morning. My legs are *tired*." For a second, they sound very young. I am struck by the sudden memory of being much smaller, back before Dad was sick, whining just like Jax so that he'd lift me up and carry me on his shoulders.

"You'll look after Dad, right?" I say.

Jax snorts. "Who d'you think I am?"

"Say it," I press. "I'll give you some of my share if you look in on Dad, make sure he eats."

"Much as it pains me," says Jax with a heavy sigh, "I can't take money from you for something me and the others already plan to do. And it does pain me. Deeply. In fact, make the whole offer again, and let's see what I come up with this time."

I blink, wiping what must be stray sand from my eyes. "So you'll take care of him?"

"'Course," Jax says. "Least we could do for a friend, even an utter fool such as yourself."

"That's really—" I swallow hard and cast my gaze to the sky, where a pinpoint of light is quickly approaching us.

"All right, curtain's up in five," says Jax, stretching and standing.

"What curtain?"

Jax throws me a lopsided grin. "For the rotting *show*."

3

The days before my big trip slide into nothingness like water evaporating on the sand.

We're three days out, and Dad and I are eating our nightly Pink Dream when Jax bursts through the door, breathing hard, an awkward bundle under one arm.

"Cass," they pant. "You've gotta get out of here. Theron, he found out about the watch. Says he's gonna kill you."

"Over a watch?" says Dad.

Jax shakes their head. "He's really angry, Cass."

"What's that gasser gonna do? He'd never get his hands dirty enough to—"

"Cass, listen," Jax interjects, pale under their tattoos. "I don't know how he convinced them, but he's got port security looking for you. There's a ship heading for Ouris in ten minutes, and then nothing for hours and hours. You've gotta leave *now*."

Cold dread bubbles through me. Port security never bothers itself over our affairs. I have to break atmo, and fast. I grab Mom's old rucksack and the jewelry I've stolen to wear at the ball—three rings, a bracelet, and a square silver pendant. Dad throws me half a jar of Pink Dream and a skin of water, provisions for the trip.

"I need the dress," I say wildly. "It's not finished—"

Jax shakes out their bundle, a carefully tailored mix of black and red, plus a reinforced black slip. "Mita sewed the last stitches this morning."

I stuff the fabric into my bag and hug Dad goodbye, squeezing tight. "Love you," he murmurs into my hair. "Keep your eyes open and your wits awake, you'll be all right." His voice trembles slightly and I know he's struggling to believe his own words, but there's no time for anything else.

"Pav's waiting at the port," says Jax.

I hadn't planned an elaborate goodbye to Sarn, but it's surreal to get my last glimpse of it as Jax and I tear across the sandy stretch of land on the way to the port, our lungs on fire. We pass the market where Dezmer and Mita work, Jax's place, the old schoolhouse, and then I see Pav standing a ways from the loading dock, his back to a large crate and a demagnetizer in one hand. I run harder, using up stores of energy I didn't know I had, and then Pav is jogging out to meet me.

"Theron," says Pav gravely.

"I heard," I tell him. Behind me, Jax is doubled over, catching their breath.

The three of us sprint to the crate. I glance back and see Theron in the distance, yelling in some portworker's face, no doubt demanding my whereabouts. Two of his cronies are tossing the market, and they're coming this way.

"You'll protect Dad, right?" I pant.

Pav and Jax nod. "Of course, you fool," says Jax. "Security's not gonna charge him for the bullshit his daughter did, and we can take Theron on his own."

"Get in," says Pav. "Take this." He shifts to shield me from view as I grab the demagnetizer and climb inside the crate, tucking my bag beside me. Pav and Jax grab the lid.

"Tell the others—" I start.

Pav shakes his head. Unaccountably, he's smiling a little. "They know, Cass."

"Tell them drinks are on me when we get back," I say.

Pav says, "Got it," and then every bit of light leaves the crate as they fasten it shut. I swallow hard, surrounded on all sides by cheap, creaking plastic. The floor of the box jolts as Pav and Jax lift it onto rollers and then I can feel the rumbling as they roll it across the packed dirt of the port and onto what must be the intake ramp for the ship.

I hear a distant voice say, "This on the manifest?"

"Not yet. Last minute switch-up," Pav grunts. "You wanna take it up with our boss?"

"Always some new bullshit," says the voice, resigned. Then a shout, and the muted thud of approaching footsteps.

"Hey," says a different voice, one that makes me clench my fists. It's Theron.

"Hey, man," says Pav.

"You seen a girl pass by?" says Theron. "Looks like this?" The pit drops out of my stomach. If he flags my face, he could create a problem that will follow me all the way to Ouris.

"Nah, sorry," Pav says. I still have the dress, I remind myself. Until the moment when I disguise myself as a servant to gain entry, I can pass myself off as a wealthy noble. Nobody will have the audacity to compare my features with those of some petty fraudster from Sarn.

"Tell me if you see her," Theron says. "There's five hundred drocks in it for you." And then Theron's footsteps are receding.

"Safe flight, old girl," Pav mutters.

"What?" says the portworker from before.

"Just talking to the ship," says Pav. He pats the side of the box. "All right, let's get out of here."

I spend most of the trip to Ouris sleeping fitfully. It's not at all comfortable inside the crate—I have to keep my neck and knees bent in order to not hit the rough, unyieldingly hard sides—but I've been burning so much time plotting to get to the ball that I am running on a severe sleep debt.

I'm in the middle of a dream about Theron chasing me through dunes of shifting Pink Dream when the jerking of the ship jolts me awake. We must be landing. I change into a new slip, my stolen jewelry, and Mita's elaborate gown as the wheels roll to a stop, thinking I'm lucky Mita gave me long sleeves because I bang my elbows black-and-blue against the crate walls.

Eventually, we dock and I do the thing I've been waiting the last seven hours to do—I pick up my demagnetizer and extract myself and my satchel from the crate.

The cargo bay is enormous, dimly lit overhead by strips of white lights that seem to bleach the color from the whole space. It's packed with crates of what's probably silica, stacked six high, and sacks of what smells like sulfur, everything carefully strapped and magnetized to the floor.

I hear the whir of the cargo bay doors opening, which gives me ample time to shoulder my bag and hide at the back of the bay, behind a row of bolted-down tanks. Above the roar of the noise outside, I can hear two portworkers unloading the ship, and after a minute or two I'm able to divine their rhythm. One walks with a limp, slow to enter and slow to leave. One strides forward impatiently, quickly shifting the crates onto a conveyor line.

Every time both of them are out of the bay, I sneak a little closer to the bright square of the exit. The trickiest part is going to be getting off the ship. My window is only about thirty seconds, and even then, they'll still see me right by the bay. I take a deep breath, straighten my dress, and when the limping portworker turns his back, I creep behind him, covering as much ground as I can without making a ruckus. Dezmer's dance lessons, all those lectures about footwork and stepping lightly, are suddenly the most valuable training I've ever had.

Halfway to the doors, the portworker pauses and glances to the side. There's no cover left. I step toward the wall, to the meager shadows that won't be enough to hide me, and then the other portworker cries, "Gant, c'mon! We've got three more ships after this, get a move on!" and Gant limps forward, cursing to himself, one of his legs creaking mechanically as he hurries to catch up. I give myself one more breath and then take off after him.

At the doors, I check that neither of the workers are turned my way, and finally I slip out of the ship and into all that sunlight. I start down the path, but just my luck—one of the portworkers ahead catches sight of me.

"Hey, what are you doing there?" he calls out. Judging by his stance, he must be the one with the limp. The other worker looks back to see who Gant is talking to. Both are in identical work uniforms, with the ship's symbol emblazoned across their chests.

Luckily, I've prepared for this. I draw myself up to my full height and get ready to do my best impression of an affronted tourist when something clips my shoulder.

I duck out of instinct and see a floating platform heaped with luggage pass overhead. At the back of the platform, a couple in clothes finer than anything I've ever seen sit on a cushioned bench. Someone races in front of the platform, guiding it along.

"Careful!" the guide calls. I dodge to one side just as the guide and their platform zoom by at an impossible speed. They must be wearing flyboots or something, to go that fast. Three more platforms whisk past with their own guides. I dart over to a paved walkway that swarms with people, nearly colliding with a figure who glows as bright as a watch face. I jerk back.

"How much faith do you have in your staff?" she says in the accent I've been studiously copying for half my life.

She's clearly some sort of holotech, but far more advanced than anything I've ever seen. Her eyes seem to be following me. I stand, frozen in place as she drifts in my direction. The sunlight filters through her like an eclipse, leaving crescent shadows in her wake.

In the same smooth accent, she says, "Invest in Asipis for all your surveillance and micromonitoring needs. Asipis, for the savvy employer."

When I don't do anything more than gape, the woman directs her speech at another person, who walks straight through her. The crowd is thick enough that I can disappear into it, so I do, moving with the flow of people until I can finally take a breath and look around.

Ouris is—there's no other word for it—splendid. Ships blur back and forth in distinct layers: zippy little personal ships at the top, bulkier transports in the middle, and floating platforms below. Neatly uniformed attendants in their polished flyboots weave through the ground traffic, wing insignias flashing as they glide past.

Everyone's hurrying like they're running from a sandstorm. Some rush into glittering buildings that stretch as high as clouds in the sky, while others race to catch a transport. A few people throw me looks of vague distaste. Of course, now that I'm here, I can see that whatever references Mita had to work from, they weren't exactly the latest fashion. Compared to their sleek and beetle-shell-shiny clothes, my gown, with its puffed shoulders and numerous ruffles, must look distinctly out-of-date and out of place.

But this gown is getting the job done. No one can possibly think I smuggled my way here. I only wish I'd thought to ask Mita for a jacket, too, because for the first time in my life, I'm walking in the sunshine and I'm freezing. My next goal, I decide, is to sneak into a warm building for a few minutes while I strategize where to tap into the city's nav feed and get the lay of the land. I knew the transport to the palace space station was docked somewhere in the city, but I'd assumed it would be visible from anywhere, the way you'd be able to spot a ship that grand from almost any vantage point on Sarn. But here, the towering architecture is packed together tight, and I can see only as far as the next crosswalk.

Up ahead, I spot a clearing among the throngs on the walkway. I can catch my bearings there, I figure. As I near the gap in the crowd, I see the cause of it: an older woman around Dezmer's or Mita's age stands on a crate like the one I recently escaped from. She's shouting to anyone who will listen.

"Bion! Markarios! Damokles! What am I meant to do without my children, alone in the world? Please, spare a drock for a woman who will never see her beautiful sons again!"

The well-dressed hurry around her, desperately avoiding eye contact, but several people stop to listen, frowning. A young man in a worn but neat suit lays a few drocks on her crate. One of his pant legs is cuffed just high enough to reveal wired machinery where his ankle should be.

"Bion! Markarios! Damokles! My children, all gone, lost to the fighting on Kore, and for what? To swell the coffers of the nobility, to expand our reach beyond what any of us will ever see, all while their mother starves!"

I think of my own mom, running supplies for the war before her ship went down somewhere on the other side of the Aeschylus Belt sixteen years ago, when I was about two. All we got when she died was a bill for her uniform. That's how Dad found out she was gone.

"All right, that's enough," says a man in sturdy white-and-bronze armor, a railgun at his belt. There's a fancy insignia on his chest, one that matches the gold shooting star on the largest and shiniest building in my sightline. "You're blocking these good people from getting where they need to go."

The mother jabs a grease-stained finger at him.

"They want us to forget!" she shouts. "They want us to move

37

on but how can we? Bion! Markarios! Damokles! Dead, on a planet at the far edge of the galaxy, and your precious imperial crown didn't even care to send their ashes home!"

We never saw Mom's ashes, either. Nobody ever even told us the circumstances of her death, where exactly it happened or what became of her ship. It's just a blank, like when I try to picture her face.

The guard steps forward, hand on his weapon. "I'm warning you. You can't obstruct a major thoroughfare like this."

"There's room to walk around her," says the young man with the mech leg.

"You'll want to stay out of this," says the guard.

"Bion! Markarios! Damokles!" cries the woman.

The guard draws his railgun and points it at the young man's chest.

"Please," the man pleads. He turns wildly to the crowd and then his eyes land on me. "Please, madam. Tell him she's not bothering anyone."

"Sir, there *is* room to walk around her," I hear myself say, and the accent comes out credible enough, but the guard doesn't even look in my direction.

The old woman raises her arms to the sky. "Bion! Makarios! Damokles! This war is a meat grinder, and we are the meat!"

Railgun still trained on the young man, the guard grabs the old woman by the arm with his free hand, clearly about to wrench her off the crate.

"You'll hurt her," the young man protests, starting forward.

The guard gestures with his railgun. "Stand back."

"Stop this at once," I try in my poshest voice. It comes out thin and tentative.

The guard yanks the woman to the ground, and a middle-aged couple in simple clothes rushes forward to help her back up. The young man starts forward again, but he's held back by a stocky woman with a holo glass over one eye.

"Careful, Nestor," she says to the young man.

The guard sheaths his weapon. "Everyone move along," he says.

"Void take you, you rot-moraled cud," spits Nestor, and the guard backhands him so hard he falls prone, then rears back to strike again. Eyepatch yells what must be profanity in a dialect I don't know and leaps forward to seize the guard's arm. As she struggles with him, someone in the crowd throws something—a lunch tin, by the looks of the greens flying—and it smacks into the guard's temple. The guard recoils, hand groping for his rail-gun.

I see the space to execute a lift and I do it, snatching the rail-gun from the mag catch and ducking out of arm's reach. I've scrapped so many of these things, I know how to do it fast: click the settings to safety, tap the sequence that opens the hatch, snap the wires that send the electromagnetic current. It's a useless hunk of metal in seconds, and I let it drop to the ground, kicking it backward into the crowd.

The guard spins around. "Where the Void is my gun?" he growls.

I'm holding my breath, scanning the area for exits. Nobody says a word. The couple, Nestor and his friend, the old woman, and the rest of the onlookers are all stone-faced.

The guard presses a small glowing panel on his helmet. "This is security unit 351 requesting backup, linking coordinates to all port zone patrols. Send backup immediately, we have a code 89-A." He looks back at us. "I'm going to need to see ID from everyone."

Well, shit. That's something I don't have. I left my ID, the one that identifies me as a nobody from Sarn, at home, and anyway, there's no way I would show it to anyone on Ouris.

The people on the walkway dutifully line up, reaching into purses and pockets to produce a small iridescent card, or just holding up their wrists. The guard scans each of them with a wave and a badge on his suit beeps obligingly. I join the line, my mind racing with escape routes.

When it's my turn, the guard turns to me. "Your ID," he says.

"I think it's in my bag," I lie.

"Then get it," the guard snaps.

Slowly, I reach for my bag, which holds nothing but a skin of water, my old clothes, and some Pink Dream. I have about six seconds before this becomes suspicious, and in those six seconds, what I need to do is jam this bag over the guard's head and run before he can get a good look at my face. I'll be hungry and thirsty, but the most important thing is to lose this guy. Five seconds. I'll need to be quick. Four seconds. I unfasten the clasp. Three seconds—

"What appears to be the trouble?" says a deep, resonant voice and the guard immediately stands straighter and bows. Clearly this is not the backup he'd asked for.

"There was an altercation during which my weapon went missing," the guard says in hushed, respectful tones. "I was questioning the suspects when this—this *citizen* refused to comply with an ID request."

"I'm sure it's a simple misunderstanding," says the stranger as my palms sweat.

I reach into my bag and feel around. "My ID is gone," I say, eyes wide. "I was pickpocketed earlier today. The thief must've taken my card along with my wallet."

"Sounds like you're having a bad day," the guard says, clearly not buying my story.

"Madam, could you turn this way, please?" the stranger asks. "Your voice sounds familiar."

Slowly, I turn around, the sun in my eyes stinging like alcohol in a cut.

"Oh!" says the stranger. "Captain, don't worry about it. I know this woman." Then, to me, "Nephthys Drakos, what are the odds, running into you here? It's been a while."

The guard sputters. "I need her ID."

"She just told you it was stolen," the stranger tells him. "And I can certainly testify as to who she is," he adds with a chuckle. "You've done your duty here, thank you. Now if you'll excuse me, I'd like to get caught up with an old friend."

To my amazement, the guard nods.

Gently, the stranger leads me by the arm down the sidewalk. With the sun no longer slicing into my eyes, I turn and get my first good look at my rescuer.

"So," he says quietly, "mind telling me your real name?"

4

I freeze midstep but the stranger lightly tugs me along.

"That guard might still be watching," he says. "Best to act casual."

I will my feet to keep moving and throw him another sideways glance. He's wearing a dark teal military-style jacket nicer than any I've seen before, with a series of bronze clasps running down one side and a full bronze shoulder piece, something that usually takes a decade to earn. He can't be more than four or five years older than me. You'd expect such a display to be worn with a perpetually puffed-out chest, but his posture is loose, relaxed.

He tilts his head to the side, still waiting for my name. Nothing about him screams *threat*. Yet.

"My name's Iola," I tell him. "Iola Galatas."

Iola was what I was almost named before my parents settled on Cassandra. And Galatas is such a common surname across so many planets and moons that it's almost impossible to trace. It's also Mom's family name. I like hearing it out loud, in present tense. But the important thing is, it's clean.

"Well, Iola," he says, "where are you from?"

"Yorgos," I say, because it's the least interesting planet I can think of. "My family sells minerals for hydroponics. Thrilling, I know."

"So, what brings you to Ouris?"

"I'm here visiting my Great-Aunt Berenike," I lie. "It's a little out of the way, but her partner passed away a few years ago, so we all take turns coming to check on her."

"And will you be accompanying Great-Aunt Berenike to the greatest ball of the century?"

I laugh. "Oh, no. This right here is my best dress. I'm afraid it's sadly out-of-date already on Ouris."

"The fashions move too quickly here," he says, nodding. "It gives people an excuse to focus on the constant scrabble for the new and novel over what actually matters."

"And what is that?"

"Change," he says. "Doing something to improve the way this city is run."

That could mean any number of things. "Of course," I say. "Couldn't agree more."

"Case in point, that guard back there," he continues. "Bothering a lady like you about your ID. Disgraceful."

"I really did lose mine to a pickpocket, but I suppose he didn't believe me," I say.

"You disarmed his weapon, though, didn't you?"

Somehow, I manage to keep my voice level. "What are you talking about?"

"I saw you kick the railgun behind you, and when I went to

pick it up, the wires were snapped. You were the only one close enough to get to his mag catch."

My thoughts spin out in a thousand directions. Am I about to be blackmailed? But the man quickly adds, "No, no, you misunderstand me. As a trained soldier, I know the value of decisive action in the heat of the moment. The guard was behaving too impulsively to be trusted with a weapon."

In all my years scamming tourists, I've learned that one of the golden rules of the con is you never complain about the wealthy to the wealthy. Even if they openly despise each other, it's too risky. So while I agree with him, what I say out loud is, "Perhaps he was having a bad day."

The man shakes his head. "Come on, you must know that's no excuse." His face grows somber. "I didn't lose half my comrades on Kore just to come back and watch other people get pushed around by a pedestrian bully like that."

Kore is Helia's main front against the Zarinels. I remember that much from Pav's reports of portside news. It's a major source of cobalt and a few other substances that fuel the weapons that keep this war between the Helians and the Zarinels going. Since it's so valuable, Kore's been changing hands back and forth for decades. I don't know who controlled it originally. Probably neither of them, if Pav is to be believed. I certainly don't know enough to say anything about it to this man.

"It's hard," I say instead. "Losing someone."

"Phaidros, my superior officer, was like a brother to me," he says, "and General Macedon was my uncle in all but name. Now . . . I think I still haven't wrapped my mind around the fact that I won't see them again. I keep turning around and expecting them to be right there. But I'll never hear another of Phaidros's stories or Macedon's jokes."

"It's an open wound," I murmur. Something about the way he catches my eye spurs me to add, "And you keep expecting it to heal someday but instead it keeps reopening at the worst times."

"Well put," he says heavily. "And then to come across someone in power, using that very power to terrorize other people . . . Well." Lightness creeps back into his tone. "It's a good thing that guard was so moved by the sight of me. Punching a man in armor can be satisfying, but it is hard on the knuckles."

"Thank you, by the way," I tell him.

"You seemed to be handling yourself just fine," he replies.

"Oh, I grew up with railguns. We need a little incentive sometimes to keep pirates off our supplies. What's your name?" I ask, before he can come up with any inconvenient follow-up questions.

"Altair," he says, flashing a quick grin. "Sure you aren't going to the Ascension Ball?"

"I have a feeling I'd know if I were," I say drily.

"Ah, yes," says Altair. That smile again. "Suppose I had an extra ticket?"

I stop walking. "You can't be serious."

"I'm not serious," he says. "But I am honest. How would you like to attend the event of the season?"

"I'd love to," I tell him. "But I think my great-aunt would keel over in shame if I showed up to the event of the season in a dress like this."

"Not to worry," Altair says. "It was my invitation, and so it is my responsibility to make sure you secure something to wear. We happen to be walking in the direction of Callidora's, the best modiste in the city. I'll cover the cost."

He says this like it's nothing, like he's lending me an old hat or a couple of drocks. Maybe this is life for the very rich. They can afford to be so thoughtlessly generous. I'd be a fool not to jump on this opportunity, I think. If there's a catch later, I'll figure things out from there.

"Very well," I say. "Then I accept your invitation."

We pass a wide square where children play, and I try not to stare. It's not just the towering, verdant trees and the emerald expanse of grass that I'm not used to seeing. It's the enormous, tiered fountains gushing water in roaring falls and the kids tossing coins into the water by the fistful. Glints of metallic color dance in the air, and one of them lands on my hand. It's a mechanical insect with large iridescent wings. Some kind of drone, maybe. It flits away before I can shake it off.

"I've grown fond of walking," Altair remarks. I don't know what to say to that. It seems like a bizarre comment, along the lines of "I sure do appreciate needing to move between one place and another."

Then he adds, "It's a good way to get a sense of the city," and it occurs to me that someone with Altair's resources no doubt has a private ship to bridge these sorts of distances in seconds. "Once you've been beyond atmo for long enough, you gain new appreciation for feeling the ground beneath your feet. Never thought I'd miss dirt, but here we are."

I think of Sarn, our soil carefully parceled off and sold away. I've missed dirt my entire life without realizing it.

"I know what you mean," I say.

Away from the happy families, a group of haunted-looking young people with very short hair congregate, watching a tournament projected in the air. Some have prosthetics like the young man I saw earlier. A child shouts something across the way and one young person flinches so hard, they almost lose their balance.

"Soldiers?" I ask quietly.

Altair nods. "The latest campaign in Kore has been very hard."

Privately, I thank the fates that the skyforce doesn't bother to recruit on Sarn. I'm sure they think we'd make rotten soldiers, and they're not wrong.

As we approach, the group looks up and stares at us—at Altair, specifically. The sight of his jacket must bring back sour memories. Altair reaches into his pocket and produces a fistful of drocks. A pair of zeroes glints briefly in the light and I realize I'm looking at a pile of hundred-drock coins.

"Here," Altair says, gravely offering them to the assembled group. They take the money quickly, as if he could change his mind at any moment. "Buy yourselves something warm to eat," he says. "It's cold out today."

We walk away and Altair doesn't look back, as if he does this sort of thing all the time. Between this and the dress, maybe he does. Maybe I'd be a philanthropist, too, if I could give so freely.

We reach the end of the square and turn left down a long avenue.

"Not too much farther now," says Altair. I scarcely hear him. "Ah," he adds, "you've never seen it in person before, have you?"

At the end of the avenue of silver and bronze buildings is a massive ship, shaped like a ring and bubbled with skylights. The inside of the ring is dotted with ports where smaller ships are docking or zipping away. The whole grand affair is hovering soundlessly about twenty meters above the ground.

"Built nearly a hundred years ago, the transport ship to the Imperial Palace station boasts two dozen singing crystal chandeliers from the mines of Ishael," Altair reels off in a tour guide voice.

"Oh, and also more stuffed shirts than you'd ever care to see in your life," Altair adds. "Seriously, surf down the banister of the ballroom staircase once, and they'll hold it against you for the rest of your life."

I know I need to stop staring at every new thing I see, but I still can't get over the sight of the palace station, floating in the air like something from a children's story.

I wrench my gaze from the grandeur. "Did you really?"

"It was my first ball," says Altair. "And the staircases are—well, you'll see tomorrow, I suppose."

"I'll try to fight the temptation," I tell him.

Altair laughs. "That's no fun. Here, this way."

We turn away from the ship and trail down a narrower street where the sidewalks are less crowded. The shop windows flaunt a world of luxuries so foreign to my life, I can scarcely comprehend them. I spot a display of special serums promising to eat away and regrow the surface of your face. It must take a fortune to maintain a rich person's skin.

I can tell which shop is Callidora's even before I can read the quaint hand-carved sign above the door. The windows are filled with elegant garments that bob gently on their floating manne-quins, in delicate pastels and deep jewel tones. It reminds me of the flowers in the park—so much unapologetically brilliant color.

The door chimes pleasantly as we step inside.

"Anyone there?" Altair calls, and a birdlike woman with a cloud of dark hair, a laser pen tucked behind one ear, and a whirring eyepiece pokes her head out of the back.

"I'll be a minute," she says, "I'm in the middle of—" Then she gets a proper look at Altair and hurries toward us. I'm not certain if it's the crisp military jacket or just the dimensions of his face—he *is* handsome, I suppose.

"What will it be?" she asks breathlessly.

"My friend Iola here needs a new dress for tomorrow's ball," says Altair.

The woman clicks her tongue, all business. "Short notice," she says. "Everyone else got their orders in weeks ago."

"I'll make it worth your while," says Altair, handing her a shiny card. When she holds it to the light, it beams out a ghostly image of a majestic ship sailing through a starstorm.

"Well then," the woman says briskly, "let me just scan you into the system." She retreats to the back room.

Altair turns to me and inclines his head. "I hate to leave you like this, but I've got an incredibly dull work matter to attend to."

"Wait," I say. I have to be sure this favor isn't going to bite me in the ass later. "Why are you—"

"Ah," says Altair, "yes, I'm no doubt a fool to assume you wouldn't wonder."

"You said it, not me."

"Put simply," he says, "you seem likely to shake things up, and these functions are, I won't lie, incredibly boring."

"This is a lot of trouble to go to, just to slake your boredom,"

I say.

"Then you have never truly been bored," says Altair. "That reminds me, you'll need new jewelry for your new look. Here." He reaches up behind his neck and removes a thin gold chain, his only necklace besides the diamond-shaped pendant worn by most men. "Not the showiest thing, but it'll do."

I take the delicate chain, only partly wondering how much I could pawn it for.

"Do you mind if we get started soon?" Callidora interjects from the back room. "The clock is ticking."

"Right." He produces a small flat disk shaped like a teardrop and edged in delicate silver, taps out a short sequence, and hands it to me. "Your pass to the ball," he says, pressing it warmly into my hands. "Place your thumb on the edge to code it to your DNA."

I do so, and the disk blinks to life. Green rays of light crawl over my features. A ghostly still of my face appears, looking lost and just a little bit frightened, and then disappears.

5

"All right," says Callidora, clapping her hands together. She turns to me. "Hello, Iola. Are you ready to look better than you've ever looked in your entire life?"

"Bold words," I say.

Callidora raises her eyebrows. "Well. I am the best. And I can see what you're wearing."

I bristle despite myself, thinking of the hours and hours Mita put into this dress. Her work got me this far, into this shop.

"Don't get me wrong," Callidora adds. "It's gorgeous and clearly, it's expertly hand-tailored, none of the mass-fabbed nonsense that designers are trying to pass off as high fashion these days."

"Hand-tailoring makes all the difference," I say primly, as if ninety percent of my clothes don't come secondhand or from the portside shop that sells mass-fabbed rejects.

"Exactly, that's what I tell all my clients. Now, let's get you into something that's not desperately out of date. Gown, suit, or something else?"

A suit would be more maneuverable, but a gown affords you infinitely more hiding places. It's not a hard choice.

"Gown."

"Any preferences as to color, pattern, style, cut . . . ?"

"Pockets," I say instantly. "I want pockets."

This earns me an approving look. "Practical, I like it. We can certainly make that happen."

"And I'd like it to be easy to move around in, and the fabric should be quiet." And then, in case this is too obviously a pickpocket's wish list: "I just hate rustling around, you know?"

"And as for the rest, you're relatively flexible?"

I nod.

"Whatever you'd like," I say. Then, remembering Mita's words, "Maybe something in gold?"

"Good choice, that should suit you nicely," says Callidora. "It would be best if you could stay in the area tonight so we can perform fittings as needed. Will that be a problem?"

I've been eyeing a low-slung cushioned bench on the other side of the room.

"I can cancel my hotel and stay here if that's easier," I say. "I know I'm putting you out significantly."

She lets out a relieved breath. "Thank you," she says. "That will make this considerably easier. Would you like something to eat or drink in the meantime?"

As it happens, I would.

After putting away several pieces of herbed bread and a cup of spiced tea, I feel much better. Callidora even delicately offers use of the shower upstairs, and embarrassment over how I must smell gives way to amazement at the feeling of hot jets of water and luxurious citrus-scented shampoo in my hair.

We're maybe two hours into the dressmaking process and my hair is just starting to dry when Callidora produces the first version for me to try on.

"This is nothing like the final product," she says. "Obviously, the skirt will be much longer. I just want to get a feel for the draping and—what's on your *feet*?"

I glance down at my scuffed, worn-down boots, barely held together with grubby knotted laces. Right. I'd had a plan here, and the plan had involved never lifting my skirts.

"They're comfortable?" I offer.

Callidora mutters something that sounds like, "Fates preserve me from rich people and their bizarre affectations," and then says, more audibly, "Well, for the sake of not showing up to the biggest event in decades in something that belongs on the scrap heap, can I lend you some footwear? We keep sample pairs in a range of sizes for fittings, and, let's be clear, when I say 'can I lend you some footwear,' what I mean is 'please take them because I have a reputation to maintain.'"

From there, I entertain myself either practicing my gait in a pair of sleek, supple flats, or lying on the bench and getting some rest.

"Are you certain you're comfortable?" Callidora asks at one point, frowning at her machines—she has several going at once.

"I'm fine," I say, and then I prove my point by dozing off to the mechanized hum of needle and thread chugging away.

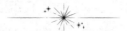

When I wake, the sky is just starting to glow bright again, and Callidora is in the other room with someone else, talking in a low voice. I drag myself upright, grimacing at the stale taste in my mouth, and help myself to another cup of tea. At the sound of the liquid pouring, the conversation ceases and Callidora emerges with a person around my age with short black hair and a simple yellow jumpsuit—fitted on top, loose and flowy on the bottom. It's no ball gown, but the effect is eye-catching nonetheless. The shade brings out the gold undertones of the newcomer's skin and complements her dark eyes. Her square pendant appears to be carved out of wood and has a navy-blue finish, and her dangling earrings are an intricate crisscross of fine lines.

"I like your earrings," I find myself saying. "Is that a map of the city transports?"

"Close," she says. "Root systems. You know, you're the first person who's ever tried to guess. What's your name?"

"Iola." I hold out my hand to shake, and she grips it briefly.

"I'm Amaris."

"Nice to meet you."

I glance back at Callidora, who's muttering over a dress form.

Amaris follows my gaze. "I'm a regular at Callidora's. I just dropped by to pick up the final piece of my outfit," she explains, holding up a shopping bag emblazoned with Callidora's signature curly *C*. "I have a sea of errands to cross before the ball tonight." Amaris smiles ruefully then. Something in that soft, easy expression makes me sharply aware of my out-of-date dress and—I reach up to check—my sloppily braided hair.

"Your dress is nearly finished, Iola," calls Callidora. "I just need to see to some last-minute touches and figure out what in the world we're going to do about the rest of your look."

"I'm decent at braiding," Amaris offers. "It'll be half an hour before the rest of the shops are open. I've got time."

"That would be amazing," I tell her, as if striking women with beautiful smiles offer to do my hair every day.

Callidora produces a small chest full of combs, bands, ribbons, and hairpins, and Amaris settles down onto the bench and sets to work, dividing my hair into sections.

"I take it you're also attending the ball?" she asks.

I start to nod, then remember the name of the game is holding my head still. "I am. First imperial ball ever."

"Excited?"

"Worried shitless," I say before I can stop myself.

"Don't be," says Amaris. "Everyone there will be focused on themselves. Making the biggest impression, that sort of thing. If you run out of things to talk about, just ask them who they think will get the crown. Everyone has an opinion about that, of course."

"Of course," I echo, making a mental note to develop an opinion on the topic.

"What do you do?" she says.

"My family sells hydroponics minerals on Yorgos," I say, in case she happens to run into Altair. I find myself wishing I had come up with a more interesting lie. "What about you?"

"I'm not sure yet, to be honest," she says with a small laugh. "I just finished my studies."

"Three years ahead of schedule," Callidora calls from her sewing machines. "She's a bright one."

I never had much use for school. On Sarn, we got the six standard years of Basic Education, taught by a rotating cast of young volunteers who would drone on about the many glories of the Helian Empire while the dust clouds rolled by outside. I spent most of my lessons in the back of the room, practicing Dad's little magic tricks and other sleight-of-hand techniques I picked up at the market. I can do my sums and read okay, but university is about as far from my life as the Aeschylus Belt.

"What are you studying?" I ask.

"History," she says. "I specialized in the third epoch, specifically the years leading up to the founding of Helia."

I try to think of an educated-sounding question and can't. "Something tells me you'll have a more interesting angle on it than my teachers did. Tell me more?"

As she braids, Amaris recounts to me a story about the dread pirate Flavia Felice. We learned a little about this in school: to combat the threat of roving marauders, General Vitalis brought together various allies to form what would later become the Helian Empire. Somehow Year Three lessons and a thousand years of distance made even intergalactic piracy sound dull and boring. But in Amaris's telling, Flavia Felice was less a one-dimensional stock villain and more a complicated, tragic figure who turned to piracy after a terrible drought left half of her planet barren.

I'd never heard of Flavia by name, and certainly nothing about the famine or how well-matched the pirates and General Vitalis's forces were. It's strange—the way Amaris lets the story unfurl, it almost feels like Flavia was the hero.

"—so that's how General Vitalis realized one of his most trusted soldiers had been working for Flavia Felice the whole time," Amaris says as she expertly pins up the final braid.

"What did the general do?"

"Mm, I'm afraid you'll have to tap into a library base to find out," she says with a quick grin. "I've finished."

Amaris leads me to a giant mirror, and I take a look at her handiwork. She's carefully secured all my braids into an elaborate crown that coils around my head, interwoven with a delicate thread of golden leaves, which peek out from between my braids. The effect is stunning, almost regal. For a moment, I don't know what to say.

"Thank you," I tell her.

"Not a problem," she says. "I used to do this for my friends when I was young. They were older, and getting good at things like braiding was how I convinced them I was cool enough to tag along. It was nice to revisit that." She picks up her bag. "So I'll see you at the ball?"

"I'll be there," I say. "Maybe I can hear the second half of the story?"

"If I can steal you away from your crowd of admirers." Amaris smiles, and I can't help but smile back at her. "Are you going with anyone?"

I shake my head. Altair might have given me my ticket but I'm clearly his amusing diversion, not his date.

Her smile widens just a little. "Me neither."

A giddiness sparks through me. I have no idea what to say, but Iola Galatas would be used to this kind of attention.

"Well, I look forward to seeing you there," I tell her, sketching a bow.

"Save me a dance," says Amaris, calls over her shoulder.

"Final fitting," Callidora says, and I jerk my gaze away from the doorway.

I slip behind a screen, and Callidora passes the dress over to me, a shimmering confection of gold. I feel like I'm still asleep as I pull it on, like I'm in a dream where clothing fits perfectly without altering and I can openly touch something so fine without fear of getting caught.

Standing in the mirror is a lady who belongs in a palace. The bodice of my dress is embroidered with brilliant rays of bronze. The sleeves are made from a lighter fabric, slit from the shoulder to the elbow, where they end gracefully in a gather, and my skirts cascade lightly to the floor, concealing six pockets, one so deep I can fit my whole arm down it.

If I encountered this woman on the street, I'd get out of her way. If Amaris encountered this woman on the street—well, I find myself wishing she was still here. I study my reflection from one angle and then another. Nothing breaks the illusion.

Fates, I think. I just might be able to pull this off.

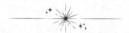

I leave Callidora's shortly afterward, borrowed shoes on my feet and the dress carefully wrapped in layers of soft paper and tucked into a shopping bag. I managed to score several more pieces of bread, two of which I've slipped into my bag and one I eat slowly as I trail down the side streets. Other shops are just starting to open, and the walkways are far emptier than yesterday.

It's bizarre to see so much variation in the light of the heavens. On Sarn, either the sun is up or it's down. There's little of these glowing pinks and oranges. Even the sky is luxurious here.

The pass to the ball thankfully displays a countdown until 19:00, when we're meant to meet at the transport ship. I've got time to explore.

I burn a few hours wandering around the shops. With Callidora's bag swinging from my hand, people are noticeably friendlier to me, no doubt taking it as proof that I can afford the finer things and my antique dress is just an eccentric fashion choice. The shopkeepers hop to attention, begging me to try this serum or that nanotech exfoliant. The fawning makes me uneasy, but I appreciate the chance to practice my high-class accent on them. If I can literally give off the scent of money, I'll seem that much richer, and so I allow them to rub lotions into my face and hands, although strangers touching me, even this delicately, makes my skin crawl.

By the end of it, I do smell amazing, though.

I manage to dress myself in a nearby hotel bathroom without incident, and I'm standing by the transport ship, trying not to stare at the fleet of uniformed guards, by 18:49. At 18:53, the guards extend a long gangplank from the main doors of the ship, which is still hovering in midair. It seems like it would be easier to just land the thing, but apparently it's more important to look impressive. At 18:54, the gangplank lights up with a holo loop of a spinning nebula. At 18:56, we are allowed to ascend the incline to the ship doors. I keep my gaze fixed ahead as I pass through the display of glimmering stars. Some of the guests totter up on heels so lofty, they require assistance on either side. I am glad to have my flats.

The doorman scans my invitation, and then we're ushered into one of several rooms, outfitted like the fanciest lounge I've ever seen, complete with a stocked bar and huge plush chairs and couches. I look around for Altair or Amaris but clearly we've been placed in different sections of the ship. Waiting on each seat are small bags tied off with silvery string. I shake one out and find what appears to be a white powdery candy bar, a bottle of purple liquid with swirls of gold, and an eye mask that emits a gentle, pulsing warmth. It's a far cry from banging around in a crate for hours, I think.

In one corner of the room, a holo display lights up the space.

"For the last one thousand years," an announcer says in a voice like syrup, "the Helian Empire has sought to shine its light on every planetary body that turns in the barren darkness of space."

"This year marks the fiftieth anniversary of the day our beloved Emperor Hyperion took on the mantle," the announcer continues, "and his administration has faced stunning challenges, from the deadly Zarinel incursion on Kore and Gree to outer planetary uprisings, all met with bravery, determination, and the will to continue our own ascension. Our vision remains, as ever, to sweep away the shadows and wrap even the darkest, coldest corners of space in the light and warmth of civilization, of progress, education, and technological advancement. But now comes the time for a new era . . ."

The narrator goes on to explain how Emperor Hyperion will personally train his successor for the next five years and blah blah blah. Nobody around me is listening. I can only imagine what Dezmer would say about this display. She always seems to know what's going on. I suspect she hacks into the skyforce feed somehow, and the end result is it makes her spitting angry. Me, I've never seen the point of following the crown or the court that closely. They have about as much to do with our lives on Sarn as Amaris's stories about General Vitalis and Flavia Felice, and they're way less interesting.

I'm about to take a bite of my complementary white bar when I notice a few people rubbing it on their necks. I follow suit, trying to look natural about it, and the powder dissolves on my skin. I touch my neck, and suddenly it's soft as a baby's bum, with a clean, herbal whiff to it. Weird. I make a mental note to check before assuming anything is food, even if it's on a plate and covered with gravy.

Finally, our arrival is announced with a solemn voice that sounds vaguely familiar—must be some celebrity on one of the shows Pav likes to watch.

We're led down a series of narrow corridors and into the docking area of the imperial station. The walls are covered in the slight shimmer of an intricate design. When I look closely, I realize the design isn't a pattern, but the full transcript of the Helian Founding Pledge. *Protection from incursion in exchange for friendship and service . . .* Would have been great if my classroom walls were like this—I would've passed my history exams no problem. A pair of uniformed personnel stand by the station entrance, checking everyone's pass one last time.

When the person at the door takes my invitation, I am half prepared for them to see right through me, smell the poor on me like a rotten perfume, like sweat and sickly-sweet protein slurry, like desperation. Instead, they bow and motion me through the grand double doors. We trail down another long hallway and then into a richly carpeted room where we're scanned for what I assume are security purposes and an attendant takes our purses and coats.

I feel a jolt of panic about surrendering my rucksack. When you own only a few things, you're bound to get weird about them. I have to remind myself that if tonight goes well, I don't need to walk out of here with anything more than my full pockets.

Another attendant opens yet another set of double doors, and I descend a curving flight of stairs. I hear the music first, just a few swooping notes, and then I see it laid out before me: the Ascension Ball.

6

The first thing I notice is the color. Endless stretches of shining, shimmering fabric, along with gems of every hue, swish along the dance floor, reminding me of the dizzy iridescent rainbow of a fuel spill on a rare rainy day on Sarn. The result, I suppose, of a hundred people with unlimited budgets each carefully calculating how to make their outfit stand out in the crowd. Any worry that this dress might be too gaudy seems ridiculous now; the glimmering threads feel almost demure. I run my gaze over the throngs of people, looking but taking in almost nothing. Eyes were not made for this.

The next thing I notice is the ballroom. Blue-green vines curl along the walls, with starbursts of delicate blossoms at regular intervals. A canopy of greenery hangs from the lofty ceiling, and when I crane my neck, I realize there is a small forest of trees above me, trained to grow upside down apparently. The space surrounding the dancers is vast, shining floors polished to a mirror-like sheen, populated with an oasis here, a waterfall there. Servers and bots slip through the crowd discreetly, expertly navigating the hybrid holo-and-greenhouse landscape.

The third thing I notice is the sweet buttery smell of freshly baked pastries, a visceral reminder that I've eaten nothing but bread from Callidora's today.

Dad always says that when something weighs heavy on his mind, the stress squashes his appetite. At the end of the day, I'd find him frowning intently at a delicate piece of engine, something designed to discourage pickers like us, with a mechanism spring-loaded to explode if tapped the wrong way, and he'd look up at me with a wan smile: *Aw, Cassie, did I miss breakfast? And lunch?*

But that's Dad. I've never had this problem. My stomach rumbles.

I hope that Jax and the others are reminding Dad to eat. I should've been more specific before I left about what to watch out for, should've bothered to bribe someone, should've—I swallow the thoughts down. My worry can't help Dad now. My focus might.

Across the ballroom, a magnificent banquet table is weighed down with more food than I've ever seen in one place: tureens of steaming soup, intricately fashioned pastries of all kinds, an array of cheeses, platters of rare fruits. All of it is arranged into works of art, made to look like something more than food—star systems, palaces, circlets of flowers.

There's no point in trying to remove valuables from the guests until the drinks have started flowing. Not to mention, it's hard to strategize on an empty stomach. I set my sights on the feast and head over.

On a platform to my left, a quintet of musicians with gold-inlaid cellos are sawing away at some sort of fashionable waltz. They're all sporting the same sharp undercut, bare skin dotted with a lace of electrodes. It takes me a few confused seconds to piece together that this is probably some experimental mindlink tech like what we've heard about on the short-wave. Even without a conductor, these musicians are more synced than is humanly possible. Dad would be fascinated. I'm just getting a headache.

A few couples are already perusing the pastries. I take a gilded white plate, so thin that it lets some light through, and help myself to several slices of sharp, crumbly cheese and some berries—at least I can identify those. For want of anything better to do, I watch the dancers as I chew, and then take several pastries filled with herbs and a soft, creamy cheese. When I'm certain nobody is watching, I add a few more pastries to my plate and slip them from my flowing sleeve to one of my waist pockets for later.

There seem to be three or four basic dances, all following what Mita showed me but with the steps somewhat simplified, since so much of the crowd is weighed down by various forms of frippery.

At first, I can't spot any security equipment, but after scanning the area several times, I realize each of the twinkling blue lights dotting the edges of the room must indicate that a feed is being recorded. A lack of blue lights in the center of the ceiling means that I should still be able to execute my lifts in the crush of a full dance floor, shielded from the palace security team by these very convenient guests. And worst-case scenario, if I'm within range of a feed, I always try to render my sleight-of-hand so sleight as to be invisible.

Footsteps pause behind me, and I turn.

"Madam?" murmurs a server. She's young, maybe my age, holding a tray of ornate flutes filled with a golden sparkling liquid and dusted with something ruby-red along the rim. For a second I can't tell what about her makes me nervous, and then I realize— her eyes are carefully downcast, trained halfway between my face and the floor. I'm not used to people addressing me like that. I suspect I'm expected to pretend that she doesn't exist. I'm not about to dull my senses or slow my fingers with drink, so I make a gesture of refusal with my hand. The server nods and scurries away as I pop a berry in my mouth. The juice is richer than anything I've ever tasted.

"Are you sure?"

A middle-aged man in peacock blue lifts a goblet. I don't know why, but in all my hours of careful planning, I had not seriously considered that these perfectly coiffed socialites might try to talk to me.

"Yes," I say, once I've chewed and swallowed, trying to pitch my voice a little lower, a little more refined.

"It's the good stuff, though," says Peacock. "None of that grape-grown swill that you find in the farthest reaches." I wonder how far into the farthest reaches he has actually been. The hand gripping the stemware looks baby-smooth, the light skin unblemished by sun or labor. On his tie pin, a sapphire the size of an unbroken thumb nail glitters. "Apple ambrosia," he continues. "A vintage from years before the war, back when we could spare our best ships to move fruit from Gree with the orchard's morning dew still on them." The man sighs. "A shame about the war, but we must all make sacrifices."

I think of the sea of exhausted, angry faces at the station, of the old woman screaming the names of her dead children over and over. *This war is a meat grinder and we are the meat!*

I take another bite of bread and cheese, chewing contemplatively. "Sacrifice makes heroes of us all," I say in my most studied posh accent.

"Quite right," says the man. "Have you met my wife yet?"

Peacock nods to a woman decked out in shining greens. Her dangling earrings and her square pendant hang heavy with emeralds, and a matching headpiece is woven so elaborately into her fair hair, I'd need a pair of shears to retrieve it.

The woman raises an eyebrow. I realize I have been staring through her entire introduction, titles and all.

"I love your dress," I say for cover. "The color is—" I search for some overheard scrap of fancy language that I've picked up since I began moving among these people, finally landing on "marvelous, like something from the orchid conservatories of Tyche."

"You've a good eye," she tells me. "This gown is made entirely from spider silk."

I don't need to fake my surprise at that. We have plenty of spiders on Sarn, but they don't make more than wispy cobwebs. Even the bugs of Amphor are more glamorous. I realize with a lurch that my reaction might have blown my cover, if such things are common on the mainworlds, but the woman in green looks delighted by my ignorance.

"Do you know how we get most of our silk?" she asks. "Most people don't."

Dutifully I shake my head.

"Silkworms," says Emerald. "We wait until they've spun their cocoons and then boil them to unravel the fibers, with the worms still alive inside. It takes two thousand to three thousand cocoons to weave just one pound of silk." She sniffs.

"My Ligeia has a soft heart," says Peacock, patting her hand.

"Three thousand," says—Ligeia, apparently. "That's three thousand dead baby worms for nearly every dress in this room." She nods toward the dancers still swirling on the polished wooden floor. "These people are swimming in blood, and they don't even know it."

"That's a shame," I manage, "about the worms. So, these spiders—?"

"The beauty of the system is that they live in the wild," she tells me. "Every three months, they're retrieved by hand, so as not to harm them. They're brought to a facility where they're sorted by color, and then they're milked for thread and returned to their homes. We need over three million spiders to make a single gown."

"How long does that take?" I ask.

"Oh, it depends," says Ligeia. "When I received my inheritance, I came into possession of a very small planet called Telay. Really, an insignificant place. The only thing it had to its name were a handful of mines. Amethyst, a trifle out of date, of course. But," says Ligeia resolutely, "I am not one for sitting around."

I nod again. Her hands are every bit as smooth as her husband's.

"And so," she continues, "I invested in spiders. People thought I'd lost my mind, of course—" She and Peacock titter. "And the locals were *very* resistant. The spiders bite, you see. One bite does very little, but if you get a few dozen, apparently your hand can swell up and become unable to bend. So, unfortunately, we are compelled to ship in extras from time to time to replace those who do lose full use of their hands."

Unbidden, my fingers curl in my fine sleeves.

"But it worked out in the end," she continues cheerfully, "and without harming a single silkworm to do it."

"May I?" I gesture toward her dress, and she holds out an arm for me so that I can touch her sleeve. She's wearing an emerald-studded bracelet that clasps at the underside of her wrist, which is to say, at the most sensitive part of the arm, but with the right distraction I think I could take it.

Just then, the musicians start a new song. Another waiter scuttles by, bearing a tray of empty goblets.

"I love this one!" says Ligeia, finishing her brandy and adding it to the tray in one fluid motion. "Gennadios, shall we?"

"My feet," says Gennadios apologetically. "You know how I struggle with these faster numbers."

I've been watching long enough to get a feel for the adjusted steps, and there is no time like the present. Judging by the pink in her cheeks, Ligeia's had quite a bit to drink. Her jewels sparkle green under the chandeliers. One of her long dangling earrings is starting to come unhooked.

"I'll dance with you," I say.

I place one hand on Ligeia's shoulder and the other at her waist. She does the same to me. For the first half of the song, I take nothing. I am planning my movements carefully, choreo-graphing them in my head. Well-executed theft is its own kind of dance. I think of Dad's magic tricks, making the screw or bolt that I need appear here, disappear there. *Watch carefully, Cassie.* Seeing how the trick was done never spoiled it; it only made me marvel at the artistry.

"A truly splendid party," I say.

"Certainly," says Ligeia. "Even compared with last year's summer solstice gala, Emperor Hyperion and Empress Thea have really outdone themselves."

"Very much so," I reply. And then, to keep her from asking me any questions, "Who do you suppose the Emperor will name?"

Her face lights up. "Now that you mention it," she says, dropping her voice to a near whisper, "his brother is the most obvious choice, of course, and I know most are saying it will indeed be Mynos, but—and don't go spreading this around—my Gennadios actually has a minor claim to the throne."

"Does he?"

"Shh! He is perhaps not the frontrunner, to be sure, but one has to think the empire must be grateful. I was just telling Ambassador Zahur of Khonsania—see the distinguished individual with the purple and yellow sash?"

I scan the crowd and see a person with dark brown skin and an immaculate towering hairstyle of braids, surrounded by a fleet of uniformed aides. I nod.

"I was just telling them of Gennadios's accomplishments," she continues, and here, she veers into an elaborate monologue detailing the many ways in which she and Gennadios have served the crown.

As the music's tempo speeds up and she continues to talk, I take a careful breath. Very slowly, I allow the fingers of my left hand to drift up and upset the earring that is now barely hanging off her earlobe. It is in my hand and down my sleeve in seconds. She turns her head, faltering, feeling the change in weight before she understands it, and in that moment, I transfer the earring to my right hand, and into the pouch at my hip.

"My earring!" she cries, her hand flying to her bare ear.

"Oh! Have you lost it?" I say.

"It must have fallen out!"

We drop to our knees, Ligeia surveying the floor intently, jostling the other dancers as she goes. A slippery dress shoe stamps on her palm, and as she cradles her hand to her chest, I slip the other earring off her right ear.

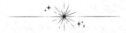

From there, I dance with others. An arrogant young lad, the son of someone important, asks me to join him in a minuet. As he explains why Mynos is the logical successor, I trip over the steps, bumping into him several times and apologizing for my clumsiness as I pocket his opal-studded golden cuff links. I waltz with a pretty but rather distant blue-haired lady who is wearing so many golden bracelets that I liberate three of them without her noticing, slithering the chains off her wrists as she airily hints that Empress Thea favors Mynos. An extremely stuffy mustachioed man asks me to join him for a treacly slow ballad and what turns out to be a lengthy reflection on brotherly duty. As we part, he unknowingly also parts with his pinky ring, heavy with a sparkling purple stone.

Palace politics are screamingly boring, but with the right fence and a bit of luck, I have bought perhaps ten years of easy living for Dad and me.

Ten years is not enough.

I have spent every day of my life weighing every decision by our lack of money, by the endless concern of scraping together enough meager coins to survive for another day. I want to be free of the sucking force of poverty entirely.

I want to go to the market and buy food for the week without worrying for a second how much anything costs. I want a home far from the desert, free of the grit that drifts through every corner and spoils everything—our beds, our drinking water, our lungs. I want to buy hearty broths and meds that will make my dad well again. I want one damn day without struggle, and then another, and another, and another.

I make my way back to the refreshments table. Someone has set out a steaming five-tiered fountain filled with some sort of tea even fancier than what Callidora served me, fragrant with spices I can't begin to name. One mouthful is likely worth more than an entire day's toil on Sarn.

I drink two helpings, balancing the small teacup against my pinky and letting the warmth of the tea settle me. If I play my hand correctly, I'll be enjoying this brew every morning from my private balcony.

"Hello again," says someone to my right as I consider a third cup. I turn, and standing beside me in a brilliant red-and-orange dress, like sunlight shining through the petals of a rare flower, is Amaris.

7

"Amaris!" I blurt out. "Good to see you."

She smiles. The red and orange suit her even better than the yellow did. The dress makes her eyes look almost amber, luminous in the warm light of the ballroom.

I'm on the job, technically, but I could use a short break from thieving. Staying locked into a pickpocket's mindset for too long can fry your focus, make you sloppy. I can spare the length of a song for a conversation, I tell myself. This is fine. Everything is fine.

"Do you have time to tell me the rest of that story?" I ask before I can think better of it.

She folds her hands. Her elbow-length lace gloves must also be from Callidora's because they are exquisite. For the first time, I wonder how a very recent graduate could afford such finery, which is to say, I wonder who her parents are. She never did mention her last name.

"You are at the event of the century and you want a history

lesson?" she says.

"I'm famously studious," I say.

"Fair enough," says Amaris. She holds out one hand. "Would you happen to have that dance free now?"

I do. We take our places. "We left old General Vitalis and Flavia Felice in quite a tricky dilemma," I say. Despite the gloves, I am very aware of her hand on my shoulder, her other hand resting lightly on my waist. I nearly fumble my opening footwork but thankfully, I'm saved by the reflexes I acquired during Dezmer's dance lessons.

"We did," she agrees. "What do you think?"

"Of this rather dramatic cliffhanger? I think I want to know what happens next."

"What do you think of the story itself?" says Amaris. "The great clash of the general and the pirate."

"I had hoped General Vitalis would show a little more sense," I tell her. "As a former spy, he should've known sooner not to trust the people under him. But that's just my take. What does a trained historian say?"

"Depends on the historian," she says wryly. "Do—"

She breaks off as a couple in striped chartreuse, their faces flushed, nearly careen into us. Amaris whirls us out of harm's way with truly impressive speed and grace.

"Are you all right?" she asks.

"I'm fine," I say. "And suppose, just for example, the historian I was asking was you, the person who is absolutely triumphing at the double waltz."

"Years of dance training," she replies. "It's mostly a matter of practice, unromantic as that sounds."

"Still, you're remarkably nimble," I say. "Dodging feet, dodging dancers, dodging questions."

I twirl her, and when we've resumed our places, Amaris says, "I don't like to let my thoughts color the narrative."

"I'm asking for your thoughts," I remind her. "But if you must, I'll take my answer in the form of a neutral statement of facts."

"There's no such thing as neutral," she says. "Every story ever told is about two things: the supposed topic, and something of the teller themselves. You can't escape that, any more than you can taste fruit with someone else's mouth."

She frowns thoughtfully, biting her lip for the briefest moment. "But I think that General Vitalis's success was always tempered by his hubris. He would achieve something great, then reach too far and fall again. His arrogance was his vice. And unfortunately, even the smartest and most talented among us can make a mistake, overextend ourselves, and find ourselves in an unenviable position for which we never planned. Don't you think so?"

Her eyes meet mine.

"Perhaps," I say. "But isn't that why it's important to stay flexible and not overthink things? People can bounce back from all sorts of setbacks so long as they keep on moving. It's just like dancing. The only thing you can really do wrong is freeze up."

"Always keep moving," Amaris murmurs.

"Something like that."

"Sounds tiring."

"It beats the alternative," I say.

I wait for her to fill the silence with more opinions or reasoning. She does not. A lull in the conversation opens like a bottomless pit, murky silence all the way down.

"Did you know there is a woman here tonight whose dress was made using nothing but spiders?" I find myself saying.

She blinks, looking genuinely taken aback. "Is that so?"

"Engineered to spin in all colors."

A pause.

"Are they engineered to organize themselves by hue, too?" she asks.

"Workers do that," I explain. "They catch the spiders, and release them when the silk is spent, to recuperate for a few months."

"And the spiders don't mind this?"

"Oh no, they bite. Hard."

Her face is impassive but I can feel her hand tighten slightly on my shoulder. "Then don't you suppose the dress was not made by spiders alone?"

The strings swell and she spins me in time to the music. We resume our positions.

"Three million spiders," I say, "to make one dress."

"And how many people?" she says, a little too sharply.

A hundred. A thousand. I don't know, and the person I am pretending to be wouldn't care. There is no way to bluff, or divert course, or cobble together a good lie. I say nothing at all. Part of me wants her to believe that this fiction I'm projecting is still capable of shame.

She clears her throat and softens her tone. "It must be terribly fine, spider silk."

"It makes the silkworm stuff look like cotton," I tell her.

"Well, it sounds . . . innovative. It could very well be the way of the future."

"It could."

"An investment," she says. The slightest of pauses. "And perhaps a better investment even than gems."

"Do you think so?" I say. The music swells again. We're reaching the end of the song and it's almost time to spin her.

"I would say so." She moves a half second before I can, dipping me in one heady move, then reels me in close enough to smell her subtle gingery perfume. My gaze drops to her lips, which part ever so slightly. Then she leans in and whispers in my ear, "There is a jewelry thief running around tonight."

I do the worst possible thing then—I freeze. Amaris reels me out again, sending me spinning back into place. I focus on the dizzying dance of lights on the marble floor. We're surrounded by other dancers, all whirling away around us. I can't break away from Amaris without making a scene.

"How terrible," I manage. "I will keep a sharp eye out."

Amaris gives me a look. "There are worse people than thieves," she says.

My blood runs cold. I breathe out through my nose, willing myself to remain calm, to sound playful as I ask, "And who can be worse?"

"Those who catch thieves," she says, eyes fixed on mine.

The song ends.

"Thank you for the dance," Amaris says gravely.

I nod, mouth drier than it has ever been. When I turn to leave, she squeezes my hand in hers, a viselike grip on my fingers.

"I hope to have the pleasure again someday," says Amaris, meeting my gaze with those luminous brown eyes. She smiles as if nothing at all is amiss, as if we've just shared a pleasant but uneventful waltz. All around us, the couples are bowing and complimenting each other and dissolving back into the crowd. Amaris bows, light catching on her fire-colored dress, and with the thumb of her beautifully gloved hand, she traces three letters into my palm:

R-U-N

8

Amaris disappears into the crowd before I can ask any of the thousand questions suddenly swarming my mind. Was that a warning, or a threat? She didn't sound in league with the thief catchers, but I have no reason to trust her on the basis of a smile and a story. And where exactly does she expect me to run *to*? The royal station may be docked in Ouris, but it's not as though I can beat a quick exit through all the layers of security I went through to get here.

Well, that's not exactly true. I always have exit routes in mind. But there's no way I'm leaving this ball before I've gotten what I want. I'm on a devious, criminal mission, thank you very much.

I stumble off the dance floor and, in my haste, step hard on a trailing pale-blue skirt. The owner of the skirt whirls around. It's the drunk woman I met on Sarn, the one who got me into this whole mess in the first place. She'd said she wasn't going to the ball, but apparently she'd scored an invite after all. She appears to be sober this time and looking directly at my face. There is a long moment where my whole brain screams at me that this is it, I am caught, everything is over, and then I scrape together enough of my phony accent to manage, "Terribly sorry."

"They let anyone in nowadays, Duchess," she says to her companion with a sniff.

The duchess replies, "It's truly shameful. You can *sense* the lack of imperial blood . . ."

I watch them glide away. Several heartbeats later, I put together that the woman in the light-blue dress didn't recognize me, and her imperial companion was calling me out not for being common, but simply for being more common than a duchess. It's clear the woman has no clue who I am. No need to panic.

But my hands are still shaking. I can't have that, for professional reasons if nothing else. I need a moment to collect myself again. And I will do it in the company of the grand-looking foreign official Ligeia pointed out to me earlier, Ambassador Zahur. If anyone has a thorough understanding of the lay of the land, surely it's someone who has to sweet-talk everyone for a living.

They're tall and broad, easy enough to track down, and I find them standing beneath a majestic tree with feathery leaves growing down from the ceiling. They're wearing a dangling triangular pendant, which catches the light off the chandeliers as they talk to a dour-looking man with dark slicked-back hair and a simple black suit.

The dour man's hair is too long for him to be security, but he has that look about him—his gaze twitches away from Ambassador Zahur's, sweeping the ballroom, as if he's on high alert. His plain suit and undecorated diamond-shaped pendant stand out here in a way that only a very confident or foolish person would risk. He must be someone important, and I want to know who.

I wait for a pause in the conversation, and when the ambassador glances over at me, I bow.

"Ambassador Zahur, may I have this dance?" I ask in my best phony accent.

I wind up leading. It's a sedate dance, one that leaves room for a lot of conversation, and drifting through the ballroom, I attempt to get Ambassador Zahur talking about their mysterious companion, without letting on that I have no clue who he is.

"Sorry to have swept you away from your conversation," I say. "It looked absorbing."

"It was," says Ambassador Zahur. "I appreciate the opportunity to talk to anyone with such a keen intellect, but going to a ball and not dancing is like going to Palenth and not trying the garvoshé." They smile and so I smile too, privately wondering if garvoshé is a dance or a food or zero-gravity charades.

"It's important to do a thing right, really get the most out of an experience," I say.

"Full agreement," they say. "What's the point in doing something if you're not going to immerse yourself in it?"

"Still," I say, "my apologies for interrupting you."

Ambassador Zahur tilts their head to one side. "To be fair, I think my exchange with Perseus was likely reaching its natural end. An ambassador and a member of the emperor's council are bound not to see eye to eye."

The councilors must have some degree of power, if Ambassador Zahur is willing to devote their time to talking to one. Then again, they are dancing with me.

"I suspect his nerves have undergone quite a journey anyway," they add, "given the ascension and his candidacy. One struggles to get a sense of whether or not he even wants the crown."

Fates. I just walked up to the possible future emperor and poached his conversation partner.

"It is a tremendous responsibility. Mynos seems to be the favored candidate," I say instead. "What do you think?"

"I can't say," says Ambassador Zahur. "Palace politics will leave even a seasoned expert guessing, so I think I would prefer to wait until after the successor has been crowned, then offer my triumphant words on why it was bound to happen the way that it did."

"Very wise."

"Oh, I intend to be."

"So, what precisely does your job entail?" I ask. This feels like something that Iola Galatas from Yorgos should perhaps already know, so I laugh and add, "I'm afraid I must've dozed off on the day we covered ambassadorships."

"It's a challenging role, one might say," Ambassador Zahur says. "Although most jobs are challenging in their own right. What we endeavor to do is create and maintain relations with our receiving party, in this case the Helian Empire, and to promote a foreign policy strategy that will be conducive to the well-being of both the planets within the Khonsanian Collective and the rest of space."

This has the ring of a well-rehearsed answer. "So, how many times a day do you have to say that?"

"It comes up," says Ambassador Zahur, "on occasion. Our

goal is to arrive at a solution that is satisfactory to everyone."

"If your job is to make everybody happy, you must put in long hours," I say.

"I chose this line of work," they reply. "I find it fascinating. Of course, as far as satisfying our own people, the fact that the heart of our territory lies within the Gamallian Radiation Sphere provides a certain degree of insurance when it comes to negotiation with the Helian Empire."

"And why is that?" I ask, adding for safety, "I suppose I was asleep on that day as well."

"You may wish to visit a doctor," says Ambassador Zahur mildly. "Falling asleep that often may be a sign of a serious condition."

"I took my lessons in a warm, stuffy room, with comfortable chairs," I say. "And I can't resist a good nap. But tell me about the Gamallian Sphere. I'm genuinely curious."

Something a petty crook like Theron hasn't yet worked out: a good con is as much about listening as it is about talking. You never know what a person might volunteer in the rosy glow of someone else's attention.

"Stop me if I cover something you already know," Ambassador Zahur says. "I don't mean to condescend."

I smile. "I'd like to get the entire picture, and anyway, you may be seriously underestimating how soft those chairs were."

"The main planets of the Khonsanian Collective are located within a zone of rather strong radiation and protected by strong magnetic fields," says Ambassador Zahur. "It was settled by a group of engineers who had developed ships with incredibly good shielding. After many generations of building on previous successes, our spacecrafts can spend up to a decade in the Sphere without damage to anyone or anything living inside, while Helian and Zarinel ships frequently need our assistance once they've entered the region. Not every time, of course, but frequently enough that it must be factored into one's plans." The slightest of wry smiles. "Thus, should people of any empire or federation wish to pay us a visit, they must do so slowly and carefully."

"And respectfully," I add.

Ambassador Zahur's smile widens. "We do have a liking for manners," they agree. "Of course, it also helps that we're located in the middle of several crucial trade routes, and anyone not on good terms with a planet in our collective must take the long way around or chance the radiation without our aid."

"Who doesn't love a shortcut?" I say.

"Who indeed."

When the final notes of the song fade away, we return to the upside-down tree, underneath which Perseus is still standing.

"So, am I to assume you are done?" Perseus asks Ambassador Zahur.

"My dancing partner and I are both finished, yes," says the ambassador. "She expressed a strong interest in interstellar politics, so I'm certain she would love to hear more about your stances on trade, perhaps over a dance of your own? If you'll excuse me, I must pay my respects to Councilor Iraklidis." Then, after a deep bow, they're gone.

Perseus grimaces as his gaze falls on me. There's something familiar about his face, but I can't figure out what it is, and he of course doesn't offer any information of his own.

Something I have pieced together from my evening so far: Ligeia and her husband must be quite low-ranking, to feel the need to announce their titles to me. The genuinely important seem to give no introduction at all, assuming that everyone is already familiar with them.

I guess it's not such an unreasonable expectation. Their faces are on the news. Their faces are on money. It's strange to think about—I don't follow gossip from other planets, and prior to landing on Ouris, I'd never held in my hands anything higher than a fiver, so while their slightest whims could at any moment ripple out to upend my life, as individuals these people are nobody to me. Until tonight's holo video in the transport ship, I don't think I could've picked Emperor Hyperion out of a lineup. Every so often, a recruitment flier will surface featuring his tiny, blurry face but the man on the paper seems far too young to be the one who has ruled us for fifty years.

"I'll take the next dance with you if you have no others," Perseus grits out. And because I am playing the part of a socialite who would never turn down the chance to hobnob with a potential emperor, I incline my head and take his arm.

"What were you and the ambassador talking about?" Perseus asks as we begin the steps.

I blink, taken aback by the abruptness. "Khonsania."

"Ah," says Perseus. We spin. He volunteers nothing else.

"Big night for you," I try.

"Maybe," says Perseus.

"Well, a big night for whoever's named successor," I say.

"Maybe," Perseus repeats.

"Certainly a big night for the empire," I say at last.

There is something naggingly familiar about his face.

"What do you do for fun?" I ask.

"Systems administration," comes the terse reply. As conversational footholds go, it's a single loose rock.

"Care to elaborate?"

"It's very technical."

"Ah."

We spin again, and while we are separated, just for a moment, I see Perseus standing by the snack table, looking much more carefree in a brightly embroidered green jacket and a skirt that sweeps the floor. Then I return to my position, and he is standing in front of me in his black suit once more. I throw a glance over my shoulder and there he is, once more by the table, waving at us.

"Something the matter?" asks the Perseus I am dancing with.

It's not as though I've never heard of twins. Maxie and Moxie work at the port in Sarn, and their faces are identical, but Moxie's got a scar down one side of her neck from a junkpicking maneuver gone wrong, so it's never unclear which one you're talking to.

"I just saw your brother by the buffet," I manage.

"Which one?" Perseus says flatly. "My little joke. Obviously, you couldn't tell us apart at this distance. That's the thing about being one of the emperor's clones."

Clones. I've seen Perseus's face before on war recruitment fliers, I realize, because it's the same face as Emperor Hyperion's, only younger and more tired, with defined worry lines along the forehead and a perpetually pinched mouth. I'd heard that the emperor had no living children. I hadn't considered that he might have found another way to pass along his genes to the next generation. I wonder what it was about Perseus that has put him in the running for the throne. He clearly didn't get there through charm.

"Allow me to answer all of your questions," he drawls. "No, I don't feel pain when they feel pain. No, we don't share one another's thoughts, dreams, or nightmares. Our nervous systems are decidedly separate. Yes, I am asked these questions with some frequency. No, they are not the most foolish questions I am asked. Yes, I can tell us all apart, primarily because we are different people and secondarily because most of us are different ages. And you can stop looking over my shoulder for more clones. Only Theseus, Orpheus, and I are in attendance tonight. The rest are either too young, or in the summer palace, or recovering from surgery. Does that cover it?"

"Surgery?" I ask. "Are they all right?"

"It's a minor procedure, or so we've been assured," says Perseus. "His Imperial Majesty wanted new kidneys before the party, and it's still not advisable to go without, so two of us were tapped to donate."

I can't imagine rearranging your insides as casually as trading lunches.

"Sorry to hear that," I say after a moment, unsure how to proceed.

"If you're checking me for missing parts, everything is in place, brain to toe joints," he replies.

"You draw the long straw a lot, then. That's lucky," I say.

"Oh, I haven't been up for surgery since my coming-of-age," says Perseus. For a moment, his face hardens further, and a muscle in his jaw twitches. When he finally continues, his voice comes out bland, as if all his emotions have been sanded away. "A Councilor would be of considerably less use without a spleen."

If Perseus were a friend, I would suggest we con whoever put him in this position and split the take, but I suspect the one who put him there is Emperor Hyperion. And even if it wasn't high treason to plot against the emperor, I still don't have any reason to think Perseus would react well to the proposal. But there's something about the way his eyes narrow that tells me that he's bitter, furious even. I don't know whether to acknowledge that or let it pass.

Mercifully, the song is drawing to a close.

"I wish your brothers a speedy recovery," I say. As we part ways, Perseus gives me an odd look, his brow creasing even more. Maybe he considers the other clones to be rivals for the throne. Maybe he assumes this is so obvious as to be common knowledge. I have no idea. At any rate, I don't have time to let those thoughts marinate because he suddenly pivots to regard the grand staircase.

A stately-looking older couple is slowly descending, a man and a woman, dripping with riches and drawing murmurs from the guests all around them. They are clearly not the emperor and the empress, but they are just as clearly someone important.

"Can you believe it?" whispers a tiny, white-haired elder beside me, who is craning her neck to peek up at them. "Fates, they look even grander in person." She must be talking about their clothes specifically, because to look at their faces, they could be any person you see on the street. The man has such fair eyebrows, they nearly disappear into his face, while the woman's most prominent feature is the very thin line of her mouth, one that suggests gritted teeth. Her dress is so encrusted with jewels, she appears to be struggling to move, like a fly covered in engine oil.

"King Dorus and Queen Lena of Leithe," breathes a younger man to my right. "With the prince!"

A train of people I assume to be aristocrats and other

high-ranking officials lines up to greet them, bowing respectfully. The duchess from earlier and Ambassador Zahur are among them, I note. With what looks like laborious effort, the queen reaches out one arm to the young man following at their heels, who I hadn't even noticed at first in the wake of all that finery.

I could retire on a fourth of what the queen alone is wearing, but for once, that's not what's drawn my eye. I'm looking straight at her son, at the utter lack of family resemblance on display in the dimpled chin and bright-green eyes of the man who had introduced himself to me as Altair.

He looks up, scanning the ballroom, and for just a second our eyes connect. I remember how immediately the guardsman had stood down when ordered, the stunned gratitude of the veterans, how flustered Callidora had been upon seeing him, and only then do I put together that this was not just appreciation for a handsome man in uniform. They were showing proper respect to a member of the royal family, a man I—oh yes, that's right—called a fool, to his face.

I chance a friendly little wave. It may be a tremendous breach of etiquette, someone like me openly greeting someone like him, but given that he's the one who put me in this situation to begin with, I decide that he might as well at least say hello.

He grins. A small group of extremely stuffy-looking people, including the man whose pinky ring I liberated earlier, are beginning to swarm around him. There are benefits to being a nobody, I think. But Altair—if that is his real name—ducks out of the crowd and jogs down the staircase.

When I glance around the room, I notice Perseus is no longer next to me. He's beating a hasty retreat from the ballroom.

The Prince of Leithe is suddenly at my elbow, only slightly out of breath and still smiling widely.

"You weren't kidding about those staircases," I say. "Although I'm a little disappointed that you took the steps instead of the banister."

"It's a bit early to be giving these poor citizens a heart attack," he responds.

"As opposed to you, as the prince of an entire planet, inviting random women off the street to the most historic ball of the past fifty years," I say. "I may be the esteemed grand-niece—and between you and me, the favorite grand-niece—of my Great-Aunt Berenike, but I was not prepared for the honor. Your Majesty."

"Oh no," he says with a laugh, "please don't start with the Majesty business. I can't tell you how refreshing it was to go without it for a few minutes."

"You could've mentioned it," I point out. "Between telling me you enjoy walking and allowing me to call you a fool. You might've found the time—"

Altair holds his hands up. "Do you know how hard it is to work into casual conversation that you're in line to rule over a planet? Try for a moment. I'll be you, Iola, and you be me." He tilts his head slightly to the side. "Oh, I'm just here visiting my Great-Aunt Berenike," he says, watching me expectantly.

I consider this. "Relatives are fascinating, aren't they," I say. "For instance, my parents happen to the royal heads of a planet you might've heard of—"

He laughs again. "Masterful. What a very graceful and efficient way to alienate the first interesting person I've met since arriving on Amphor."

"So instead you invite me to a ball," I say, "where the instant you arrive, it's extremely clear who you are."

"Who my parents are," he corrects. "I am not them."

"What was your long game?" I ask.

Altair shrugs. "Not sure I had one," he says cheerfully. "I tend to go by my gut, since the alternative is trusting a series of pompous upper-crust types and ingratiating advisors, each of whom—" He lowers his voice slightly. "Well. You've been here. You've seen. Everyone here has an agenda, and much of that agenda is to keep things going exactly the way they've gone before. Which I think we can agree is no fun."

My long-held rule against complaining to the rich about the rich is at war with the temptation to vent about some of the absurd people I've met.

I settle for nodding. "Not a great time, no."

"My instinct said, 'This ball will be better if someone can shake things up a bit,'" Altair continues. "I'm not certain yet how, but I feel that extending an invite to someone from outside this world—someone who can render a Centura Magnetic Rifle useless in under ten seconds—will greatly improve this evening in one way or another."

"I hope I don't need to disarm any weapons tonight," I say. "A weapon of that caliber doesn't go with this dress at all."

"I think the main risk you face tonight is terminal boredom," says Altair with another quick grin. "But I trust you'll have that in hand." He glances down at his watch and sighs. "Unfortunately, much as I'd love to stay and chat, I have—"

"Royal duties to attend to, right," I finish. "I understand completely, Your—"

"Don't say Majesty, don't say Majesty," Altair mutters fervently.

"You're . . . forgiven for letting me think you were simply a mysterious, wealthy eccentric," I say instead. I'm not even lying. The thought of holding a grudge against someone for concealing their identity—exactly what I'm doing, except for far sketchier reasons—is laughable. "Say hello to those ingratiating advisors for me."

"I'll be sure to—"

The sound of chimes cuts through the music and the general din of one hundred people talking.

"What in the worlds," Altair murmurs, as the entire wall is suddenly eclipsed by the towering image of a glowing blue figure. In the nose and the high forehead, the face bears some relation to the clone I danced with, although it is obviously not Perseus, nor the emperor. The lips are too thin, the skin too smooth and untroubled, the eyes pale and piercing instead of dark and somber.

Mynos. The emperor's brother and possibly the next emperor himself. "Honored guests of the imperial ball," he intones, "I have some—some terrible news."

I glance around the room at the wide-eyed, upturned faces.

Mynos swallows and shakes his head, almost convulsively. "My brother, His Imperial Majesty, our beloved emperor and the guiding light of the Helian Empire, is dead."

9

A crash to my left—one of the servers has dropped a huge tray of glittering crystal goblets, which shatter against the intricately tiled floor in a glassy hailstorm. For a long moment, everyone in the room watches the shards scatter. Almost robotically, the server drops to their knees to gather the pieces, scooping the jagged glass with their bare hands until a stark splash of red is added to the picture. Nobody speaks. Nobody stops the server, until another server jogs out with a small silver device, which quickly suctions away both the glass and the blood.

A frantic murmur rises among the crowd, growing louder and louder with every passing moment.

"I have to go," Altair tells me, his mouth a grim line. I watch him swiftly maneuver through the throngs of people, ducking out of the way of elaborate headpieces and sidestepping skirts with long trains.

The floating image of Mynos raises his arms to quell the swelling chatter. A roomful of faces stare up at the massive hologram.

"Worse than that," says Mynos. "This is no medical catastrophe, no failure of organs or sudden onset of lurking illness. It is neither time nor nature that took him from us, but a person, someone with cold hatred in their heart and imperial blood still warm on their hands. Emperor Hyperion has been murdered!"

The image of Mynos blinks out, replaced by the wide angle of a surveillance feed showing a cavernous hall. In the center is a huge, shining pool of water, surrounded by ivy-covered stone columns and twinkling with tiny lights. The translucent image shudders, blurring briefly, then refocuses. A man in a military jacket dense with gold braid is lying facedown in the middle of all that illuminated water in a dark cloud of dissipating blood.

There's a collective gasp from the ballgoers.

"As you can see," Mynos continues, voice echoing through the vast ballroom, "the culprit has tampered with the station security feed, but the stab wound is unmistakable. What happened here tonight was an act of treason."

Which means there's a murderer somewhere on this station. The realization breaks over the crowd in waves. Someone screams, their shriek piercing the sudden chorus of panicked murmurs and shouted questions.

"We have every reason to believe," says Mynos, "that the party responsible for this unimaginable tragedy is affiliated with the treacherous insurgent group that calls itself the Voyria. At least one of their agents has bypassed our security systems and infiltrated the palace."

Mynos lowers his head, as if collecting himself. He's clearly waiting for the commotion to die down so he can speak. I get the sense he's enjoying the attention.

"We have entered a state of total lockdown. All outside comm feeds have been cut. The station has departed its docking port and is heading into open space. We apologize for the inconvenience, but given the unfortunate circumstances, we have no choice. Guards will be circulating to take your account. Those of you with nothing to hide have nothing to fear." He sweeps an arm out over the crowd.

"But to the murderers that have struck this terrible blow against us on this sad night, know this: the light of Helia may flicker, but it will never be extinguished. A plot of this scope suggests what we have suspected—that in their hunger to devour all that we stand for and steal what is rightfully ours, our enemies the Zarinels have decided to work with the Voyria, putting resources and power behind these unknown assassins in the hopes that we will falter and lose sight of our mission. But in our hearts, we know that our skyforce will prevail over the so-called Zarinel Federation, and the shadows of their influence will be swept away.

"Again, I speak directly to the ones who committed this foul deed, and I say, know this as well: we will find each of you. We will root out every liar, every imposter, every criminal in our midst, and you will face the full wrath of the Helian Empire!"

A scattered cheer goes up, but when I look around, I see many more ballgoers looking ill or at least shaken. I don't feel so good myself. I've only seen a few dead bodies in my life, and never ones involving that much blood.

"All members of the imperial family or a mainworld royal family, please come with me," yells a guard in the center of the ballroom, flanked by two more guards. "We have orders to take you to a secure second location." I see King Dorus and Queen

Lena all but dragging Altair in that direction, and then they're lost in the throng that surges forward, all loudly asserting some minor claim to royalty. Others swarm the guards stationed at each exit.

The guards step away from the doors, trying to herd the guests toward the center of the ballroom for questioning. Despite all the finery, it reminds me of the woman on the crate down in Ouris, when she faced the guard. There's a palpable sense that at any moment, something might break. A riot of very well-dressed people is, at the end of the day, still a riot.

Across the room, I spot Ambassador Zahur talking to Perseus with their heads bent together, looking strangely unaffected.

I need to think calmly, I remind myself over the thud of my heartbeat. I can't afford to be searched with my loot still on me, burning a hole in my pockets. Mynos had said that the security feed had been tampered with, and when I turn a slow circuit of the room, I can see that the little blue twinkling lights are no more, suggesting that for the time being, nobody in palace security has eyes on the whole station. If that's the case, then what I need to do—and fast—is find a discreet place to hide my haul and return to the ballroom in time for questioning. And if I'm very, very lucky, I might still be able to retrieve my stash once all this is over. But priority one is now survival.

I scan the room, wishing hard for a distraction, and then someone in an all-white suit backs directly into the table bearing the boiling fountain of tea, all five tiers of it. There is a tremendous crash. Every guard except the three who have departed with the royals starts toward the commotion. In the panic that follows, I extract myself and dash across the ballroom to a set of double doors opposite the ones we entered from. If anyone asks, I'm looking for the restroom. A fine lady such as myself can't be expected to hold it, after all.

The double doors yield a gleaming hallway, each surface more polished than the last, lined with more doors. I try the first one. It's locked with an eye scanner I can't hope to hack. The second door is also locked. The third is illuminated from the inside, likely meaning people are inside, meaning no good. The fourth door is much older, with a thumbprint screen I've seen many times before on salvaged ship parts. The previous user would've left enough oils from their own print that breaking in is just a matter of readjusting the pressure settings on the sensor. Using the post of a stolen earring, I manage to pry up the lid of the panel enough to cross a few wires. The door clicks open, and I replace the panel and duck inside, locking it again as I go.

The only light source is a set of glowing emergency lights around the perimeter of the floor. When my eyes finally adjust, I see that the room is lined, floor to ceiling, with shelves stuffed with books. It is not just more books than I've ever seen before. There are more books than I have ever imagined existing. If I can locate a few volumes that I'll be able to find again, I should have a place to hide my stolen bounty behind. I reach into my pockets, past the pastries and into the jewels at the bottom. The point of something sharp catches on my thumb. Carefully, I grab the object and hold it down to the light.

By the artificial glow of the floor, I can make out the shining surface of a densely engraved dagger. It's a bak dagger, one half of a pair of ceremonial knives made only in Sarn, and I know for a fact I didn't steal it.

My blood runs cold for the second time this evening. Someone has planted a knife on me. If I let my guard down long enough for that, what else have I missed? I am swallowing a sense of tremendous unease when I hear the slightest click behind me.

The handle on the door is turning.

10

There is absolutely no cover in the room, not so much as a couch to kneel behind. I grab the dagger and race to the other side of the entryway, so that the opening door will hide me. I watch the slice of light on the floor widen. The door is starting to swing shut, which will render me fully visible if this person so much as turns their head.

I feel the weight of the knife in my hand. The door closes with a *snick*. Whoever it is makes no motion to turn on the lights. I hold my breath, my eyes readjusting after the brief burst of light from the hallway. I can see the outline of a person facing away from me, and any moment now, they'll turn and see my face. I can't let that happen.

I strike, darting behind the intruder and throwing my right arm tight under the figure's chin. My opponent jerks backward, knocking me hard against a wall, but I've thrown down before on Sarn, and I know how to hold on. I can feel two gloved hands grab my arm and start to twist. The most important thing is to be frightening. If I scare this person enough, I might not have to deal any real damage.

Very lightly, I bring the knifepoint to their clavicle. I have no intention of stabbing anyone—for one thing, I don't want to deal with the mess—but my opponent doesn't need to know that.

"Walk out the door right now," I whisper.

Only then do I make out the shining fabric of the stranger's dress, still brilliant orange and red in the dim light.

My grip falters just for a second, and then the person stomps the heel of her shoe down on my foot, grabs my arm, bends at the knees, and flips me forward over her shoulder.

When I look up from the floor, Amaris is holding my dagger. She's not even winded.

"I told you to get out of here," she hisses.

Slowly, I hold up my empty hands, palms out.

"Look," I say, "you're sneaking about sending secret messages to strangers like me, which suggests to me you've got something less than savory going on, and if you kill me, I'll do everything I can to get blood on your beautiful gloves, which will raise a lot of questions for you. So in the interest of no complications, why don't we consider this a case of wrong place, wrong time and get on with our lives? You can even keep the dagger. I'm not all that attached to it."

She shakes her head. "I can't let you go."

"Why not?" Still holding up my hands, I scramble to my feet. I glance behind her. She's between me and the door, but it's not far if I put on a burst of speed. "I've already forgotten your face, and I probably never knew your real name. Ships in the night. If you'll do me the same favor, I promise I won't tell a single person about—"

"My real name is Amaris," she snaps, "and look, as much as I hate to say this, I need your help."

"My help?" I say, eyes wide. "Are you sure you've got the right person? I'm just a tourist from Yorgos, I don't—"

"Cut the act," says Amaris. "The reason I know you didn't do it is because I've been watching you all night."

"I'm flattered," I say, grinning.

Amaris rolls her eyes. "Not really. You didn't harm a soul. You didn't leave for any period of time. You just ate and danced and stole thousands of drocks' worth of jewelry from some of the galaxy's most prominent citizens."

I swallow.

"If I searched you right now," she says softly, "would your pockets be stuffed with jewels? Or did you already find a place here to stash your loot?"

"Pretty good fighting skills for a noble," I counter. "Who trained you? What, are you with the Voyria?"

"Yes," says Amaris.

"I—what?"

"Yes, I'm with the Voyria," Amaris repeats casually. It's surreal, like hearing someone admit they're a ghost. My first thought is that she's lying or deluded, a clueless rich person playing games. The Voyria have plagued the empire for more than fifteen years. They are the reason shipments are delayed sometimes. They are the main suspect anytime a high-ranking official goes missing. The Voyria are joyless extremists. They don't go around dancing at balls or wearing gorgeous dresses, or smiling like they know a wonderful secret they're about to let you in on.

My tailbone twinges. She did not flip me lightly.

The dress could be stolen, obviously. Smiles can be faked. What I'm stuck on, irrationally, is that she braided my hair. But then, I don't pretend to understand the revolutionary mindset.

"I think someone's looking for you," I tell her.

"Someone always is," she says. "But we didn't kill the emperor."

"Why are you even here, then? Don't tell me you just really love to dance."

"I was scoping out the political situation, obviously," says Amaris. "Don't you think we'd have some interest in who the next emperor might be?"

"Aren't they all the same to you?" I say. "Vile imperialist scum and all that."

Her lips tighten. "There's bad choices and worse ones, but this, *this* is bad. This is the excuse the empire has been dreaming of. They might even know we're innocent of the murder, but that doesn't matter. If the empire can pin the crime on us, they can charge anyone even suspected of supporting us." She glances at the carpet, then back at me. "Regardless of how you feel about us, that's a lot of innocent people."

The only innocent people I know live on Sarn, light-years from this mess. "What's this have to do with me?" I say.

"The only way I can see clearing the Voyria's name is solving the murder before the empire can collar some poor fool they claim is one of us," she says, and for the first time I have a moment to take in the significance of a mysterious knife showing up on my person the night the emperor dies of a stab wound.

I take a shaky breath. "That thing's not—"

"Yours?" She raises her eyebrows, eyes trailing pointedly to the knife in her gloved hand. "The handle must be covered in your fingerprints by now."

"And yet not a drop of the emperor's blood," I retort with more fire than I feel.

"Ceremonial bak knives," says Amaris levelly. "Primarily found on Sarn. Used in holy blood oaths, where the parties involved prick their fingers at the exact same time."

A shiver passes through me. She did say she was a student of history.

"You recognize it, then. Which means you know they come in sets of two," she continues. "There was another announcement while you were sneaking off. The murder weapon was found by the reflection pool. Do you want to guess what it was?"

Shit shit shit.

"I was in the ballroom the whole time," I say. I don't try to keep up the posh accent, don't round out the vowels of the fourth-condition *I* like I've been laboriously doing all night. "You saw me."

"Yes," she says, "but do you think they'll care? Do you think they'll stop there, in the attempt to frame you? It wouldn't be the first time an innocent has gone down for the empire's convenience."

"I'm not some revolutionary," I protest. "I don't believe in anything." I consider this. "Well, money." I pause. "And free snacks, I definitely believe in those."

Something in her face seems to harden. "Whoever planted the other knife on you knows where you're really from." I think of Theron flagging my face, all the people I danced with, the amount of time I spent in the thick of that crowd on the dance floor.

"They know you don't belong," Amaris continues, unfortunately echoing some of my more frantic thoughts. "Keep in mind that given how the empire's treated Sarn for the past few decades, it would be quick work to invent a rebel backstory for you."

"There are no rebels on Sarn," I tell her. "Revolution's a game for rich kids. We're too busy trying to scrape two drocks together to survive."

Amaris shrugs. "There are rebels everywhere. And, more importantly, there are rebels everywhere in the empire's imagination. It doesn't have to be true. It just needs to sound good."

I nod. Those are con artist rules. I'm back on familiar ground.

"Look, I'm not going to blackmail you," she says. "But I could use someone with your skills, and you must see it's in your best interest to work together. Don't tell me you don't believe in *that*."

I'm not sure I do. I certainly don't have any reason to trust that Amaris is who she says she is. She could just as easily be a palace spy, or a professional liar like me. But she's the one with the knife, and anyway, it's clear that I'm out of other options.

"So," I say, "all we have to do is evade capture and solve the emperor's murderer, with no resources and no leads, all while we're trapped with the real killer lurking somewhere on this very station?"

Amaris sighs. "Again, I won't force you to help me. But if you truly wish to sit idly by while someone springs a trap made just for you—"

I shake my head. "Oh no, I was saying it out loud to keep from screaming," I tell her, carefully stowing my sparkling tangle of ill-gotten gains behind a thick dark-blue book. "I'm in."

11

"If we move fast," says Amaris, all business, "we might be able to make it to the med bay in time for the autopsy."

"The what?"

Amaris removes a small glass from a pocket in her gown, quickly illuminating the flat, shiny surface. I've seen these before, but only at a distance, in the hands of tourists. They can conjure nearly any image or publically available information, if you know what you're doing.

"The medical examiners will be inspecting the corpse to verify the time of death, things like that. Details we sorely need." She gestures as if drawing out an invisible string and the default image on the glass is replaced by a schematic of the entire space station. It's way too detailed to be meant for tourists—though, clearly, neither of us are tourists.

"How did you get ahold of that? Is this standard Voyria tech?"

Amaris doesn't dignify that with an answer. "Help me find the med bay."

I squint down at the dozens and dozens of tidy little floating labels.

"This place has its own reservoir?" Thinking of a huge body of water makes me antsy. Nobody I know on Sarn knows how to swim. As much as I don't want to be ejected into deep space as a traitor to the crown, I also really don't want to drown. I glance at the map again, searching for something less horrifying. "Panic Room, do you think that's where they're keeping all the royals? A room just for panicking?" Looking closer, I see it is in fact a suite of rooms. Fates forbid our rulers should be cramped in their time of personal catastrophe.

"Focus, please," says Amaris. She trails her finger along the outline of a hallway to a small room marked MED BAY AND DIAGNOSTICS LAB in tidy little floating letters that look almost handwritten. "We need to get there from here, and we need to do it quickly and without being noticed."

"What are those?" I ask, pointing to a series of small channels running from one room to the next.

"Internal vents," she says. "For circulating replenished air throughout the station. Back to the matter at hand—"

"Could a person fit inside them?" I press.

She knits her brow, dubious. "The map's to scale. It'd be a tight fit."

"Not exactly worried about comfort right now," I say, scanning the room for an entrance point into the vents. I find one embedded in a bookshelf, about two and a half armspans from the floor, decorated to look like an engraving. "Give me a boost."

"A boost," Amaris repeats incredulously. "Am I meant to balance you on my head, or to stretch up like an octopus?"

I peer up at the grate, only a little distracted by wondering what in the Fates an octopus could be.

"Fine," I say, "shoot down my ideas without offering any of your own. If that's how the Voyria operate, no wonder you've never overthrown—what are you doing?"

Amaris has moved to the closest bookshelf, which she is carefully tapping at odd intervals.

"The decor in here is old-fashioned enough that anything but a manual ladder would clash with the style," she says. "It would've retracted into the wall when the station took off, but there should still be a way to deploy it."

"Seems awfully considerate of them to leave one in here."

"To reach the highest books," says Amaris. "Honestly, have you ever been in a library?"

"On Sarn? Yeah, but it was less floor-to-ceiling shelves and more of a . . . shack," I say.

Amaris turns to me, eyes soft. I make a face at her. She can save her pity for some other nowhere-planet lowlife.

"Hmm," she says. "I wonder how much use this room gets. Most of these books are caked in dust."

I glance around. "That's not true," I say. "This fat little gray book is pristine."

Amaris appears at my shoulder. "*Being a Full Account of Monogeneric Insectoid Creatures Found on Kantos,*" she reads. "Who's reading—"

I pull the book from the shelf. To my left, a tall, thin strip of wood emerges from where the shelf supports meet and folds sideways out into a ladder, which Amaris grabs and floats along a cunningly concealed magnetic strip to the grate. She gestures for me to climb, so I climb.

"*Gosh, Cass,*" I say as I reach the top, "*I am overcome with gratitude! I am filled with thanks! In fact, I am moved to poetry! Thank you, genius Cass, for saving my sorry a—*"

She's not listening. "Can you get the grate?"

"It's screwed on tight."

"Well, do you have any thieves' tools on you?"

"Like what," I say, "hands?"

"A lockpick disguised as a hairpin?" says Amaris hopefully. "A laser needle? Some kind of electromagnetic scrambler—"

"I'm a pickpocket, not a burglar," I snap. "Trust me, there's a difference."

"You could lecture me on the taxonomy of common thieves, or you could just say no."

I open my mouth.

"And don't you dare," she goes on, "claim you're an *un*common thief. There's nothing worse than someone who's convinced they're charming."

I close my mouth, then open it again. "Are you having an argument with your own imagination right now?"

"We need to focus," says Amaris. "We don't have much time; we should—" She glances down at the bak knife in her other hand. "Hang on a minute." She hands me the knife. "The edge of this should be flat enough."

The screws come out easily with a twist of the blade tip. I wipe the handle with my sleeve and slip the knife behind a large brown book on an upper shelf. A dagger could be useful but the thought of carrying around a murder weapon, even a fake one, unsettles my stomach.

The vent is not as wide as I'd hoped, but not as narrow as I'd feared. Peering down the length of the polished white tunnel, I can see glowing panels, likely for the maintenance crew. I place the grate to the side, since we have no hope of screwing the thing back in from the inside. When I clamber in, I can just about fit. It's a little chilly up here, with a breeze that must be the air cycling through the ship. I crawl forward and crane my neck behind me to see Amaris following, her mouth a grim line.

"Okay back there?" I whisper.

"I'm fine," she snaps.

She doesn't sound fine, but that's her problem. I creep forward until we come to a point where the vent branches out in opposite directions.

Behind me, I hear Amaris stop crawling, then a rustle. She must be checking the map. I'm pretty sure I remember the way, but I have a feeling if I open my mouth, we'll just start arguing. I take the left branch.

A brief pause, and then I hear the swish of Amaris's dress as she follows me.

Slowly, as silently as we can manage, we make our way down the length of the vent, from one glowing service panel to the next. I get the sense the vents were designed for engineers to pop into and out of, not for spies to crawl throughout the station wearing fancy evening gowns. It's not comfortable, but neither is hiding inside the exhaust vent of a ship to get away from a mark who didn't see the humor in Bad Mook, Good Mook, and I've done that more than once, and with Jax, who has the boniest knees and elbows this side of a skeleton.

Behind me, Amaris is clearly doing worse. As we creep along,

I can hear her breathing growing louder and more ragged. She's clearly trying to keep it under control, and for a few breaths she does just that, but then she gives kind of a gasp and is right back to struggling to take in air.

"Sure you're all right?" I whisper.

"Yes," she hisses back.

"Because it sounds like you're about to pass out."

"I won't," Amaris manages. A shaky exhale. "The truth is, I've never enjoyed small spaces."

I'm so surprised by her admission, I almost stop crawling. We've reached a place in the vent wall where a series of slits allow for airflow. From the other side, I can hear brisk voices and the buzz of comm lines. Security personnel, I think. Talking here would be disastrous, so I say nothing as we keep moving forward.

Once we're safely out of earshot, I whisper, "Maybe stop focusing on where we are?"

"What else am I supposed to focus on?"

We pass another series of slits, careful to move as quietly as possible.

"What's an octopus?" I whisper when we're in the dark once again.

"Be serious," she whispers.

"I *am* serious," I reply, "and I have never heard of a rotting octopus before."

"This can't possibly be what you're thinking about right now," says Amaris.

"No," I say, "what I'm thinking is that my partner-in-crime is about to faint, which means not only will you be useless to me, you'll also block the way back and I'll be stuck here for the rest of my short life. Think. Of. Something. Else."

"I'm dealing with it." I can almost hear Amaris setting her jaw.

"Very badly," I say. "I can feel the misery wafting off of you. It's starting to make me sick. Come on. Anything else. Think of how good I look in this dress." I wiggle my backside a little.

She huffs out a strained laugh. I decide to take the victory and move on.

"Cat or worm?" I whisper.

"What?"

"From context, the octopus is a thing that stretches. Does it stretch like a cat or worm?"

"Neither," she says. "More like a diltav. Do you have those on Sarn?"

"Never heard of it."

"Imagine eight worms, joined at a central fleshy knob like spokes on a wheel, and the resulting creature can move in any direction."

"*Why?*" I whisper.

"That's for the Fates alone to know," she whispers back. "Don't worry, you won't see one tonight. They live deep underwater."

"Ugh," I say. These octopus creatures are just getting better and better. On the bright side, we've come to a join in the vents that is slightly larger, enough that I can pull myself to my knees for a moment. If I remember the map correctly, that means we're finally coming up on the med bay. Behind me, Amaris pauses to pull up the map again. I open my mouth to make a comment about her love of maps but think better of it.

"—much longer is it going to take?" someone is saying from

far away. The voice is familiar to me, I realize a second later, because I've heard it reverberating through the ballroom. Mynos.

"I'm happy to liaise with one of your aides if you have somewhere better to be," someone else replies, in a calm tone. Another familiar voice: Ambassador Zahur.

Up ahead, I spot the slightest slice of light, and I crawl toward its source, a series of small slats in the vent wall. After a second or two of inner debate, I decide it's worth the risk to take a quick look. The slight echo tells me we're high up, likely far from their line of sight. When I cautiously peer through the grate, the room below is so shiny and brightly lit that my eyes water.

Amaris inches close to me to look through the grate, too. She crouches with uncommon stillness, as though she spies on royalty all the time. And maybe she does—she's Voyria after all. In the chill air of the vent, I can feel the heat of her body beside me, and her hair has the faintest whiff of ginger and vanilla. I don't know why I notice. Maybe I'm still hungry.

There are five people in the med bay. Mynos, who's pacing back and forth. Two aides in Helian colors. And Ambassador Zahur, with a single aide to their right busily taking notes with sharp gestures over a hovering screen.

And in the center of it all is the body of the late emperor, laid out naked on a metal table and looking almost rubbery in the extravagant light. A jagged stab wound zigzags across his neck and down to the clavicle on one side. His face is set in a horrible grimace and his hair is still damp from the reflection pool.

"My staff of imperial doctors have scanned and examined the emperor to my satisfaction," Mynos snaps. "I am the acting head and heart of the empire at the moment, and I'm telling you that your medical examiner isn't required."

"And as I've told you, this must be a joint investigation, if the legitimacy of your throne is to remain intact," says Ambassador Zahur. "This in your people's best interest, as well as mine."

"I don't know what your game is, but you're testing my patience, Ambassador—" Mynos breaks off as the door to the med bay slides open with a chime. A figure in a lab coat steps through, pausing briefly as a strip of red light pulses in the doorway. This newcomer is slight, but with impeccable posture and a neat gray beard. Everything about this person radiates competence and confidence.

Amaris whispers in my ear, "The light's for disinfection." I nod, trying my best to ignore the way her breath stirs my hair.

"Doctor Galen," Ambassador Zahur says, inclining their head.

"Ambassador," says Doctor Galen. A med bot glides over with a tray of tools. The doctor produces a compact black bar and plugs it into the med bot before turning to Mynos. "Apologies for the delay. Your guards were incredibly unhelpful."

"Do you understand that your discretion is of the highest priority?" Mynos snaps.

"I understand," Doctor Galen says. I'm so focused on trying to register the words through the lilting accent—completely unlike Ambassador Zahur's—and trying not to pay attention to how close Amaris is sitting, that I almost miss the fourth-condition *I*, the one for women. "Now let's take a look at the deceased, shall we? Our first step is to verify the identity."

"Fates," Mynos says, lip curling. "This is my elder brother, Emperor Hyperion Castellanos, second of his name, seventh in our genetic chain, and the shining light of the Helian Empire. Good enough for you? Do you need a DNA analysis, too?"

"Your medical staff already provided one," says Doctor Galen, "and as is widely known, clones are not uncommon in the Helian palace, so DNA doesn't carry much weight. I'd prefer to have the late emperor's wife ID the corpse, if possible."

"She's too distraught to leave her rooms," Mynos says quickly.

"Very well," says Doctor Galen. "Let's assume this is the late emperor. Now one thing I found odd was the blood in the water. Had his throat been cut while he was alive, the arterial spray would have been tremendous. There simply wasn't enough blood in the pool to support a knife wound as his cause of death."

"What are you saying?" demands Mynos. "Are you trying to imply that Hyperion was killed and then stabbed after the fact? Ambassador, this is absurd."

"This whole night has been, as you say, absurd," says the ambassador. Again, that curiously remote tone I heard when we danced, as if they were discussing the weather and not an unsolved murder. A shiver runs down my spine.

"I'm just telling you what I've observed," replies Doctor Galen, stroking her beard. She produces a case of small silver objects, which she removes one by one and passes over the body. The second-to-last item emits a series of beeps, and she studies it for a moment, turning to check the readings on the med bot's screen. "Interesting."

"What?" Mynos says.

"He tests positive for CNNP," says the doctor, "a strain of neurodegenerative nanotech pathogens that was banned by agreement between the Zarinel Federation and the Helian Empire before talks collapsed two years ago. Only a very well-connected person would have access to this."

"Or a criminal," puts in Mynos. "Any piece of filth could have procured this on the black market."

"I doubt it," says Ambassador Zahur. "If CNNP is truly out of circulation in the Helian Empire, then there wouldn't be any for the black market to trade. Unless you mean to say that CNNP is still being manufactured in your system. That would be a major violation of the Klethykas Accords." Their voice takes on the slightest note of menace.

Mynos must notice because all he does is snort and gesture for the doctor to continue.

The doctor passes one of her tools over the body again. "I'm not getting a reading on a possible injection site. Aside from the recent kidney surgery your staff mentioned, I'm not getting any alerts."

"Because there isn't an injection site," Mynos says.

"You may be right. But perhaps an orifice on the face . . ." Doctor Galen taps her tool and it flashes blue. She passes it over the corpse's head again. "Of course. The ear canal," she says.

"The *ear*?" I hiss to Amaris. In the dim light of the vent, she presses a finger to my lips.

Not now, she mouths back.

"Poison through the ear," muses Ambassador Zahur. "That's a new one. But why go to so much trouble to conceal the injection site?"

"The time of death might answer that," says the doctor. "Based on the extent of the nanobot infiltration throughout the body, the infection must have occurred about an hour and a half ago."

"That doesn't prove anything," Mynos says. "The guards have verified that the Asipis system started malfunctioning hours ago. My brother was murdered then. He was stabbed in the neck by the pool, and that is all there is to it."

"Unlikely. Once infected, the late emperor would have lost control of his nervous system almost immediately. He would have been unable to walk on his own. What's strange is that if you check the body scan, you'll notice microscopic hairs from a hand-woven caulwood tapestry rug under his toenails, indicating he was dragged across it."

"The palace has many rugs," says Mynos. "Your collective keeps giving them to us."

Ambassador Zahur clears their throat. "There is only one such caulwood rug on this station. I remember when our delegation presented it to the emperor."

"Where are you going with this?" Mynos says, almost growling now.

"The rug was placed in His Imperial Majesty's private chambers," says Ambassador Zahur.

I nudge Amaris with my shoulder, but she doesn't respond. She's staring intently at the scene below. This doesn't seem like much of a revelation to me, especially compared with the proof that Hyperion wasn't killed with a bak dagger. But Doctor Galen shakes her head.

"Well, shit," she says.

"Yes," says Ambassador Zahur. "Quite."

"So this means," Mynos starts, then scowls. "What does this mean? Why is this necessary?"

"It means that your brother was killed in his private chambers, via an injection of a banned nanotech pathogen," Ambassador Zahur says. They shrug. "Not an auspicious start to the next Helian era."

"The imperial medical examiners will have to verify this," says Mynos. "I know the Khonsanians like to style themselves as a neutral party, but it's clear where your true loyalties lie."

"Right now my loyalties lie with a strong cup of tea," says the ambassador. "If you'll excuse us. Doctor Galen will meet with your medical staff shortly."

"Fine, go," says Mynos, flicking his hand at them. The ambassador, their aide, and the doctor file out of the med bay.

Mynos turns to his aides, who come forward and bow. "Tell the head physician to report to me after they meet with the Khonsanian doctor. I'm going to check on the empress. Have the kitchens prepare something for her to eat."

"Yes, Emperor," the aides say in unison. The med bay empties and the emperor's corpse is left alone in the room beneath the cold glare of the overhead lights.

I'm about to suggest to Amaris that we head back to the library when I hear Ambassador Zahur speak again. Their voice is coming from another grate farther down the vent. We stealthily crawl over and see Ambassador Zahur leaning against the wall in another medical suite, this one thankfully corpse-free. They let out a long sigh.

Then they tap the side of their jaw and say, "Memo to base." Ambassador Zahur massages the back of their neck. "I continue acting on prior orders," they say in a low voice. "Although the Helians make it difficult.

"There is no delicate way to put this." They close their eyes for a moment before continuing. "The emperor was killed in his chambers, behind a door recently fitted with a new generation of bio-lock. You can easily imagine the implications, so I won't belabor the point. We will be treading carefully here. It's unclear who, if anyone, our delegation can trust."

They pinch their nose. "I hardly need to say that the conflict between the Helians and the federation has escalated since the last round of talks failed. They insist on answering the Kore question with increasing amounts of bloodshed. But if this latest development destabilizes the Helian governing body, the Zarinel Federation may take the chance to strike. An all-out war between the two giants may pull Khonsania into Helia's and the federation's orbit and consume us. Our delegation will proceed with the objective to ensure a smooth transition of power, regardless of which party involved did the deed."

Another long exhale, followed by a dry laugh. "Shit indeed," they murmur. Then they tap their jaw again, straighten up, and smooth their tense features into a look of polite distance.

Back in the library, Amaris makes a circuit around the room, clearly deep in thought.

"Can you retrieve the screws for the grate?" I ask. "You've got gloves."

Amaris startles. She looks at the grate like she's never seen it before.

"What?" I ask. "Please don't say, 'Oh, Cass, we need to work with that nice Khonsanian official,' because I highly doubt they'll want to join hands with a thief and a rebel."

"Obviously we don't work with Ambassador Zahur," says Amaris. "As you noted, we're not ideal allies for an ambassador. Not to mention, having to work through the official channels will slow them considerably. We don't have time for that. And clearly, they're looking out for Khonsanian interests, which aren't necessarily ours."

"And what about Voyrian interests?" I say, half teasing.

Amaris ignores me and continues, "But even if we don't work with the ambassador, we may be able to use what turns up in their investigation. I'm still not certain what to make of that bio-lock. On the one hand, it nicely narrows the number of suspects, but the implications—" She shakes her head.

"Hang on, how does the lock narrow our suspect list? This is news to me."

"The emperor's personal quarters are the most protected place in the entire station," she explains. "Are you familiar with what a bio-lock is?"

"Assume no."

"It's a lock programmed to your DNA. The trouble is, it's not that hard to get a sample of someone's DNA, even without them knowing. We leave traces of us everywhere. But the newest generation of bio-lock solves that major flaw. It takes a full body scan to get in, so a sample of blood or spit won't be able to bypass it. As far as we know, it's unhackable."

"And the emperor has this new type of lock."

"Correct," says Amaris. "The bio-lock should be coded to respond to Hyperion's DNA sequence and his wife's. Only a member of the Helian imperial family can enter the emperor's private chambers. And that's where he died."

"So . . ." I remember the pained twist of Emperor Hyperion's lips, almost grotesque in their stillness. "That means—"

She nods. "Hyperion was killed by a member of the royal family."

12

I take a deep, shaky breath. This might explain Emperor Hyperion's awful grimace: he was betrayed by his own flesh and blood. I can't begin to fathom my family—Dad, Jax, Pav, the whole crew—selling me out, much less murdering me. Then again, maybe Emperor Hyperion's face just looked that way.

"So," I say, "someone from the Helian royal family wants to pin a murder on me, a random kid from a minor moon who didn't even know what the emperor looked like before today." I laugh a touch wildly and attempt to run my hands through my hair. They meet immediate resistance—my braids remain in place, still mostly pristine after everything that's happened.

"Welcome to Ouris," says Amaris dryly. "The ambassador was right. This is a political conspiracy with intergalactic ramifications. This isn't even just the Voyria's safety on the line. If someone doesn't solve this soon, the Zarinel Federation moves in and the resulting war swallows up the whole galaxy. We need to start investigating the family, and we need to start now."

She pulls her glass from her dress pocket and waves a hand over the flat, translucent surface. It goes opaque, quickly populating with messages, feeds, and, inexplicably, an image of a small dog with huge floppy ears.

"I thought all comms were cut," I point out. "Nothing in or out."

"Right, but the intracomms within the palace are still up. They have to be to keep the station running," she says distractedly. The glow from the glass illuminates her face in the dim library as she makes quick gestures, pulling up a new series of message chains. "I've got a source in station security. I'll check on the status of the surveillance feed. Once it's back up—"

"We're dead," I finish.

"I was going to say severely compromised in our ability to freely move about the station," Amaris says. "It sounds like we're good now, but we need to work fast and be strategic. So we know that a Helian imperial is responsible for Hyperion's death. Who do we look into first, and how?"

I think of running Good Mook, Bad Mook with Jax back on Sarn. "Whoever the murderer is, they must've had help. Killing the emperor isn't a one-person job."

"Agreed," Amaris says. She smiles at me, and I feel like I've just won a prize at a festival. "So we start with what we know and work from there. Who planted the knife on you?"

"Anyone I danced with could've done it," I say. "Hate to say it, but with my mind focused on the take, I might've given them a window."

Amaris pulls up a blank sheet on her glass. "Make a list of all your dance partners."

I bite my lip, thinking. "There was the woman with the spider silk dress, I told you about her. A stuck-up guy around our age. A blue-haired woman who didn't seem to be paying much attention to anything. A stuffy man in dark green with this huge mustache—"

"Who, Iraklidis?" she says. "About this tall, wearing a ring with a purple stone?"

I cough. "Well, not anymore."

"Okay," says Amaris, shaking her head. "So you stole from Councilor Iraklidis. Good to know."

"What, is this guy important?"

"He's a ranking member of the Council, the second-highest governing body in the empire, so yes."

"Nice." I grin at Amaris, who rolls her eyes. "So does he go on the top of our suspect list?"

"Well, I can't think of a reason someone like Iraklidis would want the emperor dead," she says.

"Why not? He seems as likely as anyone else."

"I don't think so. Recent politics plays a crucial role here," says Amaris. She straightens up, and it's clear she's going into lecture mode. "The Council started out as a group of high-level advisors who served as a guiding light to the emperor. What people don't know is that the Council is also a counterbalance to the crown. If they rule unanimously, they can overturn an imperial order, no matter what that order may be."

I let out a whistle. "Some counterbalance. Why haven't I heard of this?"

"Well, normally the Councilors are supposed to elect their own successors, but Hyperion found a loophole that lets the emperor appoint a replacement if a Councilor is found to be unfit. So he had all his most vocal opponents swapped out for sycophants who wouldn't dare cross him. Iraklidis is one of those Councilors. He owes all his wealth and power to the Helian crown and has proven his loyalty countless times. Iraklidis is a dead end."

"I danced with Ambassador Zahur, too," I tell Amaris. "But we heard their transmission in the med bay. They're not in on it. Probably."

"Highly unlikely. The Khonsanians stand to lose as much as the rest of us if the Helian Empire descends into chaos. The problem with war, among many other things, is that you can't isolate its effects. It's felt everywhere," says Amaris grimly. "Can you think of anyone else you danced with?"

Mentally, I go over my list. "Hang on," I say. "What about Perseus? I danced with him, he's on that council, and he's literally a clone of the emperor, right? He'd even have access through the bio-lock."

"Remember my source in security?" says Amaris. "Their job was specifically to watch Perseus. He's in the clear."

Someone clever enough to pull off a high-stakes murder on a royal station is likely clever enough to evade surveillance, but there's no point in arguing with Amaris right now. We'll just have to go down the list, and when she's ready to admit I'm right, I'll bask in sweet, sweet victory.

"You know what," I say slowly, "maybe we should look at this from the other side. Almost everyone I danced with said Mynos was the favorite for the next in line. And sure enough, he's emperor, at least for now. Let's start with him."

"The highest-ranking royals—" Amaris starts.

"—are all sequestered," I interrupt. "I know, I heard. But if you bring up your map again, we can figure out how to get to them and do a spot of spying."

Amaris is already pulling up the palace schematic. "The vents are here," she says, pointing, "and here. But that's near the entrance, where the guards will be. We can't risk being discovered."

"Well, do you have a better idea?" I say, crossing my arms.

"I do, in fact," Amaris says. "An imperial ball is one of the few places where we can easily mingle with people who know the royal family personally. We need information and we need leads. Gossip can get us both of those things." She smiles grimly. "Time to go back to the party."

"Hey, cheer up," I tell her. "If the bio-lock proves an imperial was involved, that's gotta clear everyone from your little club, right? Nobody would suggest your people are in league with Hyperion's family. At least, not with a straight face."

Amaris shakes her head. "The Voyria are known for their hacking. Anyone setting you up as a member could claim that you hacked the bio-lock. My people, as you call them, are far from safe."

"The lock you just told me was unhackable," I remind her, but Amaris isn't listening. She's staring into the middle distance, picking at a thread on her dress. "Hello? You still there?"

Amaris starts, but says nothing, eyes still focused somewhere else. I'm starting to get jealous of the middle distance.

"Don't you want to—I don't know, lecture me on the importance of revolution, or remind me not to try to steal anything?" I say.

"You'd be amazed how little I care about these people or their ill-gotten wealth," says Amaris, snapping back to reality. "But obviously don't go around *pickpocketing during our murder investigation*—what's wrong with you?"

"It was a joke," I retort. "Now come on. We've got lots of mingling to do."

When it's safe, we exit into the hallway, then slip back through the doors to the ballroom. I can see Ligeia's emerald spider-silk dress from across the room. Given her personality, she seems like a good place to start.

"Lady Ligeia?" I say, tapping her on the shoulder.

Ligeia whirls around. "Oh, it's you," she says. "Iola something or other, right?"

"Galatas," I say, inclining my head. "How are you holding up? This whole affair is simply ghastly." I can feel Amaris giving me a look. Maybe I'm laying on the posh-society-lady act a little too heavy, but Ligeia seems to be buying it.

"Absolutely devasting," Ligeia agrees. "Why, my Gennadios nearly started weeping at the news! I only wish they hadn't blocked the comm lines. I can't get through to my friends at all."

"It's for our safety, dear," Gennadios says, patting her arm. "The imperial guard is handling this nasty, nasty business." He turns to me. "Have you been questioned yet? Our questioning was quick. I told them, I said, 'Let me know if there's anything I can do to help.'" He taps the side of his nose. "Had a few misadventures in my youth, and let's just say I know how to handle myself." He executes a gesture that may be an attempt at a sword thrust, or maybe just shaking out a cramp.

"Yes, well, I'd still like to contact the Nicolis and the Gatakis. They must be worried sick. Don't you think the palace should make a few exceptions?" Ligeia sniffs. "I'm certainly no member of the Voyria. And the way the guards have us packed together in this ballroom—" Ligeia looks between me and Amaris. "Iola, I didn't see you earlier, or your lovely companion. Did you manage to sneak out?"

I feel Amaris stiffen beside me. For all her talk of not getting distracted, she's the one acting like she's never run a con before.

"We did steal away, just for a moment. We had to get some air," I say, fanning my face. "We were both feeling faint after seeing the emperor's body." The excuse sounds thin to my ears, but the rules never apply to the rich. I'm sure we're not the only ones who managed to give the guards the slip.

"How funny," Ligeia says, eyes narrowing. I hold my breath, but then she gushes, "I just adore how couples get in sync like that."

"Oh, absolutely," I say, taking Amaris's elbow. "Everyone says we're quite the matching set." I make eyes at Amaris, who manages a tentative smile. "You should've seen us giving our marriage declarations," I tell Ligeia. "It's as if our hearts became one and the same in that moment."

"Oh, I love declarations!" Ligeia claps her hands together. "Where was yours listed? Which feeds?"

I'm adrift now. I don't know a thing about wedding feeds. Sarn has only the one primary feed and the short-wave. It's too small for anything more. I glance at Amaris again, but she volunteers nothing. If I didn't know better, I'd think she was struggling not to laugh.

"It was, um . . ." I cast about for something to say, but Ligeia interrupts.

"An unlisted wedding! Did one of your families disapprove of the match?" she guesses eagerly, pulled in like a pressor beam toward potential scandal.

The more people there are talking about us, the more people there will be to poke holes in our stories. Best to seem as boring as possible, I decide as I take Amaris's hand in mine and beam back at Ligeia.

"No, our families were delighted. But we just couldn't wait any longer, so we dispensed with all that," I say. "You know how it is." To sell the lie, I bring up our linked hands and brush a kiss across Amaris's knuckles. At that, Amaris manages a very convincing blush, and my brain briefly short-circuits at the sight.

Luckily, Ligeia rushes in to fill the gap. "What were we discussing? Couples being attuned to each other? Gennadios and I can look at each other and just *know* what the other is thinking," Ligeia says. "The other day, we were talking to Bakchos—have you met Bakchos yet? You simply must! He knows *everyone*—and I thought to myself, 'We should ask him to put in a good word for us with His Imperial Grace,' and then, like magic, Gennadios says, 'And do tell His Imperial Highness that we continue to serve him faithfully in all we do.'"

"The empire is lucky to have you," says Amaris, finally pulling her weight. "Especially after such a tragedy. We were just talking about that awful footage, how horrible it all was."

"You know," Ligeia goes on, "I had a premonition this might happen. As I was getting ready to go, I had just the worst feeling in my temples. It reminds me of when Empress Thea lost her baby all those years ago. Stillborn, the poor thing. Quite a shock for everyone, in this day and age, and in the heart of the empire, of all places. And I knew—I *knew*, tell them, Gennadios!—that something terrible had happened before I'd even looked at the feed."

"She did say so," says Gennadios dutifully.

"Still, we soldier on," says Ligeia. "And speaking of which—"

"So, this Bakchos character that you mentioned we should meet . . ." I interject. A bit too blunt, but Ligeia is already nodding in the direction of a man in a lemon-yellow suit at the very far side of the ballroom.

"He is the head of the media—the legitimate media, I mean. Impossibly well-connected."

Gennadios starts in on a long and rambling story, which seems mostly designed to highlight just how close he is with this Bakchos, who must be a big deal to merit this level of name-dropping.

After trying and failing to get a word in three times, Amaris and I offer our goodbyes and cross the room.

"Guess we're married now," I say, just to needle her.

Amaris, to my surprise, squeezes my hand. "So it seems. Nice work back there."

"Say that again?" I can't help it. I want to rub it in, after Amaris doubted me earlier, but she takes me seriously.

"You did well," Amaris says. "I didn't expect your acquaintance to notice we'd left the ballroom, and I panicked. And then you started saying all those absurd things . . ."

"What, like that we're united in our hearts and our souls are bonded for all eternity?" I tease.

"You're lucky those two were so gullible," Amaris says.

"Give me some credit. It wasn't luck," I say. "My dad says that whenever skyforce enforcers tried to search my mom's ship, half the time they'd hand her the lie she needed. People believe what they want to believe. You just have to figure out what they want, and I'm damn good at that." Amaris nods, and before she can ask, I explain, "My dad wouldn't tell me, but I think my mom was smuggling on the side. A lot of haulers do."

"I imagine," says Amaris. "Helian tariffs make life impossible outside the mainworlds. The farther you go from the center of the empire, the worse the conditions are."

"Yeah," I say. "So you do realize that we have to pretend to be happily married and passionately in love for the rest of the night."

"The thought occurred to me, but I believe we can manage," Amaris says.

"I can if you can, cuddle muffin."

Amaris shoots me a glare that could melt steel. "Absolutely do not call me cuddle muffin."

"Fine. But we need some kind of nickname if we're going to sell this. What were those pointy little pastries on the silver trays?"

"Cream horns?" says Amaris. Pure dismay washes over her face. "Oh no, under no circumstances—"

"It's that or something even worse, no doubt," I say, my tone dead serious. "Take your pick, my darling cream horn."

Amaris lets out a sharp exhale, her mouth quirking briefly. I almost break my stride but manage to keep going.

"Was that a laugh?" I ask.

"Of course not," Amaris says. She nods at Bakchos in the crowd, unmistakable in his yellow outfit. "So how do you want to play this?"

"My plan was to act very stupid, say a lot of obviously wrong things, and wait for him to jump in and explain why I'm wrong."

"You're betting a lot on arrogance," she says.

I shrug. "People *love* correcting others."

"That's true," Amaris says, "but we need a more focused approach here."

"Well, what do you propose? A history lecture? A treatise on politics?"

Amaris slips her hand out of mine and rolls her shoulders, like she's about to walk into a prize fight. "Follow my lead" is all she says.

Bakchos is deep in conversation when we sidle up to him, holding court at the edge of the ballroom. Over his shoulder is an enormous window displaying nothing but darkness and distant pinpricks of light. It's disorienting, a glimpse of the yawning maw of space right there in the middle of a fancy party. Forcing my attention back to the matter at hand, I can see Bakchos is surrounded by hangers-on, each in a more outrageous getup than the last. One woman's skirt ends in a translucent bubble filled with water in which real fish appear to be swimming back and forth.

"My sources in station security tell me that we'll be headed back to Ouris in an hour," Bakchos is saying. "Now I'm taking bets: who thinks the Zarinels put the Voyrians up to this?"

"I do," says Amaris loudly. "Voyrian scum will take money from anyone."

"We have our first bid!" Bakchos motions with his hand for some of his entourage to part and make room for us.

Someone in a gauzy floral suit says, "I'll bet a hundred drocks the Voyrians aren't even real. They're a Zarinel conspiracy.

Completely made up."

"How do we know they aren't a Khonsanian cell?" Fish Skirt puts in. Soon, everyone is arguing over what exactly the Voyria is and who they're backed by. Only Bakchos stays silent, watching the people around him with a little smirk on his face, his nose ring glinting as he turns this way and that.

Amaris looks right at Bakchos and says, "My money's still on the Zarinels."

"That they're working with the Voyria, or that they invented the Voyria?" says Bakchos, raising an eyebrow.

"The former. The Voyria are very real," says Amaris. "Or so my sources tell me."

"I wonder if our sources are the same," says Bakchos. "And who exactly are you?"

"Dalia Galatas," she replies, reaching out her hand. He takes it and kisses the tips of her fingers. "And this is my wife—"

"Iola Galatas," I say. I don't feel like having his slimy lips on my hand, so I do a quick bow.

"All right, Galatas, what do you want from me?" Bakchos says. "And don't play coy, everyone wants something from me."

"I wouldn't dream of playing coy," Amaris says primly. "I just have a favor to ask. You see, I report to a certain illustrious friend, a patron with a shocking appetite for rumor, whose pieces feed out to only the most exclusive circles."

"You mean—"

Amaris gives a slight shake of her head. "I can't say."

"Ah," says Bakchos. He winks at Amaris. "I'm familiar. So what can I do for you?"

"I'd like to speak with someone close to Mynos, who might be willing to share some insights on our emperor regent. He hasn't played an active role in politics before, after all. Interested parties want to know how he will govern." Amaris lowers her voice. "And, of course, whether he has any skeletons in the closet that we should know about."

"All due respect to your patron but I can't refer you," Bakchos says, waving a hand. "Mynos is off-limits."

I take a careful look at him and his perfectly tailored clothes. The Agata watch peeking out from beneath his sleeve is fake—I know that much from working with Jax—and I suspect his cuff links are too. His shoes are clean, not a speck of dust on them, and clearly new. They look too new, in fact, like they came mass-fabbed from Danae. I'm pretty sure Babbit wears a knock-off of this knock-off when he goes to work.

"Of course Dalia's patron and all their clients would love to hear of your money troubles," I tell him, and his eyes go wide. "Is it gambling or poor investments, would you say?"

"Clever," he says with a forced laugh. "It's a good guess, I'll give you that. Does it work on other people?"

"It works because it's true," I counter.

"Tracking down the finances of someone like you would be quick work," says Amaris. She slips out her glass. "Just a few well-placed questions . . ."

Bakchos glances at his friends, then back at us. "No need for that. Let's talk over there."

He leads us to a shimmering fountain in the center of a holo array depicting a spread of lush greenery. The sounds of the crowd fall away, dampened by the roar of water. The void of space is blessedly not in our line of sight anymore.

"Zona Fotos," he says, turning to us. "The tall woman in the silver dress talking to those guards over there. She was Mynos's head of communications, long, long ago."

"And she'll speak to us?" says Amaris.

"Zona'll speak to you if she knows I sent you," says Bakchos. "She wasn't too happy about being cut off. I've always suspected that she came too close to some secret or other and was let go as a result."

"I see," says Amaris. "That's good to know. We appreciate your help."

"You won't tell your patron about—" Bakchos glances around.

"About?" Amaris says, her voice dropping a note. It's ever so slightly menacing.

"The thing is, the markets are so volatile right now, with the war on Kore. They haven't taken such a plunge since the intergalactic summit on Leithe. But I hear things are supposed to get better soon."

"Perhaps," says Amaris. She offers her arm to me, and I take it. "Well, thanks again for your time."

"And good luck with your finances," I say.

Once we are safely out of earshot, I turn to Amaris. "All right," I say, "that wasn't half bad. You've conned before."

She shrugs. "I came up with a plan, and I executed on it."

"Pretending to be a jumped-up gossipmonger is quite the plan," I say.

"The best lies contain a trace of truth." Amaris lowers her voice slightly. I have to lean in close to hear. "The Voyria know the power of a good story better than anyone. We have our own gossip feeds—"

"The illegitimate media?" I say. "Fascinating."

"You're mocking me," says Amaris.

"Actually, no. It's interesting." I'm not even lying. "What happens when some poor gripe is unfortunate enough to run afoul of those feeds?"

Amaris smiles ever so slightly, showing just a flash of teeth.

"Remind me not to get on your bad side," I say.

We find Zona clutching an empty glass and deep in conversation with a familiar dark-haired man. As we approach, I take a glass of brandy off a server's tray.

"Sorry," Zona is saying, "you're looking for—"

"Perseus," says—well, not Perseus, apparently. "I'm Theseus."

"Ah, right," says Zona. "You're the handsome one."

"And the charming one," Theseus adds with a wink. The bags under his eyes are less severe, I realize, and the lines on his face haven't had time to settle in. He must be younger than his brother, or at least less stressed.

"He's been missing for the last half hour," says Theseus. "Councilor Teresi is hoping to meet with him, and I can't get him to tap into our feed." He indicates a white-haired woman standing impatiently to the side. Her suit matches her glowing holo eyes: gray-blue.

"Have you checked his rooms?" I say, joining them. "Maybe he's feeling ill."

"Oh, clone health is carefully monitored," Theseus says. "All of us receive the highest quality of care at all times."

Right, they watch your vitals around the clock in case Hyperion wants your liver, I think. It's not a bad motive for murder. For Theseus or any of the clones, really. I try to catch Amaris's eye, but she's turned to Theseus.

"Have you talked with Councilor Iraklidis? I know he had some business with Perseus tonight."

"Perhaps," says Theseus, looking between us. "I shall go investigate and bid you all farewell." He bows and heads off.

I hold out the goblet I swiped from the server just now. "Have you tried the apple ambrosia yet? It really is divine. Straight from the orchards of Gree."

Zona takes the brandy, eyeing us over the rim. "If you're fortune hunters looking to worm into Mynos's good graces now that he's emperor regent, you're talking to the wrong person," she says.

"Oh, no," says Amaris, glancing quickly at me. "I'm Dalia and this is Iola. My wife. We just wanted to extend our sympathies to a personal friend of the crown."

Zona knocks back a mouthful of brandy. "That's kind of you, but I really can't claim to be a personal friend. Not after the way I've been treated. A personal servant, more like."

"There's a story there, I assume?" I say.

"Mynos and I went to school together, we summered together on Tyche, and when he asked me to head up his communications office, I said yes. But ever since Emperor Hyperion announced he was choosing his successor, nothing. Not a call, not a message, not even a ping on my feed." Zona takes another long sip of brandy.

"So unfortunate," says Amaris sympathetically. "You would think an imperial would know to stand with his staunchest allies."

"And yet," says Zona wryly, raising her eyebrows, "this is so utterly like Mynos, retreating when he's needed most. It's scandalous, is what it is. Of course, not the biggest scandal to involve Mynos, that's for sure."

"Oh, Fates. What scandal could the emperor's brother possibly be involved in?" I ask, going for breathless intrigue.

"You don't *know*?" The perfectly plucked eyebrows are climbing even higher up her high forehead, like airships cut free from their tethers.

"We've heard whispers, of course," Amaris chimes in, "but you know how people talk. We'd rather get the word right from the source."

"Well, it's common knowledge that Mynos never married. They say he never got over the loss of his childhood sweetheart, stolen from right under his nose. Very sweet, very humanizing, a lovely story. The public ate it up in interviews. What doesn't get mentioned is the name of this childhood sweetheart."

Zona finishes her goblet in one swallow. "Because the woman he's held out for over all these years is Empress Thea. His own brother's wife."

13

Well, I didn't see that coming.

"That *is* outrageous," I say. "His own sister-in-law?"

Zona covers her mouth and lets out a dainty burp. "You of course didn't hear it from me."

"Of course," says Amaris.

"This is all unconfirmed," says Zona in hushed tones. "I want to be clear about that. But there's always been tension between the brothers, and I know from Thea's old personal aide—this would've been two personal aides ago—that Thea and Mynos take a lot of, shall we say, private meetings together."

"So the emperor and his brother were at odds?" Amaris asks.

"I've never personally witnessed any direct confrontations," Zona says, frowning slightly at her empty goblet. I retrieve a fresh one off the tray of a server who is circulating the room and hand it to her. "It was more of a general sense of bad blood between them. They didn't like to be in the same room together, that sort of thing. I suspect Mynos never took a seat on the Council because he couldn't bear to serve under his brother."

"How terrible," says Amaris, hand fluttering to her heart. "I had no idea there was such a rift in the royal family."

"And all over Thea," says Zona. "Who, I must say, has been positively glowing lately. I have to get her beauty routine. We can't all be lucky enough to be born with those gorgeous eyes and those perfectly shaped, completely mod-free lips, but I hear she bathes in the secretions of de-aged snails raised on rehydrated calcarnan seed."

"I heard that, too," I say. "Only the best snails for the empress. Snails that win races, even." I feel the slightest pressure on my foot. I don't have to look to know that Amaris is stepping on it.

"Exactly," Zona says, raising her goblet. "Prize-winning snails. I'll drink to that." Her gaze focuses on someone behind us, and she scowls. "Or not. My partner has caught me in the act once again. They've been on this cryo-cleanse kick. I'll just—" Zona flags down a waiter and puts her used goblet back on the tray. "Absolutely lovely chatting with you two. You've made a friend of Zona."

Zona blows a kiss to us and leaves to meet someone in a wine-red suit with a cape draped across one shoulder. The two disappear into the crowd, and then it's just me and Amaris in this corner of the ballroom.

In case anyone is watching, I fold her gloved hand in mine and lean in as if to say something romantic.

I murmur, "I was going to suggest we look into the clones next—"

"They have every reason to hate the emperor," Amaris says quietly. "But I think we have to learn more about Mynos, given this new information."

"You read my mind," I say. "I mean, private meetings with the emperor's wife? I'd bet my life they're having an affair."

"All we have right now is petty gossip, though," Amaris says, reaching up with her other hand to brush a strand of my hair behind my ear.

"It's motive," I point out. I do my best to keep very, very still as she continues to tidy my hair, her fingers gently brushing my cheek, then my ear. The lace of her gloves is soft, and her movements are sure and steady, like she does this all the time.

"Motive isn't the same thing as guilt," she says. "One can be adulterous without also being homicidal. We need proof that this affair and the murder are connected."

I free my hands and rest them at the back of Amaris's neck, hopefully looking very smitten. From the corner of my eye, I can see someone stopping not far away. I turn my head slightly and catch sight of Perseus, apparently back from his mysterious disappearance.

Amaris takes my chin in her gloved hand, and my eyes snap back to her. She's suddenly close, too close, and I can't focus on anything else.

"Maybe the emperor found out about Mynos and Thea," I say, a breath too late. "Or maybe Emperor Hyperion was planning to retire with his wife to some quiet little planet like Gree, and Mynos couldn't stand to be apart from her. Or maybe Mynos just hated his brother and wanted to take the throne with Thea by his side."

"We can come up with theories all day," Amaris says. "And one of them may even be right. But we still need something to back all this up."

I pull back. "So we ask around about their affair."

"We can't," says Amaris. "We've risked enough asking about Mynos. The point is to clear your name, not make ourselves even more suspicious poking around for the gory details of some secondhand gossip. If the feed wasn't blocked, I could look into Thea's personal aide and ask—where are we going?"

"To get something to eat," I tell her, tugging her along with me. A plan is forming in my head, and it has about two steps to it. The first step is nabbing some free eats.

She starts to laugh. "You can't be serious. Why?"

"Because a new round of food is going out. Are those *smoked meats*?"

"Your life is on the line right now," says Amaris. "You could *die*—"

"Yes," I say, "and I'll die a lot faster if I stop eating."

We reach the dining area, where servants are arranging an extravagant display of tiny slices of glistening meat balanced artfully on little crackers, alongside bite-sized pastries, these ones folded like stars.

I grab a plate and begin to pile it with one of everything.

One of the servants, a man on the short side with the customary diamond-shaped pendant and three piercings in his left ear, silently approaches the end of the banquet table and whisks away a dish dotted with mounds of sculpted foams and streaked with sauce. The servant piles this dish atop many others on a floating tray that's beginning to tilt from the uneven weight. I reach out to steady the tray, earning me a surprised look from Piercings, who must be new.

"Do you have it?" I ask. Piercings taps a panel on his wristband and the tray stabilizes. I remove my hand. "Those blue melon slices are absolutely divine. My compliments to everyone involved."

"My wife here loves fruit," Amaris volunteers with a cheerful smile.

"It's true, I do," I say. "So, I was wondering if you might help us with a wager." I trail off and give the server a hopeful look.

"A wager," he repeats slowly.

"We have a bit of a friendly bet going," Amaris says, glancing at me, "regarding where Emperor Regent Mynos was prior to the ball. The comings and goings of the imperial family are just so fascinating."

This would be easier if I still had my stash of jewels, but I know how to make do. I glance down at my hands, where my three silver rings glint under the chandeliers.

"I'll give you a ring if you'd be willing to help us out, and another ring to anyone you can connect us with." I hesitate. "Um, what's your name?"

"Elias. You can call me Elias."

"Well, Elias, what do you say?" I wink at him. "Help me win a wager and you'll get something out of it, too."

"All right. Come with me," says Elias, activating the wristband to lift the tray once more.

I pocket my remaining pastries and follow, Amaris at my heels. Elias leads us behind a thick curtain of ivy to a wall covered with ornamental panels. He presses his hand to one, and it slides open, revealing a passageway.

The tunnel is narrow and dimly lit, and the walls look to be corrugated metal. It ends abruptly in a massive, humid room buzzing with activity and smelling strongly of sweet pastries. In one corner, a tall cook supervises a dozen chopping stations. In another corner, several cooks work on batches of soup, the steam enveloping them. Other cooks rush to retrieve ingredients from freezers and feed them into sleek machines that push out trays of foam or streams of juice. Bots navigate between the cooks, ferrying dishes back and forth.

"Elias!" someone cries. They're chopping some leafy green-and-purple vegetable with one hand and adjusting the settings on a mixer with the other. "Where the Void've you been—"

"I'm terribly sorry if either of you found the food not up to your standards," the tall cook says, in a tone that manages to convey hand-wringing even as both hands stay firmly occupied.

Another cook, this one piping elaborate designs onto a plate of cookies, looks up. Their eyes meet Amaris's, and they break into a grin.

"It's okay, Pinny," they say. "As you were."

"I didn't know you'd be here, Char," says Amaris. She says to me, "Char's a distant cousin. The last we spoke, they were working at one of the most exclusive restaurants on Ouris. I had no idea they were working for the court."

"Took me by surprise, too, but they needed more hands and mine were free," says Char. They glance down at the piping bags they're holding. "Metaphorically."

"Hey, Char, where's Hess?" asks Elias.

"She's cleaning the fifth bedchamber, east wing," says Char. A look crosses their face that I can't quite parse, before they focus on Amaris. "Obviously, we need to get caught up soon."

"I'll fill you in later," says Amaris. Elias waves us across the kitchen, through another door and down yet another long, narrow passageway.

"Where are we?" I whisper to Amaris, who's just ahead of me. I don't remember seeing any of this on her map, but then, I wasn't eyeing it closely.

"Servant passages," she replies under her breath.

"Right. So the upper crust needn't suffer the indignity of laying eyes on any of the people who keep this station running."

Amaris glances back at me. "It's just like Ouris," she says, "everything in this palace shines until you scratch the surface. I wonder what it would take to make more people see that. I mean, renovating this station diverted all public construction on Ouris for five years. In that time, we had no new schools, hospitals, nothing. All so a hundred people could mince around a polished room." As she talks, she gestures excitedly with her hands, casting wild shadows on the walls.

"Imagine if any of those fancy types in the ballroom came to Sarn in the off-season," I muse. "They'd have to smell the market outhouses after a half year baking in the sun."

I scrunch up my face in a grotesque parody of upper-class disgust, and Amaris giggles. I think I like this side of her.

Elias glances back at us, and Amaris stifles her laugh, turning it into a discreet cough with only middling success.

"Hess'll be through here," he says. This particular passageway ends in a sheet of unadorned plaster, no decorative panels in sight. He traces a pattern that lights up and pushes against the surface. The metal swings out like a door. We step through into a bedchamber.

Standing in the middle of the room is an older woman in

white and gold livery. She's got one hand on a small device that seems to control a duster that's hovering above us, sweeping over a light fixture so ornate and complicated, I'd guess it was a sculpture hanging from the ceiling if it wasn't giving off a warm light. A cleaner bot whirs around her, and she steps around it without looking. The two have clearly done this dance before.

When she catches sight of us, she jumps. The controller slips out of her hand, but she recovers it at the last second, duster jerking in midair as she drops into a bow.

"Don't worry, Hess," Elias tells her. He grins. "I know that's like telling a nebula to be cool, but it's okay, they're with me."

"I'll show you a nebula," Hess grumbles. "What're you here for?"

"These two have a question or two, and they're willing to pay for the trouble," says Elias. "And Char happens to know one of them, it turns out."

"Well, if they're friends of Char," says Hess. "Go on."

We tell Hess about our wager. I get the sense that Hess can see right through us, but when I get to the part about the rings, she collapses into a chair too fancy to look comfortable.

"Nobody ever sits here," she tells us, a little defensive as she shifts on the ornate chair. "Oof, and I can see why." She gestures to the neatly made bed. "Feel free to take a load off. Surveillance is still down." Hess makes shooing motions at Elias. "Get out of here before Pinny comes busting in looking for you."

Elias throws her a sloppy salute, catches the ring I toss at him, and backs out the door. Hess turns back to me. "May I see it? Which ring?"

"Here," I say, handing her one of my remaining two rings.

"And all I have to do is tell you where Mynos was tonight during the ball?" says Hess, holding the shiny silver up to the light.

"That's all you have to do," I say.

Hess shrugs. "He disappeared."

"Do you know where to, exactly?" Amaris asks.

Hess shakes her head. "All I can tell you is that he disappeared *with* Her Imperial Grace, if you catch my drift."

"Ah yes," I say. "Any idea where they might have gone for their, uh, private meeting?"

"One of the spare bedrooms, if I had to guess," says Hess. "Couldn't tell you which one. You'd have to track down whoever made that particular bed today."

Amaris asks, "Can you estimate how many people are on housekeeping in this station?"

Hess stares at the ceiling, fingertips twitching with the mental math. "Eighty-seven are on shift right now," she says at last.

A whole army, just to keep the dust from settling and the cleaner bots on task.

"I can paint you a clearer picture, maybe," says Hess, "if there's more where that ring came from?"

"There is. Hold these," I say to Amaris, dipping into my pockets and piling pastries into her gloved hands. Finally, I find an intricate gold and jadeite bracelet that fell to the very bottom of my left pocket. I had a feeling I'd been too hasty to hide everything back in the library, and I was right. "How's this?"

"Good enough," says Hess, taking the bracelet. "I heard from someone else in housekeeping, naming no names, that about two hours before the ball, Her Imperial Grace and His Imperial Majesty had a terrible row."

"Do you know where Mynos was during this fight?" asks Amaris. Hess shakes her head.

"What did they fight about?" I say.

"Oh, they always fight," says Hess. "They've been on the outs with each other ever since she lost the baby."

"And when was that?" I ask.

"Twenty-five years ago, didn't you hear? I suppose it was before your time, young thing like you." Hess settles back in her chair. "It was on the news streams all over the galaxy. Nobody liked to say it at the time, but for whatever reason, I'm afraid they blamed each other. They'd been happy before then, you know. Sometimes grief brings two hearts closer together, and sometimes it rips them apart."

Two decades sounds like an awfully long time to be married to someone you don't get along with, even before you factor in that the empress was having an affair with her husband's brother.

"You've honestly never heard of this?" says Hess.

"Wasn't born yet, sorry," I say.

She sighs. "*Fates*, I'm a thousand."

"This fight you mentioned, was it unusually bad this time around?" Amaris asks.

"Oh yes," says Hess. "You could hear it down the halls, everywhere. They were arguing about the Ascension."

"The ball?" I ask. "It seemed like it was going fine. Well, up until the murder."

"No," says Hess, "who takes the throne. His Imperial Majesty wouldn't tell her who he'd picked."

Amaris takes that in, nodding slowly. "Any names thrown

around? Mynos, Duchess Glykeria, Councilor Makros, Prince Altair, Perseus?"

"Wait, Prince Altair's in the running?" I say.

"Along with just about every halfway-capable royal across the empire who's younger than Hyperion," says Amaris. "It would be unusual, but not unheard of, for a childless emperor to pick a young royal from a prominent line. Sort of a political marriage minus the marriage. Leithe is prosperous but not all that powerful on its own."

"Uh huh," I say, like any of this stuff means something to me. I'm starting to think I should have paid more attention to Dezmer when she told me the latest news.

"I don't know about names," says Hess, shrugging. "That's all I heard. But I had to help get Her Imperial Grace ready for the ball tonight. Her new lady-in-waiting wasn't feeling well, so it fell to me and two others to assist her in dressing."

I think back to the dizzying kaleidoscope of colors and designs in the ballroom, trying to imagine what an empress's gown could possibly look like.

"I can see how that would take three people," I say.

"It would have," says Hess. "But when we got to her rooms, she was in a terrible hurry. She already had the gown half on, and we were all running about trying to fasten all the various bits and bobs. Then she rushed out, alone. Told her staff not to follow, in fact."

"Was she going to meet Mynos?" asks Amaris.

"That's the odd thing," says Hess. "He would've both been in his bedchambers at the time in the north wing of the station. But she was headed toward the south wing."

"Strange," says Amaris.

"Not so strange," I put in. "Maybe she was making a pit stop before meeting up with Mynos."

"No," Hess says. "She didn't seem like she was meeting a paramour. She was preoccupied. Nervous."

"Do you think—" Amaris starts. A muted beeping noise fills the room. "What's that?"

Hess raises her wrist, which is glowing. She presses slightly on her skin and holds her wrist to her ear.

"Alert level seven," says a quiet, clear voice. "All palace staff is to report to Perseus Castellanos immediately. Alert level seven."

Amaris grips my arm. "Cass, we have to go."

"What?" I look at Hess, who's already out of her chair. "What's happening?"

"There's only one thing that would call for a seven," Hess says. "The palace must be looking to sniff out who on the staff has connections to the Voyria."

14

From the furrow in Amaris's brow, I can tell she's thinking the same thing I am—we can't be caught with Hess, and she can't be caught with us.

"This way," Hess says, leaping up. She opens a panel in the wall with a practiced gesture and plunges into a passageway, running like she's trying to beat an explosion.

We bolt down the corridor, shoes pounding on warped metal, as Hess takes us through turn after turn. At one point, the floor slopes down sharply, and from what I remember of Amaris's map, I realize we're running beneath the palace bedchambers. The walls are lined with pipes and levers, and over the thunder of our footsteps, I hear a steady *drip-drip-drip*. We race onward in the dim red light until Hess stops behind a roughly welded door.

"I'm through here," she whispers. "You want to head farther—"

"We've got it," Amaris assures her. "Good luck."

We take the hallway Amaris indicates, still moving at a run. Eventually, the floor slopes back up and we find ourselves at another door. Amaris somehow manages to replicate Elias's gesture that opened the last door, and we creep into what turns out to be the bathroom closest to the ballroom.

No one is inside, thankfully. The tile on the walls and floor have clearly been chosen for their soothing shades of blue and green, and the row of sinks gleam like the world has no problems. I clutch at the stich in my side and take a few deep breaths. I haven't run this hard since the time Jax got caught stealing the head from a statue in front of the Opuntia hotel.

"Are we safe?" I whisper.

She shakes her head. "We're never safe," she says. "That's not our world."

"No, I mean"—I lean in to whisper in her ear—"the surveillance system."

Amaris consults her glass. "We're clear. It's still down."

"Thanks to your source in security."

"Correct."

I sit on the floor of the fancy bathroom. "Why don't you get your friend to track down the murderer? Why are we hauling ass in ballgowns?"

"I can't ask that of them," Amaris says. "They're already risking enough sending me status updates on the surveillance system. Having them do anything more would put them in too much danger."

"Well, in case you haven't noticed, we're in danger right now," I counter.

Amaris glares down at me, folding her arms. "Whoever killed the emperor has almost certainly infiltrated the security team. And even without that particular threat, anyone found allying themselves with the Voyria is subject to exile to the outer colonies or a death sentence."

"But no one knows you're a member—"

"There's no guarantee I won't be found out. And I can't risk my source. They're a person, with friends and family and a whole future before them. Can you wrap your head around what it means to care about someone else? To not treat everyone you come across as a potential resource?"

I throw up my arms. "Oh, you mean like meeting a thief who you *know* didn't kill anybody and deciding she's nothing more than a walking multitool to help clear the name of your little rebel group?"

Amaris bites her lip. "I went too far," she says, almost formally.

"You went pretty far," I agree.

She sits on the floor beside me, tucking her skirts in neatly around her. "I'm sorry."

"Apology accepted, on a conditional basis," I say.

"And what condition is that?" Amaris says. Her shoulders are nearly touching mine, and I bridge the distance, bumping my shoulder against hers.

"Treat me to lunch," I say. "It has to be an expensive sit-down lunch, too. Cloth napkins. Fruits with names I can't pronounce. Whatever those foams were."

"When this is all over, I'll feed you," Amaris promises. She looks down at the blue-green tiles. "Fates, I hope no one walks in on us like this."

"What, sitting on the floor?" I say. "We're in love, aren't we? There's no accounting for what people in love will do. Especially Iola and Dalia Galatas."

"Especially Iola and Dalia," Amaris echoes. She hunches her shoulders and hugs her knees to her chest. For the first time since I've met her, she looks exhausted.

After a moment, I say quietly, "It came out wrong, but I'm not asking you to sacrifice your friend for us. I just think you could ask for help and let them decide if they want to take that risk or not."

"Right," Amaris says. "I just hate that I've put people in danger. It's my responsibility to keep them safe. And if the palace is doing a sweep, then that might mean someone's been caught. I failed them."

"Or . . ." I uncross my arms. "I mean, we already knew the palace was gonna try to blame the Voyria. This could just be the palace stalling for time while they find some poor innocent they can pin the crime on so they can seem like they're doing their jobs. Classic misdirect."

Amaris gives me the barest hint of a smile. "Do they teach that at con artist school?"

"Oh, I'm an *artist* now, am I? That's a nice promotion from petty criminal."

"Hey, you've earned it," she says. "For what it's worth, I did ask for help. I asked for *your* help."

"At knifepoint," I say.

"Need I remind you that you pointed the knife at me first?" Amaris says, wrinkling her nose at me.

"I guess we're even," I say, getting up. I offer her a hand. "Come on. We have a murderer to catch."

Amaris takes my hand, and I pull her up. For a moment, we're face-to-face, and very close. Her eyebrows are immaculate, thick and dark and elegantly shaped. Her eyeliner must be some strong stuff, because it is also perfect, even after our adventure in the vents and our race beneath the station. The only sign that we've been on the run is the slightest sheen of sweat on her temples.

Amaris looks away first. "Give me a moment. I think everything is catching up to me." She takes a deep breath, and then another.

I remember what Jax used to do when they got overwhelmed. "Would it help if you splashed water on your face?"

"Maybe. But I'd rather not remove my gloves," says Amaris. "They're a hassle to get on and off."

"I can help," I say.

She shakes her head. "That's all right."

"What, do you have a secret Voyria tattoo you need to hide from me?" I ask. "An embarrassing birthmark?"

"How could a birthmark be embarrassing? It's something you're born with."

"I don't know, it's shaped like a butt?"

"Are you *five*?" says Amaris, laughing a little. Watching her, I feel just the tiniest bit light and bubbly, like one of those expensive drinks out in the ballroom. "Okay, here, help me."

She extends first one arm and then the other, and with a little work, I manage to peel off the delicate fabric. Her bare hands twitch as if ashamed to be naked, and I see that her fingernails are bitten down to the barest nubs. She notices my noticing, opens her mouth to say something, then closes it again.

"Stressful, being part of the Voyria," I say.

"Sometimes," she allows, then presses her lips together as if she wants to take it back.

"Admit it," I say, "it's hard work trying to do your job when the empire wants to kill you. Only one person wants to kill me, whatever chucklehead is framing me, and I'm barely holding it together."

"I can't tell," Amaris says. "You're hiding it well."

"What can I say," I shrug. "I'm great at faking it. Now the water, come on."

"This had better not get my hair wet," she says.

"You shield your hair and I'll splash," I say. "I promise I'll be gentle."

Amaris gives me a long look, her forehead creasing the slightest bit, and nods.

I come around to her side. Of course, the sink has no handles or buttons or signage of any kind. I've seen sinks like these when I snuck into the restrooms in the Opuntia, but I'm still not used to them. I wave a hand in the general direction of the sink, and immediately a stream of water rushes out all along the length of the sink. A sweet waft of citrus rises up.

"What the Void—" I start, laughing in disbelief, but there's no time for that. Amaris has closed her eyes. I cup my hands, letting the water pool, and very carefully splash it onto her face. I do it two more times, my fingers accidentally brushing her cheek. It feels almost ceremonial, what I'm doing. She blinks, and droplets of water cling to her eyelashes. I step away and fetch her an absurdly plush hand towel from a bronze tray on the shelf above the sink.

"Better?" I ask once her hands and forearms are buttoned neatly back into her gloves.

"Good enough." She shrugs. "So I was thinking—you're

right."

"Can I get that in writing?"

Amaris ignores me. "It's too much of a risk to ask someone who's on lockdown with us in the station, but there is value in reaching out for help. I think we should contact someone in the Voyria network. Someone on the outside."

"But comms are still blocked, right? We can't get word out."

"About that," she says thoughtfully. "Citizen communication is down, but I highly doubt that applies to navigation or security. The guards should have a separate line allowing them to stay in contact with mainworld security in crisis situations. So if we can get ahold of a glass with a security comm line, I should be able to transfer the permissions to my own device. Do you think you could help me make that happen?"

"You mean, could I walk up to a guy armed with a pocket cannon whose job is to be professionally paranoid, while I'm dressed in colors so bright they nearly give off their own light, and pocket his glass without him noticing?" I say.

"Is this another joke?" says Amaris.

"No." I sigh. "I'm just—being descriptive. I think I can do it."

"I'd only need about sixty seconds with it," she says, "if that helps."

"Not really," I say. "But it's the thought that counts."

Just then, the bathroom door slides open, and a small crowd of ball guests head toward the stalls, chattering amongst themselves.

We escape across the hall back to the ballroom, where I take in our surroundings. The guards are easy to pick out in their angular, streamlined armor, their military-grade boots, and their railguns. I count at least ten guards circulating throughout the room, and another four who must've drawn the short straw, posted in each corner. They must be lower ranking, meaning better marks.

"Pretend to talk to me," I whisper to Amaris, who raises an eyebrow.

"What should I pretend to talk about?"

"Anything you want," I say, maneuvering us toward the center of the room. The guard in the northeast corner looks youngest. This might mean she's more easily distracted than the others, or it might mean she works twice as hard.

"—favorite subject is sociology," Amaris is saying. I nod along.

The northwest guard has a holo eye, likely from the war. It doesn't move along with his other eye. Maybe he didn't keep up with the payments or something. This presents a similar problem: he'll have a smaller range of vision but he's probably also jumpier than your average guard.

"—once got so absorbed by a study comparing curse words among the various galaxies, I dropped my glass in a bowl of soup." Amaris, bless her, is still talking. She sounds like a real study bot, from the little that I'm catching.

"Oh my," I say blandly, steering us southward to regard the southwest and southeast guards.

"When I took it for repairs, the technician swore my warranty didn't cover lunch-related mishaps," she continues, "but I did get it working again, except there was no way to navigate backward."

"You had to live in the present," I reply, "with the smell of broth."

She frowns. "You said to pretend to talk. You didn't say you'd be listening," Amaris says, dropping her voice.

"Turns out I'm great at multitasking," I say in an undertone. The southwest guard is the oldest, I think. That means the most experience. "Be more boring, and I'll stop."

The southeast guard keeps sniffling. I can't decide if it's allergies or something else, but either way, he's becoming my obvious choice. From across the room, he motions crossly for the northeast guard to straighten her uniform. The young guard does so, but apparently not well enough because the southeast guard motions again. Apparently, Sniffles is a bit of a prig. Perfect.

"—weather we're having," Amaris says. "Sometimes it's warmer and sometimes it's cooler—"

"Sometimes it's quite cool," I reply. "Or quite warm."

As far as I can see, the southeast guard has: a security badge pinned to his chest on the right-hand side, a chip that functions as a watch on his right wrist, a more ornamental watch on his left wrist, a railgun holstered to his right hip, a scanner of some sort on his left hip, and the glass sticking out of his left pocket. Maybe a secondary weapon like a knife at his calf, but it's hard to tell from how he's standing.

"—suppose the variability in the weather is what makes it weather," Amaris observes.

"Okay," I say quietly. "I'm going to approach Sniffles there. Corner to our left. See him?"

"Mhm."

"We're going to approach from the side. When I'm an arm's length away, can you jostle me into him?"

"Yes."

"Great. Stay close behind me."

Deep breaths. This is basically Bad Mook, Good Mook. But if I'm caught, I won't be locked up for a day in a holding cell on Sarn—I'll be shot, or ejected into deep space, or fed to a giant octopus.

When I reach the wall, I cling to it, as if too drunk to stand unassisted. I trail my fingers along the fine panels, Amaris following a few paces behind. Sniffles turns, eyeing our approach.

"Hey, guard," I say to him a hair too loud, "any leads on the Voyria scum?"

"Madam, I can't divulge that," he says.

"Can't divulge—?" I slur, widening my eyes and still lurching forward. "We know there are Voyria terrorists skulking around on this very ship, but the palace expects us to live in the grips of terror because you can't give us any asher—assurances?"

On cue, Amaris pretends to trip, sending me sprawling toward the guard. As he flails for balance, I catch myself on the front of his jacket and unhook his badge.

"Sorry!" Amaris calls.

"Oh," I say, "oh, I'm so sorry. I'm so so sorry." I pretend to readjust my dress, pocketing the badge in the process.

"My fault," says Amaris.

Sniffles straightens his jacket and frowns at me.

"Oh!" I gasp. "Your badge. It must've fallen—"

The young guard from the northeast corner starts toward him, then seems to remember she can't leave her post. Sniffles drops to a panicked crouch, and as he inspects the floor in front of him, I kneel, reach around and nab his glass. I pass it to Amaris, who hides it against the wall in the folds of her skirt. Then I rejoin Sniffles in his search. He's moved on to the ground behind him, still crouched. The next time his left wrist passes into my line of sight, I unhook the ornamental watch.

"Is that it?" I ask, pointing at a spot on the floor to his right, and as he stares and sniffs, I slip his watch off his wrist completely and add it to my bounty.

"There's nothing there," he growls.

"So sorry," I murmur, surreptitiously removing the badge from my pocket. As I pretend to comb the ground, I set down the badge, then scoot back so that my dress nearly covers it. "Where could it be?" I say.

"It's right there," says Sniffles, grabbing for his badge.

I shuffle back, jostling it to my other side and staring at where he just pointed.

"I can't see it," I tell him.

"You kicked it," says Sniffles.

Amaris nudges me, and I feel her palm the glass back into my waiting hand as Sniffles pushes at the hem of my skirts, trying to free his badge. I stand unsteadily, kicking the badge behind me and spinning around. He crawls forward. I take a step back. His fingers close around the badge, and I swiftly reach around and drop the glass back into his pocket. Sniffles stands and snaps his badge back into place.

"It's a little crooked now," I tell him, still too loud.

Sniffles stoically looks past me, and Amaris leads me away by the elbow.

"That was well-done," she says quietly once we're well out of earshot.

"Well, I am a professional," I tell her, trying not to glow too visibly at the praise. "You weren't too bad yourself."

"I happen to be a professional, too," she says.

We're halfway across the ballroom when Amaris says suddenly, "Did you take his watch?"

I smile serenely, flipping my hand to reveal the glimmer of glass and titanium. "What sort of dashing con artist would do such a thing?"

Amaris frowns slightly and opens her mouth.

"You're not going to tell me to give it back, are you?" I say.

"I suppose not," she says. "It's too late now. Let's pretend like we're going for the bathroom, then head back to the library. I can't risk being overheard, and we should probably find a better hiding place for your knife."

"It's not my knife," I remind her, but she's already ahead of me, cutting across the ballroom.

"Yes," she says distractedly.

"You disarmed me in the library fair and square," I say. "If anything, it's your knife."

"Mm." We're approaching the crowds of ballgoers now, and Amaris doesn't say anything else. Her gaze sweeps the ballroom, and I can tell from the slight crease in her brow that she's thinking, calculating, planning. I've only known Amaris for a short while, but I get the sense there's no point talking to her when she's like this.

She moves across the ballroom with an efficient grace. She walks like she always knows exactly where she's headed, like she's planned and practiced every step of her life. I'm just trailing in her wake.

As we slip out of the ballroom and head down the hallway, I search for something to say. I have no words that will bring back that moment of levity again, puff up our conversation like a loaf of airy fresh bread.

I am well versed already in wanting things I'm not going to get, and now, apparently, I want to be let in on what Amaris is thinking, too. I'm not sure why it should matter to me. We're too different. I'm not even certain she and I can really be friends, even though I find myself wanting to try. Her life is her cause, and I don't know if I've ever truly believed in anything.

It's not that I even disagree with her aims, but when I look at how the world works, I just can't see how we can change out this broken, rotten thing for something better. Life just doesn't operate like that. You can't simply crack it open and put in a new ticker, and suddenly it's as good as new.

I sternly remind myself to stop caring. I'm not here to make friends. I'm here to make a fortune and, barring that, escape this cursed station with my life intact. Amaris is welcome to her wild dreams of revolution and justice, so long as she helps me solve this murder before it's my neck on the chopping block.

15

Once we're safely in the library, Amaris retrieves her glass and pulls up a name in a language I can't read. My heart is in my throat as we lean against the door and listen to the glass chime once, twice, and then a third time. A pointed, weathered face appears, the resolution shifting between high and low so that their features come in and out of focus as they blink at us.

In a quiet alto, this person, presumably a member of the Voyria and Amaris's friend, says, "What's happening up there? Is this link secure?"

"We borrowed a sec line, and the seal on my comms is still functional, so we should be fine," says Amaris.

A fizz of static, followed by a long exhale.

"You had us worried," says Amaris's friend. "I've been trying to get through to you."

"The station is on lockdown. Nothing in or out," says Amaris. "Have you heard the news?"

"All transmissions coming from the station are triple encrypted.

Most of it we're still trying to crack, but we've got the essentials. We know he's been killed. What stage are we—"

"Reza," Amaris interjects, darting a look in my direction. "I'm with a new acquaintance. Her name is—" She hesitates, and I realize I never properly introduced myself. "Cass?" she says, half a question.

She angles the glass toward me and I wave. Reza raises an eyebrow. "Weird time to be picking up acolytes," they say.

"Oh, no," I say, "I'm just the poor cuss someone's trying to pin the murder on."

"She's been helpful," says Amaris briskly. "Listen, we need to know. Can we account for everyone in our camp aware of"—she glances at me again—"our current operation on this station?"

"I'll check," Reza says. There's a long silence as their eyes scan over something we can't see.

"Everything looks good," they say at last. "Leyda says there's nothing amiss on her end."

"See?" I tell Amaris. "The palace sweep was just for show. They're trying to trick everyone into thinking they're still in control of the situation. It's just like I said, precious."

Amaris lets out a shuddery breath before jerking her head up. "Wait. Precious?"

I wink at her. "Trying out a new nickname in case one of the guests tries to talk to us again. What do you think?"

"That sounds like a cat with a squashy face who lives on a pillow," Amaris grumbles.

"So, no?" I say.

"Absolutely not," she says. "Please restart to play again." She's smiling, though. Probably because she's just learned that everyone in her secret club is safe, but I like to think it might have to do with me, too.

She turns her attention back to Reza. "It's not looking good. Whoever's behind this wants Cass to take the fall as a representative of the Voyria. And you know intergalactic parties are poised to act, depending on how things shake out. I need you to do some digging for us so we can reach a conclusion before the Council does and act accordingly."

"Say the word," says Reza. "Unless it's literal digging. My joints are stiff as a corpse today."

"Can you check the tracker feeds and see if you can piece together Mynos's and Thea's movements from a month ago up to today? And please flag if either of them had any dealings with HasaLyk."

"Who's that?" I ask.

"What, not who," Reza says. They have several screens pulled up already, and they're swiping through them with terrifying speed.

"Hasapis-Lykaios. It's a private corporation that supplies bio-weapons to the Helian skyforce. They have a mine on Sarn, I believe," says Amaris. "The Helian Empire has a binding agreement with the Zarinel Federation not to produce any C-class neurotoxins in either territory but—"

"Let me guess," I say, "they're doing it anyway."

"There are labs outside the Helian Empire proper," Reza chimes in. "It's an open secret that if you know the right people and you go to the right place and you have the right shipload of money . . ."

"Nothing's illegal if you're rich enough," I say bitterly.

Amaris nods. "It's CNNP we're looking for specifically."

"And anything to do with surveillance feeds," I say.

"I'll put a team together and report back as soon as I can," says Reza. They fix their eyes on Amaris. "Hey," they say. "May every shadow hide you. Good luck up there." And with that, the glass goes blank.

"May every shadow hide you. Is that some kind of code?" I ask.

"Turn of phrase," says Amaris, pocketing her glass. "It's common among Zarinelans with family from the mid-level rings. Local saying, I believe."

"The Zarinelans?" I say. "Wait, the Voyria really are collaborating with Helia's worst enemy? You didn't think to mention this earlier?"

"There are dissidents on all sides who want the fighting and expansion to end," she says evenly. "We work with anyone whose goals align with ours."

I can't think of anything to say to that. I don't have any real hate for the Zarinel Federation. I know they attack supply lines and settlements on the edges of the Helian Empire's holdings, but it all seems so far from Sarn, and I've always assumed we did the same thing to them. I've never really questioned it, never thought too hard about the people on the other side. It would be like taking issue with the sun. The war just is. The empire just is. This life, and how it gets a little bleaker every day, just is.

"So what now?" I say.

Amaris settles into an armchair by the bookshelves. "We wait. Reza works fast. They'll get back to us pretty soon."

I scan the room for a distraction. There isn't much to look at except for all the books. I wonder how much I can get for one.

"So how'd you get involved in all of this, anyway?" I say.

"Hm?"

"The Voyria. How'd that all start?"

"Well, about thirty years ago, an independence movement swept every seat on the planet of Hestia, which had real leverage thanks to being the empire's major source of peatwood," says Amaris. "Hyperion responded by flooding the marshland with toxins, declaring the elections compromised, and installing a puppet government on Hestia that devastated its economy. From there, it was clear that any independence movement would have to operate underground. The Voyria began as a dozen separate movements, on a dozen separate planets. But eventually, as long haulers carried the transmissions out to the outer colonies, these groups began to coalesce around their shared goals: bringing relief to those in need, lending support to dissent, and exposing the hypocrisies of the worst royals and governors. And while the entire network is divided by planet into what we call gills, each operating independently, our commonly held aims bring us together, while our varied voices give us strength—"

"Fates," I say when she pauses to take a breath. "I didn't ask for a history report, I asked why you joined."

"Long story," she says. She blinks and rubs her eyes. "So, um . . ." She shakes her head, as if trying to dislodge her thoughts. "I guess, where do I start?" She rubs her eyes again, sagging back into the armchair she's in. Now that she's no longer waxing poetic about the Voyria, all the life seems to have drained out of her.

"Say," I say, "have you eaten yet?"

Amaris stares at me. "We're on a countdown to catch a murderer before the fallout destroys both of our lives, and potentially the lives of untold civilians, and your mind turns to snacks again?"

"Ah," I say, "one of those." And then at her puzzled look, "My dad's the same way. Gets too sucked into his work to eat. Never understood it."

"I had something before I came," she says.

I do a little mental math, factoring in the trip here. "That was ages ago. I was wondering why you weren't laughing at all my hilarious jokes." I shake my head sadly. "Hunger, it clouds the mind."

"I'll take a pastry or something once we hear from Reza," she says.

"Screw that," I say, "take one now." And, with a minimal amount of rummaging, I produce a sausage-stuffed roll, shiny with baked-on cheese.

Amaris stares in disbelief at my offering.

"Are you seriously asking me to eat food that's been knocking around in your pocket?" she says.

"Why?" I say. "What other food do you think I have? Are you expecting me to pull an entire roast duck out from under my bodice? Callidora's good but there's limits to what dress construction can do for you."

I make a show of wiping the roll with my sleeve, a little cheese flaking off in the process, and offer it again. "Take it," I say. "You need to fuel up if we're going to take on unknown nefarious villains. This isn't the time for snobbery."

"It's not snobbery to refuse to eat someone's—pocket meat," she fires back.

"If you don't eat it, I will," I say solemnly. "And I'm not even hungry. Such a waste." I take a big, theatrical whiff of the roll. "Oh wow, it smells delicious."

"This is transparent manipulation," she says.

"Yeah," I say, "but the funny thing is, if you just take the roll, you'll still stop being hungry. The *transparent manipulation* just gives it flavor."

I bring the roll to my mouth.

"I've got no morals," I warn her, "I really will eat it."

"Fine," says Amaris, "give it to me."

I hand it over, and for all her protesting, she devours the thing in three bites.

"How does it taste?" I ask once she's chewed and swallowed.

"Like the interior of a pocket," she says. "Do you have another?"

I hand over another baked good, a biscuit-looking confection studded with dried fruit.

"We have these on Haddan," says Amaris reverently. She closes her eyes to eat this one, and I have the sudden sense that this is a deeply personal moment between her and the fruit biscuit. I pace the room, admiring the neat rows of books bound in dignified shades with gilded lettering.

"If I was the kind of person who loved to read, I'd be in heaven right now," I say.

Amaris pulls herself to her feet and comes over to inspect the shelf I'm looking at. "Not necessarily. These are some boring titles."

I tip out a book and flip through it before putting it back on the shelf. "I'll take your word for it."

"Oh," says Amaris, and when I glance back at her, she looks stricken. I can almost see the gears turning in her mind, wondering whether or not it's okay to ask—

"I can read," I tell her, and her posture relaxes slightly. "If I have to. I just don't like it. The little letters are so hard to tell apart."

"Haven't you ever had your vision tested?" she says.

"At school, yeah," I say. "And I had a pair of lenses, if you can believe it. But it was almost impossible keeping them clean in all that dirt, and then I dropped out, so it didn't seem worth it to get another pair."

Amaris's brow creases, and it's clear she wants to propose a solution. She's a fixer, I can tell.

"Oh, I'm lucky," I tell her. "Babbit from back home is losing his sight altogether, bit by bit."

"That's terrible," says Amaris. "What's he going to do?" she asks, and the weird thing is, she sounds as if she cares.

"Well, he was a short-range pilot. He'd fly people down to the oasis on the Big Split and back. Do they know about the Big Split on—where are you from?"

"Here and there," says Amaris. "And no, go on."

"Right, it's not exactly galaxy-breaking news," I say. "Sarn's got this huge canyon, goes halfway to the core or something. It's all different colors and shit on the way down, and then at the bottom there's this ridiculously posh resort. Although, contain your surprise, most of us have never been. So Babbit got hold of a fiddle a while back—long story—"

"Let me guess," Amaris says. "You stole it for him?"

"I did not," I say indignantly. "I stole a cleaner bot, which my friend Pav reprogrammed and resold. We bought that fiddle with real, hard-earned money."

"How law abiding of you," Amaris says. "So what did this Babbit do with the fiddle?"

"Well, he's been trying to make the switch to busking on the edge of the resort. Normally, you can't earn shit playing on Sarn but he can make a go of it because he's got a good face for it."

"What does that mean?" she asks.

"Handsome. Sharp cheekbones, beautiful eyes, the works. And he's got a good ear for tunes, but that's not nearly as important."

"Ah," says Amaris.

"He says he likes it better than flying 'cause he can stay in the shade at least part of the time, but it's not like he really has a choice," I say. "Problem is, he won't have a way to know if the tourists are slipping him real coins or trash that happens to have the right clink, which I wouldn't put over some of those tight fists."

She nods slowly.

"There's surgery or the hybrid eye but . . ." I shrug.

"But it's for those who have the money." Amaris winces. "Sorry."

"Don't be," I say, drawing myself up. "Depending on how tonight goes, I may be about to join the ranks of the obscenely wealthy."

Amaris gives me an odd look. "Is that why you were doing this? To help him?"

"No." I scoff. "I'm just doing this to get rich. Where have you been?"

"But you just said—"

"A portion of the payout goes to every sod who got me here," I explain. "Jax, my thieving partner. Babbit's boyfriend, Pav, he covered for me when I left and he'd gladly spare the drocks for Babbit's eyes. Dezmer and Mita, they taught me to dance and made my first gown. Dad."

"Your dad?" she says.

"He and I were gonna use whatever I was able to carry out of here to disappear. Set up on someplace green, with a proper day-and-night cycle, fix up his lungs, and enjoy hot food and clean water every night for the rest of our lives."

"Just you two?" she says.

"What?"

"No significant others among all your allies?"

"Nah. Me, I'm a free agent. It's me, Dad, and the rest of the universe."

Amaris starts to say something, but she's cut off by the chirp of her glass coming to life. As promised, Reza is back.

"Any news?" says Amaris.

Reza grins, flashing a silver incisor among a row of charmingly crooked teeth. "Let's just say the case is not looking good for our beloved imperials."

16

Amaris drops to the floor, and I settle down beside her. I lean in, and she angles her glass so that I can see Reza, too.

"What are your findings?" says Amaris.

Reza's gaze darts over several sheets to their left as they read, the wrinkles in their face deepened by the light. "Thea left the station fourteen times in the run-up to the ball. The official line is that she was overseeing preparations, and twelve of those trips have been documented and verified. The other two, though—ground ops says she was seen heading south on Demetriou Street on Doukash two weeks ago."

"Hmm," says Amaris. "Any reason given for the trip?"

"She claimed she was borrowing jewelry from Sophronia Bakirtzis," Reza says.

I glance between them. "Who?"

"Heir to the Bakirtzis fortune," says Reza, waving a hand impatiently. "Her family just so happens to own the Areia Institute, which uses the latest in neuropsychology to train deadlier soldiers. The institute is a bunch of glorified butchers who think they can buy respect if they play nice with the royals."

Amaris frowns. "Wouldn't Thea send an assistant for that?"

"You'd think," says Reza. "But you know who else happened to be vacationing on Doukash at the same time? Efimia Aetos, one of the cofounders of Asipis. It would've been easy for Thea to slip down to Efimia's summer home and make the necessary arrangements to crack the security system."

"She couldn't do that from the station?" I ask.

"The palace connection is watched very closely," Amaris says. "By Hyperion's security and the Council."

"Still not ironclad evidence," says Amaris, "but it does imply we're headed in the right direction. You said there was another trip, Reza?"

"Eight days ago," Reza says. "All we know is that she took a ship out to Drivax and brought back a shopping bag from Harmonia's, but there's no shopping district on Drivax."

I mull this over. "Never heard of Drivax, and I talk to a lot of homesick tourists."

"There's nothing there," says Reza. "It's not just an unfashionable part of space, it's a dead zone. Freezing cold, hardly anybody lives there."

"Right. But quite a few corps are headquartered out there, to get around trade regulations," Amaris says. "It was empire territory for a while, but after the latest Zarinel campaign, it's neutral space."

Reza sighs. "Three months ago, some young Zarinel soldiers tried to claim amnesty from the Khonsanians there and froze solid. My partner heard about it, but only because he follows the low feed."

Amaris straightens up. "Reza, can you—"

"Yes," Reza says. "Give me a second." They fumble with something out of frame, then let out a cackle.

"What is it?" says Amaris.

"Hasapis-Lykaios, Incorporated," says Reza.

"Weren't they—" I start.

"One of the companies responsible for manufacturing deadly neurotoxins?" Amaris says. "Yes. This can't be a coincidence."

"From what we've dug up on CNNP, it's particularly volatile and climate sensitive, so it has to be transported in a specially made case that looks like this." Reza taps out something and flicks their fingers, bringing up a picture of what looks like a small, green-tinted glass valise with gold clasps and a panel screen on the top.

"If we can somehow get into Thea's quarters," I say, mind racing, "and if we can find this case in one of her rooms—"

"It would prove her guilt," says Amaris. "Interesting."

There's a garble of sound, and Reza glances over their shoulder. "I have to take this," they say. "We'll keep looking into things from our end. May every shadow hide you." And the glass goes clear once again.

"What do we do now?" I ask. Amaris looks at me. "What?"

"What do *we* do," she says quietly. "I didn't expect to hear that word so much tonight. It's nice." She smiles, one corner of her mouth quirking up ever so slightly.

I'm not sure what to do with that, how it makes me feel giddy, like I'd just swallowed down a tin full of Mita's oversteeped tea.

"Did I ever thank you for the food?" she asks.

"No," I say. "You did complain about it a lot."

"Thank you," says Amaris, and she sounds sincere. "It's still disgusting that you retrieved a whole meal out of your pockets, but I am thinking more clearly."

"I can't believe your plan was to eat nothing all night," I tell her. "At the ball of the century, no less."

"I didn't come here to enjoy myself," she says.

"Hang on," I say, thinking of what Reza said when they first picked up. "Then why were you here? Why did the Voyria send an operative who can flip someone over her shoulder just to scope out the political situation?"

Amaris grimaces. "You know I can't tell you that."

"Why not? We're a team now, aren't we? I think I've proven myself, after everything."

"I can't tell you," says Amaris. She's looking straight at me now. Her voice is low, halfway to a whisper. "Because I don't want to lie to you."

I'm not sure how long I sit there looking back at her. Long enough to clearly hear voices in the hallway. We jump to our feet and look at the door. Beside me, Amaris shifts into a fighting stance.

"Can't believe there's still guests wandering the station," someone's saying. A guard, probably. "Heli's squad has called in at least nine people who 'got lost on their way to the bathroom.'"

"People don't know what's good for them," another voice mutters. "I'm thinking of quitting and joining the skyforce. My cousin says they get the best armor, everything. You can punch through a tree, easy." They're getting closer.

The library door handle jiggles. "This one's locked," says the first voice. "Do you have the overrides?"

"Just a second."

My eyes dart to Amaris's, and I can tell she's running the same mental math I am. Not enough time to get back into the vents, not enough cover for both of us to hide behind the door.

Sorry, I mouth.

What? she mouths back, and then the handle is turning and I'm sweeping Amaris into an embrace against the bookshelf by the doorway. At first, her body is stiff and unyielding, but as the door opens, she must realize my gambit because she throws her arms around me and presses her lips to mine.

My mind races. Are we convincing? How did the guards know to look for us? What is Amaris hiding from me? How much longer do we need to make this kiss last?

How is someone like Amaris this good at kissing?

One of the guards coughs pointedly, and we spring apart. Fortunately, neither of them is the guard whose watch is currently sitting in my pocket.

"We have to ask you to come with us. Guests aren't to leave the ballroom unless it's for the bathroom," says the other guard. "If you hurry, you'll make the announcement."

"Sorry," I say with a sheepish laugh. "Newlyweds. You know how it is."

"What announcement?" says Amaris.

The first guard gives us a blank look. "The Ascension."

"But the emperor—" I start.

"He's dead," says Amaris.

"It's a recorded message," says the second guard. "Let's get a move on."

Amaris and I exchange a look. I can feel Amaris's grip tightening on my hand. I blink away the memory of her lips, the way they fit against mine so perfectly, the sweet pressure of them. Gah.

"Of course," I say pleasantly. I smile at the guards. "Let's go pay our respects to the new emperor."

17

Inside the darkened ballroom, the murmured conversations have given way to a hush as everyone watches a holo display of an hourglass in the center of the ballroom. Instead of sand, the hourglass is filled with swirls of stars, which sift slowly downward. Ligeia spots us from where she and Gennadios are standing among the throngs of ballgoers, and she waves us over excitedly, as if this were a solstice celebration and not the announcement of the next emperor following the bloody, unsolved murder of the previous one.

When the top of the hourglass is empty, the lights dim and a glowing holo of a man in a glinting gold circlet and elaborately draped robes appears.

"People of Helia, I greet you," Hyperion says in a deep, booming voice. He may have been nearing eighty, but the specter dominating the ballroom appears to be in the prime of his life—a more distinguished Mynos, or an older Perseus, or a more alive Emperor Hyperion. Of course, until recently, he had the benefit of switching out his organs for fresh ones from one of his clones any time he wanted.

He pauses, gaze flicking to the faintest hint of glowing text at eye level. Faced with the ghostly image of their now dead emperor, the ballgoers stare up at him in silence.

"He looks so young," mumbles Ligeia.

He looks nervous, I think. A tremor runs through his hands, which look broad and curiously smooth, with none of the calluses and lines that my hands bear. His gaze darts from the text to the camera to a point on his right, like he's resisting the urge to look over his shoulder. Did he know what's coming, or was his age finally catching up to him? When I look over at Amaris, she's watching intently, her fists clenched by her sides.

"The one I have judged worthy of the Helian crown and throne," he's saying, "the one who will guide our hand against the encroaching tide of the Zarinel Federation, the one who will defeat all that stands between us and achieving our destiny of uniting this universe under one mighty and noble rule so that we may all live in peace, safety and prosperity—"

I feel a squeeze. Amaris has grabbed my arm, her gaze fixed on Hyperion.

"—is Prince Altair, Duke of the Ganymede Cluster and son of Leithe. I trust him to carry out my vision, and to realize our exceptional fate, warming and illuminating the unknowable Void, so that all who move through our space may do so in peace. As our imperial song tells us, may our reach yet expand for our visions are grand. Light and life to Helia!"

His voice reverberates through the ballroom, seeming to swell on the last words. The glowing figure of the late emperor fades away, and we're left staring at one another as the lights blink on.

The ballroom breaks into raucous applause as the music strikes up again, this time triumphant and sweeping. A chant goes up, a roar of sound so loud that I have to cover my ears.

To think I'd met the future emperor, and even insulted him. I can't wait to tell Jax when I get home. I hope he'll make a good leader, though of course there's no way to be sure until he's on the throne. At least he's no Mynos.

I turn to Amaris. Amaris, who looks like she might faint, or hurl, or both. She lets go of my arm and steps back, her eyes wide.

"—have to go," says Amaris.

"What?" It's hard to hear her over all the cheering.

"Right now," she says into my ear. "You stay here, I'll be right back."

She strides away before I can say anything. A server walks by with a tray of delicate goblets, filled with something clear. I toss one back and immediately regret the way it makes my throat burn. Another server carries a tray covered in empty goblets, and as I deposit mine, the back of my neck prickles. If Thea was bold enough to kill her husband, there's no reason she wouldn't kill again. And if all the royals have been sequestered together, she might have the chance to try.

I scan the crowd for Amaris, but she's nowhere to be found in this thick and jubilant crowd. She said to stay put, but I have to warn Altair. Not just because his life is at stake, but mine is, too. Altair might be the only person at the top who'd believe that I've been set up.

As I slip out of the ballroom, I try to envision the palace layout—where was the series of panic rooms on Amaris's map, and did it connect with the vent system? I draw a rough mental map. Library in the lower left corner. Panic suite in the upper right corner.

I head to the library first, dodging two guards on patrol, and check that the bak dagger is where I left it. It is. The jewels are still there, too.

My mind races. Amaris had said the vents where the royals are being sequestered was too great a risk, and if I'm caught sneaking around in the vicinity of an imperial panic room, no cover story in the world about being a bored socialite will save me. But a spot of bribery might. I quickly repocket my stolen bounty, and then I'm climbing into the vents once more. It's just as close and uncomfortable as before. I crawl past enormous bedchambers, all empty, and cramped storage rooms. I guess when to turn based on my memory of the map, wishing Amaris was here to second-guess my choice and explain what an octopus is.

After a while, my knees ache from crawling on cold metal. I realize now that I'll have no way of knowing if I get lost until it's too late, at which point I'll have no way of getting back. Amaris would've pointed this out to me, I think. Amaris would've had that map.

I'm well and truly on my way to freaking out when I hear voices. One a rumbling baritone, the other low and steady and familiar. I crawl to the next grate.

"Are you certain, sir?" says a guard in a fancier version of the palace guard uniform.

"I need to be by myself for a moment," says Altair. "Moustakas, I'm serious. Go take a break. You look exhausted."

"That bad, huh?" The guard laughs.

"That bad," Altair confirms. "Get a bite to eat, talk to your husband. I'll be fine."

The guard steps out of the room, the door *swoosh*ing shut behind him. Altair lets out a long sigh, rubbing at his temples.

"Can't believe this," he mutters to himself. "What a nightmare. I don't—"

This is my chance. I knock lightly on the floor of the vent and peer through the grate.

"Hey," I whisper. "Hey!"

Altair starts, then looks up. His eyes narrow, and he tilts his head. "Iola? What are you doing up there?"

"Oh, just hanging out," I say breezily. "Is the surveillance feed back up yet?"

"No," he says. "Station security is working on it, but they likely won't be fully functional until tomorrow. Or so they tell me. I have so many people reporting to me now, it's making my head spin."

"In that case," I say, "can you open this grate for me?"

Luckily, Prince Altair, being a man of action, has a pocket knife to unscrew the grate, and a general willingness to climb furniture. There's a heart-stopping moment where nothing is supporting my weight except his arms around me, but I make it down without incident. I have the tremendous good fortune to have found yet another ally who works out.

"Now then," he says, barely out of breath. I'm wheezing. "This is the most diverting thing that's happened to me in hours, but I'm guessing you didn't brave the ventilation system just to say hello." He smiles grimly. "What is it?"

"Steer clear of Thea and Mynos," I tell him. "I can't prove it to you, but we've got every reason to believe that they killed the emperor. Or, at least, Thea did. Mynos probably let her do all the work. Anyway, odds are good they'll try to kill you, too. You should get out of here as soon as possible. But before you do, can you round up some important people, plus Ambassador Zahur, so you can testify that I'm innocent because someone tried to frame me for the emperor's murder, and I'd really rather not get ejected out of the hold or popped into a cryochamber headed for the barren Void." I suck in a gulp of air. I hadn't realized how panicked I was until just now. "Hey, actually, you're the new emperor. Can you just absolve me of all my crimes or something?"

"Slow down," says Altair. "What's going on?" He frowns. "And who is 'we'?"

Given that Amaris is with the Voyria and I have no idea how that will go over with a royal, even a very fair-minded one, I decide to leave her out of it.

"Me and you," I say, "once I explain to you what's going on."

"Wait," Altair says, holding up a hand. "How did you get in the vents? Is this a common practice on, what was it, Yorgos?"

"I climb trees all the time back home," I say impatiently. "My cousins make a game of it every summer. Listen, you have to stay away from Mynos and Thea."

"The empress? And the emperor's brother?"

"Yeah, those two. Listen, if you talk to the Khonsanian doctor, she'll tell you that Hyperion didn't die of blood loss from the knife found in the pool. He died of poison injected via his ear while he was in his private chambers, behind a bio-lock that can only be opened by people who share the emperor's or empress's DNA. Someone in the imperial family killed the emperor."

"I—" Altair shuts his eyes briefly, then opens them. "You're accusing Emperor Hyperion's brother and his wife of murder. Why them? There's at least seven members of the royal family on this station right now, not counting the emperor's clones. Six cousins and one aunt," Altair says, holding up seven fingers. "The emperor's aunt is quite the personality, but I don't think she's up for committing murder at her age."

"Look," I say impatiently, "Thea's hated Hyperion for more than twenty years. She's also been having an affair with Hyperion's brother, who's clearly a power-hungry tyrant. Maybe the emperor figured out what Mynos and Thea had planned, and that's why he recorded the message naming you as his successor, just in case. Maybe they found out beforehand that he was naming you, and it was a matter of revenge, or of disrupting your ascension. Either way, Thea's taken some very suspicious trips recently, including one where she might've gotten the poison used to kill the emperor."

"Fates," Altair says, dropping his head into his hands. "This is a lot take in. Remind me again why you're playing detective? Whether it's the Voyria or the imperial family who did it, it isn't safe for you to be running around like this."

I take a deep breath. "The truth is, I think I'm being framed. I think someone figured out that I'm here on your invitation and I don't belong and planted a dagger on me that matches the murder weapon." Altair doesn't need to know the full degree to which I don't belong. "My mom always said that the only person you can trust to do things right is yourself. So I went asking around to get answers."

"This is bad," Altair says slowly. "I want to help, and I will, to the best of my ability. But, Iola, the emperor's brother and the empress are innocent. I can prove it."

I stare at him. "What?"

He reaches into his pocket and pulls out a glass.

"Did the comms blackout lift?" I ask when he swipes past a flurry of message chains.

Altair smiles crookedly. "The blackout doesn't apply to the emperor-to-be. I guess that's one advantage to this whole situation." He flicks through several panels and gestures, pulling up a video that starts playing in midair. "The Asipis feed."

"It's blank," I point out.

Altair holds up a finger. "Correction. It's *mostly* blank." He rewinds and rewinds, until we reach that ghoulish flicker of Hyperion lying facedown in the pool. "We only have this one moment, but judging by the distribution of the blood, it must have been shortly after he was killed."

"I told you," I break in, "he didn't die from bleeding. The stab wound was secondary, after he was poisoned. It didn't spray all that much."

"Even so," says Altair, "it's a liquid. It would have dispersed through the pool quickly, do you agree?"

I nod.

"Right," he says. "And here's surveillance with the same time-stamp, from a different room." He brings up footage of another room in the station, this one featuring a large bed and a sparkling pool of water, with a massive pair of crossed swords on the wall. Lying in the bed, lost to the world, are a man I recognize as Mynos and a beautiful older woman.

"Is that—?"

"Emperor Regent Mynos and Empress Thea," says Altair. "Fast asleep in the emperor regent's chambers."

After Thea got dressed and went to her mysterious appointment, she must've had another surprise private meeting with Mynos, I think. Eventful day, even before the murder.

"Which places them at the opposite end of the station from the emperor's private quarters," Altair is saying. "There's no way either of them would be able to slip out, administer the poison, drag the body to the pool, stab the emperor, throw him in the water, and sneak back to Mynos's room in time."

I take this in. Given that Hyperion died on the other side of a bio-lock, that also rules out an assassin sent by either of those two.

"So Mynos and Thea didn't kill Hyperion."

"No," says Altair slowly. "But I think I know who did."

18

"Keep in mind," says Altair, "it has to be someone with motive, and access, and opportunity. If this bio-lock works like you say it does, in my mind that only leaves one person."

"Who," I say, "Perseus?"

Altair almost fumbles his glass. "How did you know?"

"The bio-lock narrows down the pool of suspects to people with the emperor's DNA, or his wife," I point out. "Hyperion had no surviving children, so who does that leave besides his clones?" I remember what Ambassador Zahur had told me in the ballroom. "Perseus was the only clone with any real shot at the throne, right?"

"Yes," says Altair. "And he's served as an advisor and a minor member of the Council for years. He knows just what it would take to throw the emperor's declaration into question. If he cast enough doubt on tonight's announcement, he could convince the Council to veto the naming and select someone else. He could even sway the Council into picking him instead. Perseus may not act like it, but he can be persuasive when there's something he wants."

Altair grimaces. "Honestly, the thought of Emperor Hyperion naming me makes me sick to my stomach. I don't want"—he gestures at the richly furnished room—"this, whatever this is. I've already made a life for myself, and now it's no longer mine. Most likely the Council pushed the emperor to do it, for political reasons, but I wish they'd picked some other sacrificial goat."

"Perseus must have a lot of access, given that he's a clone and a member of the Council," I say. "Do you think he'd be able to get the permissions to tamper with the security system and kill the surveillance feed?"

"I do," says Altair with a sigh. "I'm sure there were half a dozen ways Perseus could've caught the emperor's transmission ahead of time. I could see him unsealing the message, learning that the emperor had chosen me, and flying into a rage."

I've been looking at the facts one way for so long, considering that Perseus might be the murderer feels like standing on my head. I know I shouldn't rule out Altair as a suspect—he was the one who wound up gaining the most from Hyperion's death. But if Altair had killed the emperor, he'd have no reason to cover for Mynos and Thea. He'd be happy, in fact, to let two extremely suspicious people take the fall. Besides, he had no way to get past the bio-lock, and he doesn't seem to want anything to do with sitting his butt on the imperial throne.

In a flash, I remember the time I glimpsed Perseus out of the corner of my eye, just watching the drama unfold. I think about all his connections on the Council, and how I saw him talking with Ambassador Zahur, who has Khonsanian interests—and only Khonsanian interests—at heart.

"It would explain how the knife ended up in my pocket," I muse. "I thought it was weird at the time that Perseus asked me to dance, but it did put me in close range. I was the perfect mark. He could've slipped the knife in at any point." What I don't say is that I thought I was the only one using sleight-of-hand in the ballroom. I wasn't on my guard, like I should have been.

Altair is studying me, a faint smile on his face.

"What?" I ask.

"Nothing," he says. "You're very good at this."

I shrug. "Well, it's like they say. You never know how good you'll be at solving a murder case until your life is on the line. So Perseus could have planted the knife on me. But how did he kill the emperor? Did he just, I don't know, walk in?"

"Perhaps. As a clone, his movements are far less scrutinized than those of other members of the imperial family," Altair points out. "He could get around the station without anyone noticing. Not to mention he has two identical brothers who would be more than willing to cover for him."

I imagine Perseus using all of his contacts to suss out that I'm from Sarn and slipping me the bak dagger in the ballroom. I imagine him slinking through the hallways, dodging questions by claiming he's on official Council business. I imagine him bypassing the bio-lock, sneaking up behind Hyperion, and—

"The poison," I say. "It was a neurotoxin that's illegal in the Helian Empire. How did he get it?"

"There's one explanation. But this doesn't leave this room," Altair says gravely. I nod. "I've known Perseus since we were children. We attended the same state functions every year. One day when I was twelve, I snuck away from a banquet and went exploring. I found a vast storage hall, full of ancient relics too damaged to display anywhere. I was climbing into an old groundship when I heard this awful sound." He frowns. "Do you know what a quantar is?"

"Some kind of vintage tech?"

"Not even close. It's a little furry animal, a bit like a kitten or a duckling, about the size of your palm. Big, round eyes. Sweet, trusting nature."

"Uh-huh?"

"I'll spare you the details," says Altair, "but Perseus had found a box of chemicals and liquids that aren't manufactured anymore because they're too dangerous, and he was feeding some kind of acid, I think, to the quantar. It died right as I reached them." Altair's gaze darkens. "I wish I'd done something." He considers this. "Well, I did do something—I burst out crying and then I punched him in the stomach. But I didn't tell anyone. Hyperion could be hard on his clones. He expected them to live up to his expectations, however harsh they were. And as foolish as it sounds now, I worried what would happen to Perseus."

I think of the quantar, dead at Perseus's hand. "That little shit."

Altair holds up a hand and clenches it into a fist. "He kept insisting it was 'an experiment' but I have no idea what he was trying to prove, other than the power he held over something so small and defenseless." He sighs. "Perseus has always been a bully, but I worry maybe that was the start of something for him. The beginning of a lifelong obsession with poisons. He was always going on trips, and I suspect it was to feed this hobby of his."

"You think he might've gotten the nanotech from before the ban."

"Among other such toxins," says Altair.

"And I was a convenient target," I say. "He thought he could plant evidence on me because I'm a nobody, with nobody to back me up. I was the next quantar."

"I think it may be worse than that," says Altair thoughtfully. "He might've assumed you were with the Voyria."

I frown. "Why would he think that?"

"Perseus is fully immersed in Helian politics. He knows all the big players, every court member, every council member on every planet and every moon. He might've seen you in your gorgeous dress, dancing without a care and no connections of any kind, and figured you had to be here as a spy. And Perseus hates the Voyria more than anything. He's—well, he's a clone of Hyperion. Nothing matters more to him than ensuring power remains in the hands of the old guard. I'm sure he thinks he's killing two birds with one stone, as it were."

Altair bows his head briefly. "I got you all wrapped up in this, Iola. I'm sorry."

"Yes, well, I've got the perfect way for you to make it up to me," I say briskly. "Let's talk to the ambassador and the Council. You can testify on my behalf and tell everyone I'm just a sweet farmer's daughter from Yorgos that you met on the streets of Ouris, and I'll be on my merry way."

Altair is already shaking his head. "I can't do that. The way things are right now, you won't be safe. With his access and connections, Perseus is too dangerous. People who go against him have a history of disappearing. We won't make much headway with the Council, given that Perseus is a member, and he may find a way to kill you at any point."

"But we have to try," I say, panic bubbling up in me. "You don't really want to sit here and wait for Perseus to poison you, too, do you?"

"I can't protect you if we go together. But there's another way." He smiles ruefully and scratches the back of his neck. "Staying put has never been my style. I have a small vessel still docked in the station. I'd planned to sneak off for a little joyride if things here got too dull."

"And you want me to . . ."

"Escape the palace," Altair says. "It'll make you a fugitive, until I can settle things with Perseus. But better a live fugitive than a dead suspect."

"But—"

"We don't have a second to lose, Iola," Altair says grimly. "The sooner you get off the station, the sooner I can turn my attention to taking on Perseus."

He holds out an arm, all manners even now, and I take it.

Altair lifts his other hand toward the wall, makes a few sharp gestures, and the surface of the wall fades away to reveal a second door. We slip through it, and then we're in the servant corridors once more.

For a moment, I hesitate. I take a step back toward the vents, the path to where Amaris told me to wait. But then Altair tugs at my arm, and we're hurrying along through the gloom.

"How did the guards miss your ship?" I ask. "I thought any vessel attached to the station dock had been locked down."

"Well," says Altair, "it *is* a stealth ship." He maneuvers us around a corner and continues at his breakneck pace. "There's three ways to get past the guards," he tells me. "One, simple bribery. Two, threats or blackmail—that's something to keep in mind. The person we're working against is as ruthless as he is resourceful. Trust no one. Even someone you think you can depend on might be working for him, under duress."

"So what's number three?" I say as we descend a sudden steep staircase. My mental map is dissolving around me. The ship is a labyrinth and I have no idea where I am.

"Third," he says, "is to know every nook and cranny of this whole construction. Which I do."

The stairs give way to a huge rough-hewn metal hall lined with pipes and lit by a series of red lights. I have a feeling we're deep in the underbelly of the station. Altair guides us into a sloping tunnel, then takes us through a number of sharp turns. Another staircase. Another hallway, this one smelling of damp. I want to stop somewhere, to catch my breath and my bearings, but there's no time.

Finally, we end up at what looks like a porthole set into the floor. Altair wrenches it open, revealing a steep, dark tunnel.

"This chute will take you straight to my vessel. Once you land, tap the upper blue sign on the control panel and we'll be connected. Have you ever flown a skycraft before?"

I shake my head.

"Well then," says Altair, resolute, "this will be fun. Don't worry, you may be in for a bumpy ride but it's not as hard as it looks. Just like driving a groundship."

"I've never done that either," I say.

"There's safety restraints in the seat," he says. "Use them. And maybe pray to whatever gods are on Yorgos."

"Got it." I gather up my skirts and peer down the tunnel.

"It's not as far as it looks," says Altair. "I slid down it as a kid on a dare. Think you can handle it?"

"Of course." One more lie for the road. "I'm a champion tree climber, remember? I'm not afraid of anything. Are you going to be able to handle Perseus, though?"

"Of course," he says, echoing me. In the dim light, I can see him try to summon a smile. "Hey. We'll see each other again, okay? I'm sure of it. You're someone exceptional, Iola."

"You know what?" I say. "I really am."

Altair's laughter follows me down the chute.

I've been sliding for several seconds when I remember with a jolt that Amaris doesn't know about Perseus. She might be stubborn, a snob about food, and more than a little deluded about her chances of changing the empire, but she tried to help me clear my name. And if Perseus has a personal hatred of the Voyria, then Amaris is in real danger, just as much as Altair. I have to warn her.

I dig my heels in to slow my descent and try to clamber back up the chute, but the walls are slick with what smells like mold. All I manage to do is rip a hole in my sleeve and bang my elbow, and I can feel myself losing purchase, sliding farther down the tunnel again. Something cold splashes into my eye, and I blink rapidly, trying to get a sense of my surroundings.

I strain to scrabble upward, and I'm just getting somewhere when I hear the high, thin sound of an alarm going off, over and over. Another drop hits my face.

Then there's the scrape of metal, a resounding crash, and suddenly I'm surrounded on all sides by a sharp, enveloping cold. The shock of the impact startles my mouth open and then my throat is filling with water as I plunge helplessly down.

19

My lungs burn. My body is starting to go stiff from the cold. I can feel panic flooding through me, and I fight it with every remaining scrap of my awareness, but even as the water muffles the sound of the alarm, a new alarm is wailing over and over in my head: *you're going to die you're going to die you're going to die.*

I think of my friends back on Sarn—Jax and their colorful language, Babbit's serene smile as he plays the fiddle, Pav eagerly sharing the latest port gossip, Dezmer's loud laugh as she stirs up the thick air with her fan, Mita's oversteeped tea and crispy flatcakes. I think of Amaris, who tried to help me in her own infuriating way. I think of Dad, losing me the same way he lost Mom: no final glimpse, no last words, nothing to soften the blow, just an absence.

And then I think: *screw that.*

When I force my stinging eyes open, there is only the darkness. My shoes brush something solid, and I kick off as hard as I can, using all the strength in my legs. But something is still weighing me down, beyond the thick and nauseating crush of water. It's as if I've got rocks in my pockets.

Oh wait, I do.

I reach frantically behind myself and tug on the delicate hidden zipper of my gown, but the metal is stuck no matter how hard I yank. My lungs feel like they're twisting inside out as I claw at the fabric of my beautifully made dress, feeling the seams start to pop under my cold, clumsy fingers. It tears slowly, too slowly. With one final rip, I manage to free myself. The tangle of cloth and stones drifts down without me, an entire fortune gone, and I kick desperately again, swimming up and up and up.

When I finally break the surface of the water, an arm is reaching for me and I grab at it, coughing and hacking. Another arm joins the first and I'm lifted into the air and set on solid ground again, where I retch out the contents of my stomach and a whole lot of water. When I lift my head, swallowing the last of the burning bile, I notice two things.

The first is that the death trap I came from appears to feed into one of the station's elaborate decorative waterfalls. It burbles merrily beside me in the center of some kind of portrait gallery. The second is that I'm standing in front of a pair of palace guards, soaking wet and clad only in my slip and one shoe. I basically could not look more suspicious if I tried.

"You should really mark your bathrooms more clearly," I tell them. "I've been lost for what feels like an hour without encountering so much as a *sign*! And then I nearly drowned—"

One of the guards, the taller one, grabs my wrists in one hand and, from a thin metal tube, squeezes an ooze in a ring around them that sticks my hands together. My hands go numb on contact, and suddenly I have as much control over my fingers as I do over the weather.

The taller guard drags me out of the room by the elbow, while the shorter guard follows, railgun trained at my head.

With his other hand, the short guard pulls out a radio. "This is Enforcer Andino with Enforcer Sagona, requesting backup. We've located the source of the alarm," he announces, lifting my sodden hair to peer at my necklaces. "Lone female, approximately 1.65 meters and 77 kilos. Also spotted in her vicinity: more than fifteen pieces of jewelry in a variety of cuts and colors, at least some of which may match the description of items reported missing earlier in the night. We require another guard to retrieve the stolen goods from water tank 212."

"Copy that," says a gravelly voice, and then another, cleaner transmission cuts through the static.

"Bring her here." It sounds like Altair. He doesn't sound surprised. My relief at escaping death by drowning is draining away, leaving only horror at what might happen next. The realization is turning my veins ice-cold, and I want to run—only I can't.

Andino coughs. "Yes sir. I'll bring her after we get her scanned."

"No, bring her to me first, enforcer."

I'm wrenched up a staircase and through a hallway before my throat is clear enough to rasp out, "Where are we going?"

"Shut up," says Enforcer Andino as the other guard shoves me forward.

The farther we go, the nicer the hallways look, which suggests nobody is going to shove me out of the airlock just yet. It's more or less the only comforting thought I have.

The odds that Altair, who knew the interior bowels of the station the way I know the face of my father, would accidentally lead me down the wrong chute—they feel very slim. If Altair urged me into the tank on purpose, nothing he said can be trusted, which means Perseus could well be innocent, and Altair is likely in on the murder scheme in some way. And if Altair is involved, then it's my word against a popular, charismatic politician and war hero who's been named the next emperor.

Plus, the guards have evidence that I'm a thief. In the eyes of high society and Helian law, a thief is just a short leap to a murderer, as if a really nice bracelet is equivalent to a life.

Finally, Andino and Sagona drag me to a set of double doors flanked by guards. Enforcer Andino pushes the doors open with one hand, railgun still aimed directly at my skull with the other, and we enter a lushly decorated room. Standing at the far end of the deep, soft carpet—I can feel it all too well with my bare left foot—is Mynos. Thea is beside him, collapsed on a velvet armchair, and behind her, leaning against the back of the chair, is Altair. They look like a portrait, the three of them.

I try to read Altair's face, looking for the man who sent me plunging into a water tank, but his features are relaxed, almost blank. He's watching Mynos, who blinks his pale-blue eyes and lifts an imperious finger in my direction.

"This is who the Voyria send to do their dirty work? This is their crack operative?"

"I'm obviously not with the Voyria," I croak.

"Consider cooperating," says Mynos. "If you give a full confession, admit you were a member of the Voyria and that you killed my brother to destabilize the empire, you may have some say in your method of execution."

I think of what Amaris said, about the empire using Hyperion's murder as an excuse to crack down on the Voyria, about how badly they want to get away with such a thing.

My head is still spinning. I have no other cards left to play, so I go for it. "Please, check my purse in the cloakroom, I'm here on Prince Altair's invitation."

Altair pushes himself off the chair and steps toward me, stunningly green eyes intent on my face.

"I have never," he says, enunciating clearly, "spoken to this girl before in my life."

Since the moment I was dragged out of the water, I knew, deep down in the pit of my stomach, that this was coming. But still, I can't tear my gaze away from Altair's. My mind is struggling to summon anything that will help me get out of this. All I can think is that I've broken my number one rule: never implicate the rich to the rich. This is what happens when you don't follow the rules, I tell myself. This is what happens when you come up with silly ideas and leave your home seeking something better.

Under his breath, too quiet for even the guard standing near me to hear, Altair whispers, "Do you really think I only kept one dose?"

I flush cold all over, like I'm back underwater. I know I'm dead. It's all over for me. I had a good run—well, no, I had a terrible run. At least I got to spend the last of it in the company of someone like Amaris. But, I realize with an awful start, if Altair ever saw her with me, then he'll go after her, and I have no way of warning her—

Altair steps back to face Mynos and Thea. "You know, I do recall someone bumping into me on the street the other day. Afterward, my extra pass to the ball was missing. In retrospect, that's not much of a coincidence, is it?"

"Not much of a coincidence at all," says Mynos. He turns to me. "The only question left is, who was the mastermind of your plot? It clearly wasn't you. I mean, look at you."

I say nothing.

Thea reaches out a hand to Mynos, who pulls her to her feet. She walks over to me, her steps impossibly graceful.

"How old are you, child?"

I glance from her to Mynos to Altair.

"It's not a trap or a trick," she tells me. "I simply want to know. How old are you?"

"Eighteen," I say.

"She's only a girl, Mynos," says Thea quietly. "And likely a girl who has been raised without certain advantages, the poor thing. Before we unleash the full wrath of the crown upon her, let me talk to her." She indicates the side of the room with a flick of her fingers. Enforcer Sagona starts to drag me there. "Alone," she adds.

"Is that safe, Your Highness?" says Enforcer Andino.

"I am not afraid," Thea replies. "We will only be in the next room over, and it's clear she has no weapons. If I am in any danger, I will scream and you are welcome to intervene then, but I rather think she is too smart to try anything."

Enforcer Sagona grimaces, clearly not comfortable with the

prospect. "We really must object. Your Highness—"

"I was not asking."

Enforcer Sagona drops my arm.

"This way," says Thea. We step through what looks like a waterfall trickling along the wall but turns out to be just another holo, behind which is a door. Thea opens it, and I follow her inside. She shuts the door and gives me a long look I can't decipher.

"Now then," she says, "let's have a talk, just you and me. You know, I wasn't lying back there. You could not have gotten so far without considerable intelligence. They tell me you came from a rather remote part of space, and I can believe, without the proper influences, it would not be hard for a bright young girl to get swept up in the thrall of a group like the Voyria. What you don't realize, perhaps, is that at its core, the members of the Voyria are much like anyone else. They want power, control, and all that sets them apart from us is that they're willing to kill for it. What would truly change, if they came to power? The names of your rulers, and the lists of the dead, that's all."

I attempt to meet her eyes, but my head is still pounding from nearly drowning earlier. Finally, I manage to squint up at her. "What do you want from me?"

"Simply the truth," says Thea. "Admit your crime and give us one other member of the Voyria, and I will speak on your behalf when it comes time for sentencing."

"What does it matter?" I say. "You'll want to set an example to the rest of the empire. I'm dead either way."

"You're young," she says. "You haven't yet realized the difference between a quick, painless end and a death that lingers. But take a moment to ask yourself how you want your last moments to be." Her eyes well with feeling, reflecting luminous shades of jade and emerald, and somehow she still looks elegant, still looks stately. "Please, I am only thinking of what I would want for my own child, had I been so blessed. The hand of the law can be merciful, or it can be very, very cruel."

"A confession and a name?" I ask.

"I may even be able to make a case for your rehabilitation," she says, folding her hands. Her fingers bear several gorgeous rings, their jewels winking in the light. "Think of what is in your best interest, child, because nobody else will."

A confession and a name. I picture Amaris beside me, her hands bound with this numbing gel, waiting to be interrogated about her involvement with the Voyria and likely tortured for it. I think of her slow smile and the vanilla-ginger scent of her hair, her reluctant hand reaching for a biscuit, and her stupid, disastrous belief that something could actually be done about the state of the universe. Even knowing that, without someone else to take the fall, there is no way out of this for me, I can't make the words come.

"A confession, and the name of the person who murdered your husband, and you'll speak on my behalf? Do you promise?"

She nods.

I take a shuddering breath. "My confession is that I didn't do it, and the name of Hyperion's killer is Empress Thea. Does that help?"

Thea closes her eyes. She opens them again and exhales slowly. "I take back what I said about your intelligence," she says. "Had I killed Hyperion, I would have done it months before the ball. It would have been peaceful and in his sleep, and there would have been zero loose ends."

"You know, this really isn't convincing me that you're innocent," I say.

"I don't need to convince you," she says. "You don't have value to me. And before you get any silly ideas about making some kind of daring escape, your features are on record in every enforcer database in the empire." For a moment, from the set of her chin and the coldness in her gaze, she looks startlingly like Altair. *They're all the same*, I think hysterically.

Thea clicks her tongue. "My deepest sympathies to everyone who loves you for what is about to happen." And with that, she opens the door. I stumble out after her.

Enforcer Sagona grabs my arm again. I don't try to fight it. There's no point. Thea has made clear that there is no corner of space left where I can be safe, and there is no way I can ever see my family without putting them in danger, too.

"Nothing but vile insults to the Helian crown," Thea announces. She pauses next to Mynos and says something in a quiet voice to him. "Not worth—"

I'm straining to hear her, which is why I'm able to detect from behind the door an almost imperceptible *click*. It's a sound I've been trained to notice since I first started junkpicking. When a piece of tech is wired to blow, that click is your only warning to get as far away from the source as possible, so that you can hope to lose a hand instead of your life. I throw myself onto the ground, taking Enforcer Sagona with me.

"What—" Mynos starts, and the room rocks with the force of a thunderous explosion.

20

The force of the blast knocks us all off our feet. I awkwardly scramble back up, bracing myself on my numb hands. The guards are facing the door, and I follow their gaze. Five, no, six people stream in through the melted remains of the doors, their faces so aggressively nondescript that even I can tell they're wearing some kind of masking collar.

"What are you doing?" Mynos shouts at the guards. "Get them!"

Enforcer Andino raises his railgun, but there's smoke everywhere and the intruders move fast, darting around him. There's a shout as one of the guards goes down, and then another. Enforcer Andino rubs at his eyes with his free hand, and in that split second, the stockiest masked person charges him, snatches up the railgun, and swings it up with practiced ease to aim it at Altair.

Altair straightens up, his gaze fixed on the railgun. He glances at me and laughs. "I see. Well, go on then."

The guard to my left struggles to their feet, and one of the masked figures rushes over to me. They grab my arm and wave me on. I follow their lead, stumbling along, as we clamber over the melted and fused chunks of door.

The five other strangers follow, two running, one supporting another who is limping, and one carefully backing out of the room with the gun still trained on the royals inside.

"This way," calls one of the strangers in a deep, distorted voice. The guards who were at the door before are nowhere to be found, and together we book it down the hallway.

When we turn down a corridor, I glimpse a flash of familiar white-and-gold armor in the distance, and I hiss, "Guard up ahead!" in time for one of the six to toss a small bundle down the hall. It bursts into a thick cloud of smoke, and the approaching guard doubles over, coughing.

We run past the guard and through an open door and then we're standing in what looks like a loading bay. There is a round, still-sizzling hole in the far side of one wall, through which some-one has threaded a black door-sized tunnel ending in what looks like an airlock. The others advance toward it.

"In here!" one of them tells me. "Our ship!"

Long term, I have no reason to trust these people. Short term, they are my best friends. Still, I wait until two of them have slipped into the tunnel before I follow.

The stranger in the lead pushes a button and the airlock opens. Distantly, I can hear running feet behind us—the guard, most likely. We rush through the airlock to the other side, the stranger in the rear slaps another button, and the airlock snaps shut behind us. We're in the intruders' ship, whoever they are.

The stocky one lets out a sigh, then taps the ceiling and calls out, "Knifeshark to Meez, all present, let's go!" They press a button at their collar and their nondescript features blink out, replaced by a heavily tattooed face. They grab at a handle riveted to the wall and indicate for me to do the same. I awkwardly wedge a handle between my elbows and watch the rest of the group grasp at handrails of their own.

"Meez was born with both feet on the throttle," Tattoos tells me by way of explanation.

The ship gives a single violent shudder and we're off, so fast my stomach swoops. Nobody speaks for what feels like a long time, too busy holding on with every ounce of their remaining strength.

"That was ghastly," breathes the shortest of the half dozen. "Are you okay? It's Cass, right?"

There's only one person in all of Ouris who knows I go by Cass, not Cassandra or Iola. I had a suspicion as to who my rescuers were, but now I'm almost dead certain.

"Meez to Knifeshark," says a laughing voice. "Looking all clear behind us. Stations are bad at playing tag as a rule and our good buddy thinks he's successfully fried their scanners for at least an hour, so that's something. Think I'm gonna quit ripping through the fuel and go dark. Feel free to stretch your legs a little, and maybe consider getting a better codename, loser."

I can feel the ship slow a little then. No doubt it's still rocketing faster than anything has a right to, but I no longer feel like a force outside of my control is stirring my innards with a big dirty spoon.

The people around me sigh, relax their grasp on the handrails, and start to deactivate their masks. The bland, pointedly uninteresting features melt away. My rescuers look astonishingly ordinary. Freckles, curls, chapped lips—they are anyone I could've passed on the street on Sarn.

The shortest of the group has a gray buzz cut and brown skin a few shades lighter than Pav's.

"You've had a *night*," she says to me. "How're you feeling?"

"You just—" I say, trying to collect my thoughts. I try again, "You all just—"

"Oh, the station will be fine, don't worry about it," says Buzz Cut, misinterpreting my shock. "We reseal the hole as we disconnect, and hopefully no one's the wiser. This type of ship is called—"

"—a Remora, I know," I reply. "I used to take them apart for scraps. Where did you come from?"

"Shoulda led with that," Tattoos mutters, seemingly to themself as the door to the rest of the ship slides open and Amaris steps through.

"They're with me," she says.

The wave of relief that sweeps over me then, seeing her, is so distinct and so all-encompassing that I nearly fall over. It's as if the only thing that's been keeping me going tonight has been blind panic, and without it, even my bones aren't sure how to do their job.

Amaris has changed out of her ballgown and into boots, trousers, a short tunic, and a tough-looking dark jacket. Her gloves are nowhere to be found, bitten nails on full display. I can't remember the last time I was this happy to see someone. Back on Sarn, which feels like a lifetime ago now.

Behind me, the easy chatter has stopped. "You sent the Voyria after me," I say. It's not really a question.

"Yes, well." Amaris's eyes flick to me briefly, then drop to the floor. "You're innocent."

I snort. "Hardly."

"Innocent of murder," she says, mouth twitching toward a smile.

"Mission report," says Buzz Cut.

Amaris starts. "Yes, Kleo, go on."

"No casualties or serious injuries on our side. No casualties on theirs, either. Possible minor structural damage to the station's hull, but the Remora lived up to its name. I recommend that Tarek be treated for minor blunt trauma to the legs and trunk."

"My trunk is fine, thank you very much," says, well, probably Tarek.

"Don't be a hero," Kleo fires back. "You were limping. We treat sprains before they become breaks." She turns to the rest. "Did I miss anything?"

"Mynos has a *very* grating voice in person," puts in Tattoos. "Like two pieces of metal scraping together."

"Anything pertaining to the mission or to the safety of our crew?" says Kleo.

"I took psychic damage, hearing it," says Tattoos. "I think I need to lie down in a dim room and have Filo sing to me. Voice like a bird, that one."

"I would prefer not to sing to Osman," says a man who I assume must be Filo. "Their taste in music is abysmal."

"So," says Amaris, and everyone jumps to attention, "to sum up, the mission was a success, with no bloodshed on either side."

"Correct," says Kleo.

Osman clutches their heart. "Except that Filo just cut me to the quick! *Abysmal*, really? You couldn't just say bad?"

"The mission was a success, and our side is feeling well enough to get silly," Amaris concludes. She smiles, meeting each person's gaze in turn. "Splendid work, everyone. I know this isn't quite what you trained for, but you pulled it off perfectly. Consider yourselves officially off duty. Please, get some rest. That means you, Kleo."

Kleo laughs, and she and her five companions file out of the room, chatting amongst themselves.

"So," Amaris starts, "I should tell you that—"

I raise my joined, numb hands.

"Uh, is this permanent?" I ask, trying to match the lighthearted mood of the room a few seconds earlier but failing even before my voice cracks.

"Oh," says Amaris, "no, not at all. We just need to wash the holding gel off your wrists. Follow me." We head the same way as the rest of the Voyria, door swishing shut behind us, and dip into a darkened alcove which blessedly has a sink.

I swipe my boneless hands under the faucet until the water starts. It comes out freezing cold on my forearms, and for a second I am back underwater, the chill weight of all that liquid pressing harshly into my lungs. I jerk my wrists away. A cough wells up in my chest, even though I hacked out all the water back on the station. A phantom drowning.

I'm not sure what my face is doing, but Amaris flashes a palm at the faucet and the water begins to almost steam. She reaches behind me, my body registering the fleeting warmth, and returns to the sink with a soft cloth, which she wets with the warm water. She switches off the tap.

"Better?" she asks quietly.

I nod, and she gently wipes at the places where my wrists were stuck together. They come apart under her careful attention as if they'd never been trapped. I still can't feel my hands, but even being able to flex my arms in any direction feels like a divine gift. For a moment, I watch the gel swirl down the drain. Neither of us speaks.

"I hate this stuff," I say. "Not being able to even wiggle my fingers, it was—" I grasp for a word and come up with nothing. "Creepy," I finish.

"Rude of them, to not even pick a holding compound that smells good," says Amaris. "Spring flowers or spices or fresh-baked sausage rolls."

For some reason, I have to swallow past a lump in my throat.

Amaris regards me with concern. "Is the washcloth too hot?"

"It's perfect," I say. Her eyes soften just a little. It leaves me scrambling for words once again. "You know, I'm normally pretty good with accents, but I can't place yours."

"I'm from here and there," says Amaris.

"That's what you said the last time I asked you," I point out. Unspoken: *aren't things just a little different now?*

"I grew up on Haddan," she says. Other than her comment about the biscuits, I've never even heard of the place, which means it's either not wealthy enough to support interstellar tours to Sarn or too far away. She pauses to rinse the cloth, then touches it back to my skin. I want to tell her she doesn't need to be so deliberate, so delicate in her movements—the past hour has shown that I am not terribly breakable—but I can't bring myself to say it. "I went to school on Ouris at Othonos University," she adds. "What you likely hear is an unholy mixture of two extremely commonplace tongues."

Othonos I have heard of, unfortunately. There's no worse tourists than students of a prestigious college on break. They get drunker and rowdier than anyone else, and they've never heard the word *no*. I can't picture clever, diligent Amaris as one of their number.

She finishes with my left hand, which tingles strangely as the feeling begins to return.

"What Callidora said," I muse, "did you really finish three years early?"

She takes my right hand in hers and continues. "Yes, I was in a hurry to be done with it, I'm afraid."

"Scholarship student?" I ask, and the motion of the washcloth pauses for the barest second.

"How did you know?" she says, resuming her careful strokes.

"I've met plenty of students stopping off on Sarn for a solstice festival, the spawn of this wealthy donor or that, and they were all utter brats. I think it does something to them, to be handed everything in life. They never have to learn, so they don't. You're smart, you've clearly had to fight before." I pause. "And I'm not just saying that because the third time we met, you flipped me over your shoulder like the station's grav field was busted. I'm not light."

A wisp of a smile. "The majority of the universe would disagree with your read of Othonos, you know."

"The majority of the universe is wrong about all kinds of things," I point out. "Who cares what they think?"

"It wasn't that I worried what any individual thought of me," she says. "But it was . . . wearying to be constantly treated as less, to watch the best internships and the most exciting opportunities always go to the child of whoever sponsored the school's anti-gravball team."

I can picture how badly that would've upset someone as fair minded as her. "Their vomit's just as gross as everyone else's," I say. "I've had to clean it off my boots often enough."

She wipes the last of the gel off my wrist. "I'm sorry to hear that," says Amaris wryly.

"I'm sorry to hear you had to put up with those pukers full-time."

Amaris opens her mouth to say something, then seems to catch herself.

"What?" I ask.

"School was difficult, and not just academically," she says, "but the worst part was coming home."

"Why?"

"Millions of people on Haddan applied for that scholarship." She sighs. "And Othonos, in its wisdom, awarded it to twenty people from my planet." A trace of bitterness creeps into her tone. "Twenty. My application was very good, but thousands and thousands of applications were very good. I won a lottery, essentially. And so I would go home for breaks with a mountain of extra schoolwork, knowing none of it would put me ahead of the children of privilege, and I would see the people I grew up with, the ones who weren't taken by soldiers for breaking stupid rules or trying to make things better—and I would see how their lives were going nowhere and I would know—I would *know* that I am no better than them. The whole system is so rotten."

"Rotten to the core," I agree. "And your friends back home deserved better, just like my friends back home deserve better. But that doesn't change the fact that you are remarkable. You're remarkable, Amaris."

Amaris sets down the cloth but she's still holding my hand, palm to palm. She looks back at me, then at our joined hands, as if surprised to see them.

"I should tell you—" she starts.

"—that you're their leader?" I interject. "Yeah, I mean, I guessed."

She lets go of my hand.

"I'm not the only one," she says. "There are two others, and of them, I am the most junior."

"Wait," I say. "You're the leader of *the Voyria?* I meant the leader on the ship. You're in charge of the whole thing?" I spin the puzzle pieces in my mind, trying to make a new picture.

"One of three," says Amaris. "Of this gill, which is specific to Ouris."

"But the Ouris gill of the Voyria has got to be one of the most important."

"Well," she says, tilting her head, which is how I know I'm right.

"How did you—were you elected?" The only elections I've encountered involved choosing which of two imperial blowhards got to bathe in the money that came from selling off Sarn's resources. But clearly, this is something else entirely. "Was it a gill-wide vote? I'd vote for you."

"You would?" says Amaris, glancing up at me. For some reason, she sounds surprised.

"Of course." From the soft way she's looking at me, I can't shake the feeling I've somehow said too much. "Or, y'know, I'd wanna see what the other people had to say about you first," I mumble.

"That's fair," says Amaris.

"One of the three leaders of the Ouris Voyria," I say, retreating to safer territory. "I crawled around in the air vents with one of the three leaders of the Ouris Voyria. *Fates*. I mean, I should've known."

"Because of the way the others treat me." She hands me a towel, and I gratefully wipe down my hands and start in on my still-damp hair. Feeling anything under my fingertips is such a relief that I don't immediately answer.

"They treat you like you're in charge of the ship, sure," I finally say. "But you sent them back for me. I doubt a ground-level grunt could make that happen."

"They might, if they argued their case well," she says. "We don't really believe in grunts in the Voyria, anyway."

"Now that you say it," I tell her, "of course you're a leader of the Voyria. For a revolutionary spy, you're not that good a liar." I attempt to twist the towel in place in my hair and fail twice. It's so dry on Sarn that towels don't get much use.

"I convinced a ballroom full of people that I didn't mind being called Cream Horn," says Amaris dryly.

"Are you kidding?" I reply. "You nixed that one out of hand. I don't think we ever settled on what Iola Galatas, hapless ballgoer with no ulterior motive, actually calls her beloved wife."

"A pity," she says, and the strange thing is, I am a little sad that our ruse is up. Not the part where I was trapped on a station with someone who wanted to frame me for murder. But there was something to be said for having someone so capable at my side, someone who could be counted on and, with a little work, coaxed into laughing.

"Do you want help with that?" Amaris asks, and I look around before realizing she's talking about the hair towel.

"No," I say, "I've got it."

I don't, I definitely don't. Just when I think I've wrapped the towel securely enough to lift my hands away, it slithers to the floor. I duck down to pick it up, and Amaris does the same, and when our fingers tangle on that plush piece of terrycloth, it feels like getting my sense of touch back all over again.

"I've got it," I repeat.

"Right," says Amaris. She glances at me, then glances decidedly away, scrambles back to her feet, and adds, with sudden formality, "Shall we find you a change of clothes?"

That's when I remember I am standing there in only a slip. On Sarn, it gets so hot in the sunny season that once you're safely in the shade, nobody thinks twice about showing some skin, but of course, that's Sarn. Also, I must've lost the one remaining shoe at some point during my thrilling rescue because I am fully barefoot.

"Uh, yeah," I say. "That would probably . . . yeah."

Amaris reaches up to the ceiling and presses the comms button. "Anyone who has a moment, we need a spare clean outfit for Cass in the first bathroom. Thank you." She hands me a larger towel to wear in the meantime.

As I wind the fluffy towel around myself, I say, "So you should know that Thea's innocent. Mynos, too."

Amaris, who had been pacing the room, spins on her heel back to me. "Are you sure?"

"Unless Altair was able to fake the footage of her and Mynos sleeping at the opposite end of the station," I say, "it wasn't them."

"We did all that for a dead end." Amaris groans. "Who do you think did it, then?"

"I don't know," I admit, the shame of the betrayal making my face go hot. "Altair said it was Perseus, but obviously Altair lied about a lot of things."

Amaris nods. "You can trust Perseus," she says.

"He's stuck-up, but I hear a lot of stuck-up people go through their whole lives without murdering anyone," I agree. "And besides, Altair tried to pin the murder on both Perseus and me. I think that automatically puts us on the same side."

"Glad to hear it," says a wry voice from the other side of the room, and there, framed in the doorway and holding a neatly folded set of clean clothes, is Perseus.

21

Perseus steps inside the room and gives Amaris a questioning look. She nods.

"Wow," I say to nobody in particular, "this ship is full of surprises. Is there anyone else in here I should know about? Do you have Councilor Iraklidis stowed in the hold?"

"I'm afraid not," says Perseus. He holds out the clothes. "Apologies, I didn't know if my face would be welcome to you after the events of tonight, but Osman was indisposed."

"Indisposed?" Amaris echoes, brow furrowing in concern as I accept the bundle from Perseus. Just thinking of replacing my wet, ruined slip with something dry has me smiling.

"Sleeping," Perseus says. "You know Osman. They carry on about how they won't get a wink, and then you turn around and they're out like a light."

Amaris visibly relaxes, and I glance between them. "How long has Perseus, uh—?"

"Been a part of the dastardly Voyria?" he finishes. "It's been, what, two years? Three? Time flies when you're engaging in what's technically treason."

Amaris clearly trusts him, so maybe I should, too, but it's incredibly strange to be standing here in her ship, talking to someone with the same face as the dead emperor. It's also pretty weird to be doing it barefoot and looking an awful lot like a drowned rat.

"Is there somewhere I can change?" I ask.

Amaris nods toward a privacy screen farther into the room, and for the first time, I realize that this little alcove is probably part of her bedroom. Though there's not much to see—a rough painting of a mountain range pinned above the bed. A holo pic of what looks like the entire crew on this particular Remora. Another image of several teens about Jax's age, squinting at the camera from a worn-down front stoop and accompanied by a solemn-faced little girl who has to be Amaris. She looks about seven.

"Everything all right?" Amaris calls back.

"Uh, yeah," I say, ducking behind the screen. Whoever pulled this outfit together was considerate enough to include undergarments. I strip off the sodden slip, the last of Mita's handiwork, and change into a set of clean, dry underthings. I can almost feel my mood rising a notch. Then, a pair of trousers like Amaris's. Then a sky-blue tunic.

"Why would someone so close to the throne join up with a rebel group?" I blurt as I poke my head through the neck hole.

"I don't pretend to be the hardest hit by the Helian Empire," he says, "but still, it is easier to see the flaws in a system when that system is directly and very personally hurting you."

Perseus reels this off easily. I wonder how many times he's had to field this kind of question before.

"The organs," I say, pulling my arms through the sleeves. "The surgeries." I had been tamping down my thoughts of the implications of his tossed-off comment about kidneys, all the better to dislike him, but they come rushing back now.

"Don't forget the disposability," says Perseus evenly. "But that isn't the worst part."

"What could be worse than knowing your insides barely belong to you?" I ask, peering around the screen. "We don't have much on Sarn, but we've got that."

The look in his eyes is one I won't be forgetting in a hurry. "The worst part is that they pit us against each other," he says.

"Your brothers?"

"You don't need to talk about this if you're not up to it," says Amaris gently.

"I don't mind," says Perseus, his voice a little distant but untroubled. "Yes, we're brought up to hate one another. Hyperion saw us as a means to an end, a free supply of whatever organs or other living tissues he wanted, and a set of like-minded advisors he could mold. He knew what kind of person he was, and that meant he thought he knew what kind of people we were. He was terrified we'd form alliances and seize more than our share of power. So we had to compete for everything. Food, sleep, attention, our education—it was all a zero-sum game."

"What happens to you all now that Altair is the next emperor?" I say.

"I would prefer not to think of it," says Perseus. "Hyperion was careful to keep all of us alive, and me on the Council, as long as we were useful, but Altair has no reason to keep us around. My youngest brother is still a child, but I doubt that will stop him."

I take in all of this with a shudder. I remember the way Altair looked me in the eye and said he'd never seen me before.

"He's ruthless," I say. "He'll stab you in the back with a smile, and he'll make people love him for it." I think back to everything Altair told me, wondering how much of what he spun for me about Perseus was actually in some way about himself. "When you were young, did you ever, uh, see him hurting an animal?"

Perseus regards me with a level stare. "Which time?"

"The quantar," I say.

"Again," says Perseus quietly, "you'll have to be more specific."

"He said people in your way tend to disappear," I say, as a new terrible misgiving starts to form in the pit of my stomach. "When I first met him, he told me about his superior officer and a commander who'd died—"

"Who, Phaidros and General Macedon?" says Amaris. "Phaidros was directly above him in the force."

"When he passed, Altair was kind enough to take his place," Perseus adds, "and his rank."

"The same thing happened about a year later with General Macedon," Amaris says.

"He really has such terrible luck with his superiors, poor fellow," Perseus drawls.

"It was the middle of a war," Amaris explains. "People disappear as a matter of course. And so nobody thought to ask questions."

"Almost nobody," says Perseus.

I remember the cheers in the ballroom, the palpable sense of relief when Altair was named successor.

"The people really do love him, don't they?"

"Why wouldn't they?" says Perseus. "They have the benefit of not knowing him."

"He's charismatic," says Amaris, "he's handsome if you like that sort of thing, he knows what to say to get someone on his side, he's gotten a great deal out of being a war hero—"

"Oh, *Fates*," I interject. "He'll get away with anything he wants, won't he?"

"So you see why we had to try to prevent him from taking power," Amaris says. "He has his own ideas about how the empire should be run."

"Those ideas mostly involve wanton bloodshed and conquest," Perseus says.

Amaris grimaces. "He thinks Helia has been too peaceful, if you can believe it. He believes the Zarinel Federation, the Khonsanian Collective, and any remaining holdouts should step into the light of the Helian Empire."

"How—" I rub my face. "How does someone even end up believing something like that?"

"Well, it's not such a great leap from what we're taught from the moment we learn to sing the imperial anthem," Amaris says.

"Altair just took that philosophy to its logical conclusion," Perseus says. "He's always had a predilection for claiming what isn't his and still wanting more."

I nod, and then my brain catches up to what Amaris said earlier. "Hang on, *you* didn't kill the emperor, did you? So you could blame it on Altair? Has everyone in this room either been blamed, or blamed someone else, for killing Hyperion?"

"I wanted to tell you earlier," Amaris says. She darts a look at

Perseus, who gestures at me.

"Tell me what?" I demand.

"We—the Voyria, that is—didn't kill the emperor." Amaris worries at her thumbnail with her teeth. "But we knew Altair had killed in the past to improve his station. We knew he was impatient and short-tempered."

Perseus says, "And we knew that he could be flattered into believing the people wanted him and not Hyperion to rule during the five-year training period. He had enormous public support."

"We suspected that Altair would be Hyperion's choice for emperor. Altair had made a name for himself in the war, and Hyperion liked that. I think he might've even known that Altair killed his superiors."

"To Hyperion, that would have been a plus in Altair's column, not a minus," Perseus says.

"When Perseus accessed the emperor's files and confirmed that Altair was next in line, we knew we had to do something," says Amaris. "Altair in power would mean a continuation of Hyperion's policy of expansion, but with none of his caution or reluctance to engage in losing battles. Altair as emperor would throw not just our empire but the entire galaxy into chaos and destruction."

Perseus grimaces. "We got a taste of that a few years back, when Altair pulled a few strings, had a couple key diplomats killed, and stopped the Helian-Zarinel talks in their tracks. The war escalated quickly from there."

"So if Altair was next in line for the throne anyway, why didn't he wait to kill the emperor?" I ask.

"Enter the Voyria," Perseus says, bowing with a flourish.

"We fed Altair information through rumors and leaked files that Hyperion had chosen Perseus. We hoped to goad him into an assassination attempt and catch him in the act."

"That's pretty risky," I say.

"We didn't have many other routes," Amaris says. "Time was running out, so we bet on his previous pattern of behavior."

"Lots of murder," I say, nodding.

"Yes," says Amaris. "We assumed he would strike earlier, when we had plenty of agents in place to catch him. When the night of the ball came and no murder attempt had been made, it sent us scrambling. Our best guess is that obtaining the neurotoxin took longer than he'd anticipated. Pulling together a gown and an invite at the last minute wasn't ideal."

My mind races. "But you didn't count on the bio-lock, did you."

"No," says Amaris. "That was unexpected. We've been looking into it and our best intel says it was installed very recently at the request of Thea."

"So you came to the ball thinking you knew who would try to kill the emperor."

"Correct," says Amaris ruefully. "When you appeared on the scene, I first assumed you were someone Altair had brought on to do his dirty work, perhaps someone with training in assassination. He didn't commit all his murders himself, you know, and with a victim this high-profile, it seemed likely he would try to keep his hands clean. I made an executive decision to tail you and not him, as I'd been planning. Once I realized my mistake, I tried to signal to you that the situation wasn't safe for you. By then he was out of my line of sight, and then the news of the bio-lock came and I decided it couldn't have been him."

I try to digest all of this, but it's not going down easy. "So when I came to Altair and he lied to me about the murder, led me into a water tank where I almost drowned, and then tried to have me killed—all of that could've been prevented if you'd just told me the truth from the beginning?" My hands are shaking now, and not from whatever numbed them.

"Cass—" Amaris starts, brow knitting.

"I almost died, twice," I grit out. I'm overwhelmed with the memory of the feeling of bitingly cold water surrounding me on all sides. "And you could've—with a little warning—"

"I knew you were here on his invite, and we had only just met. Going by the clock, we barely know each other now," says Amaris, and maybe she has a point about the beginning, but I had splashed water in her face and helped her with her gloves and coaxed her into eating. She had kissed me, but more than that, I had—well, I had trusted her. For some reason.

"Am I free to wander the ship?" I say.

Amaris blinks. "Are you free to—yes, of course. The cockpit requires a retinal scan from one of us to enter, but other than that, you should be able to access everything."

"Good," I tell her. "I need to take a walk. Alone."

22

I walk past Amaris and Perseus to the next set of doors. They open into a hallway lined with more rooms just like the one I came from. At the end of the hallway is another pair of doors, and I keep going. I'd been picturing this vessel as a tiny stealth ship, but it is much larger than I'd thought, bigger than any of the Remoras I've scrapped for parts on Sarn.

I pass the kitchen, which is outfitted with what looks like a cross between our thruster stove on Sarn and the shiny machines in the palace kitchens. I walk through what looks like a room just for relaxing, lined with pillows and soft light, strewn with old books, a blanket, an unwound scarf. The whole space is open and welcoming and I hate it.

Finally, I arrive at a small, dark chamber with a window for a floor. I ease myself down to the smooth, shiny surface and stare for a long moment at the inky blackness below.

If I'm being honest, I'm angry at myself more than anything. I've always trusted my own people and no one else. I knew that allies and friends don't come easily. Nothing in life does. But I'd wanted to believe in Amaris, someone I barely knew. I'd been as willing as anyone to take it on faith that she would have my best interests at heart, and she had knowingly left me, with no hint or warning about Altair.

It occurs to me that I still have the necklace he gave me in Callidora's, tucked under the tunic that isn't mine. It had remained around my neck during my struggles in the water, and nobody had thought to confiscate it later. There's one bright spot, I tell myself. When this is all over, I've got one new piece of jewelry I can pawn, and maybe if I'm lucky, that will be enough to hire me a mercenary long enough to scare off Theron, so that I might at least end exactly where I started, with Dad, no better than before.

Then again, *if I'm lucky* is an awfully big *if*.

I'm tired of thinking this way, I realize, tired of all my sentences built around *I*. Me, me, me, like the tourists swarming Sarn in the sunny season. Maybe that's why I was so quick to buy what Amaris was selling. Maybe spinning fairy tales about some sort of designated good guys is a human need, like the vitamins you don't get from Pink Dream. Maybe it wasn't about Amaris at all. Except, I think of her warm brown eyes and her firm insistence on caring, the fact that she did eventually eat the pocket meat and even the way she effortlessly flipped me over her shoulder—

The doors behind me swish open, and I startle, but it's only gray-haired Kleo.

"Mind if I join you?" she says.

Part of me wants to say that I do mind, that I clearly chose this particular room for maximum wallowing, but there's something familiar in her accent, how utterly not stream-ready it sounds, and so what I do is lift one shoulder in a shrug.

"Lucky they found clothes that fit you," says Kleo, and I wordlessly raise my arms to show the many times I've rolled up my sleeves. "Ah," she says. "Well, that's fair."

I expect her to start in on some lofty speech about honor and duty and rebellion, but she just leans against the wall, crosses her arms, and asks, "How was the music?"

"What?"

"At the ball," she says.

"Sedate," I say. "Tame, safe. Synced up by brain waves, if that counts for anything."

"Not if they weren't any good," says Kleo. She shakes her head. "I miss live music since we took up this life. Back home, we only had a little fiddle, some guitar, a little drum, but there's an energy to it that you can't get on the radio."

I hadn't thought of this, but then, on Sarn, we've got Babbit, at least when the Oasis can spare him. I wonder how he's doing, if the tourists are treating him all right, if his vision is worse.

Then, like opening a door I can't shut, a crowd of other people to worry about streams through my mind: Pav, Dezmer and Mita, Jax, and Dad. I try to imagine explaining my trip so far to Dad, the faces he'd make, the things he'd say, the way he'd laugh or shake his head or lay a hand on my shoulder and call me Cassie. Then I have to stop; it hurts too much.

Counting in hours, I've been gone less than two days, but it's easy to feel far from everyone here, light-years away from the sun and sand of Sarn. Anything could be happening to them now and there's nothing I can do about it. I even kind of miss the scorching sunlight. This much artificial lighting makes everything feel like it's not quite real.

"Nobody wanted to go on this mission," Kleo is saying. "Walking into that station felt like walking into—not even the lion's den. The lion's mouth. A black hole where a lion used to be. Amaris volunteered."

"Food was good," I offer.

Kleo snorts.

"Food's always good, as long as it's not rotten or Pink Dream," she says. "You chew enough garbage, you learn to round up."

I blink. That chalky magenta powder's been a staple for my whole life, but out here, after the impossible glamor of the ball, I feel almost like I invented it in my mind.

"Did it taste a little spoiled to you?" I say. "Pink Dream, I mean."

"Always," she says. "My theory's they made it that way on purpose so you could never tell when it'd really gone off."

"Maybe it helps to mix the stuff with milk," I say, "but who's poor enough for stomach fill instead of food but rich enough—"

"—to have a ready supply of milk?" Kleo finishes, uncrossing her arms to put her hands on her hips. "Absolutely, it makes no sense."

I thought I'd sensed something familiar about her vowel sounds, the way she forms the fourth-condition *I*.

"Where're you from?" I ask.

"Rotting middle of nowhere," she says. "This miserable industrial planet called Danae. Factories in every direction. I didn't get to touch real dirt until I was in my thirties." I'm vaguely aware

I'm gaping at her. "What?" she asks.

"I'm from Sarn! One of your moons!" I almost shout.

"What are the chances!" Kleo reaches up and taps the ceiling. "Leyda to the observation deck! May I repeat, Leyda to the observation deck! We've got another Sarnian for you!"

Another? I mouth.

Kleo nods, crosses the room, and sits next to me on the floor, even though I can tell her joints are protesting.

"Always good to meet another person who understands life on the edge of the universe," she says. "Ouris must've been a bit of a shock."

"Everyone is so smartly dressed," I say, nodding. "And it's so cold, even with the sun! And the park with the mech insects! Even just trees—"

"Did you know half the interiors of the imperial station are made of wood?" she tells me.

My jaw drops. "What? Really?" I think back to the glossy dark walls and, in retrospect, there might've been something organic about their swirling patterns.

"They slice 'em open, polish them up, and add a varnish so they shine," says Kleo. "It took a lot of orchards to finish the station. What a waste."

Those walls could've been made of anything else, but trees? I don't know much about ships, but it seems like a terribly extravagant and useless choice for the station interior.

"They took 'em from Gree," she adds. "Spliceberry trees. The farmers were furious. It lost them seven years' worth of harvests and a good deal of the food they were depending on besides, but you know, the royals must have a grander station than the Zarinels or the war's for nothing. And that's meant to mean something to us. We're meant to be glad that—"

The doors at the other end of the room slide open, and a heavyset middle-aged woman with beautiful streaky hair walks into the room. As she does, Kleo sits up a little straighter.

"Cass, meet Leyda. Leyda's too humble to mention it with her own mouth, but she's another of the leading trio of our little organization. Where's Reza?"

"They took the left cruiser out when Amaris came in," says Leyda. "We agreed the three of us shouldn't be within bombing distance of one another."

"Good thinking," says Kleo.

"Kiss-ass," says Leyda, not unkindly, and sounding so much like Dezmer that I have to wipe my eyes. She turns to me. "So, Cass, where on Sarn are you from?"

"The port near the Opuntia," I manage.

"The Opuntia!" Leyda cries. "Wasn't too near there myself but I heard about it, of course."

"Finest establishment on the whole moon if you avoid the Oasis, and who'd want to spend any length of time with resort customers? My friend Babbit says he heard one of them try to order hot ice. They've got no sense."

"True! Wish I'd known you were coming aboard," says Leyda. "I would've saved you a bottle of grunk."

I laugh. "Fine with me. Grunk tastes like if a fistful of cheap candy farted."

"Way with words, this one," says Leyda as Kleo grins, and it's not Dad's hand on my shoulder but it's something. "Do you miss the sun? I miss the sun. I don't miss the dark season, but that much light, even when there was too much of it—"

"Yeah," I say hoarsely. "For half the year, you were never cold."

"Precisely," Leyda says, sounding wistful. Then she seems to pull herself together. "I should get going," she adds briskly. "Lots to do. Kleo, remember you're off duty, yeah?"

Kleo tosses off a half salute.

"I thought there were no rebels on Sarn," I say to nobody in particular.

Leyda taps the side of her nose. "There's rebels everywhere, Cass. Ideas know no borders, as they say, and that's all it takes to get to us: an idea."

"You said it," says Kleo reverently. Leyda opens her mouth and Kleo adds, "I know, I know. Kiss-ass."

"You said it." Leyda laughs, and the doors close behind her.

"So what brought you to Ouris?" Kleo asks me. She produces a flask from her jacket, takes a sip, and then offers it to me. "It's just water," she says apologetically, but that's what makes me reach out to accept it and take a sip of my own. The water tastes cool and clean. In a way, this feels like more of a luxury than the spiced tea or the sparkling gold liquid from the ball.

"My dad," I say. "His health." My voice sounds raggedy, unsteady. I swallow. "I thought, if I could go where the rich people are, maybe I could take enough to make him better."

It sounds so simple now, almost childish.

"A lot of sickness on Sarn," says Kleo. "When they took your topsoil and left all that grit for folks to breathe, it started doing a number on your elders. It's even worse than breathing on Danae, and we've got more fumes than sky. There was a study but somebody suppressed it, go figure."

I hadn't stopped to think of Dad as part of a larger pattern. It makes me angry, that we could be lifted or sunk by tides we have no control over, that the tragedy of his failing lungs is just a drop in the ocean. The enormity of the problem, thousands of others out there with stories as brittle and sharp as mine—it makes me want to *do* something.

The doors behind us slide open, and for a moment I'm relieved that someone might distract from this train of thought, but when I crane my neck around, it's Amaris. She's holding a tray covered with a cloth and looking distinctly uncomfortable.

"You just missed Leyda," Kleo tells her.

"That's all right," says Amaris. "Mind if I join you?"

Kleo glances between us, then, with some trouble, pulls herself to her feet. "Think I'll go check on Tarek," she says. The doors swish shut behind her before Amaris speaks.

"I hope it's okay that I'm here," she says. "I can go if you'd rather, but—"

"It's okay," I say. Amaris fidgets with the edge of the cloth, then sets the tray to the side.

"In that case, not only am I sorry for what happened on the palace station, I apologize for not coming sooner to find you," she says. "The smell of that gel, I had to wash it off. It was starting to—" She clears her throat. "Bad memories."

"They used it on you, too?" I ask.

"Yes," says Amaris. She closes her eyes and breathes in through her nose, out through her mouth. "The first time being when I was nine."

Childhood is short on Sarn, but this is beyond my reckoning. "Nine years old?"

"At my first arrest," she says.

"When you were *nine*?"

"When I was nine," she affirms, opening her eyes. "They used the holding gel on my elbows and knees." Her voice is level, but part of me still wishes we were holding hands, something. "They'd put us all in a pit, you see. I think they were afraid we might try to crawl out."

"Sorry," I grit out, "I'm trying to imagine someone using that stuff on a nine-year-old and . . . It should be illegal, and *I'm* saying that."

"Well. I grew up on Haddan," she says, as if this explains everything.

I shake my head. "What's on Haddan?"

"Not much, but it's right on the border of Zarinel territory," she says. "Hard to hold on to. The Voyria has a strong presence there." She lowers herself to sit cross-legged next to me, with notably more grace than Kleo.

"That hardly explains how you got yourself arrested as a kid," I point out.

"My parents both worked all the time, and I excelled at school, so I was given more freedoms than perhaps were wise." Her lips quirk. "I had no siblings of my own, but the older children on my block looked out for me. So when they began to grow restless at the Helian soldiers on our streets, I joined my friends' efforts."

"You were a revolutionary at nine?"

"Nothing so formal," she says.

My voice is more or less steady when I say, "An informal revolutionary? That doesn't sound like you."

"I passed messages," says Amaris. She draws her knees up to

her chest, and for the first time all night, I am reminded that we must be around the same age. "Even a very good encryption can be hacked, but I was small for my age and nobody thought to stop and question a child on an errand."

"How were you caught?" I ask, knowing I am about to snap the pleasant thread of this conversation but too curious not to.

"There was a mole in the group," she says.

"Who gave up a nine-year-old?"

The line of her mouth hardens. "He gave up everyone. The money was too good, and he needed it. At the cost of our lives.

"The soldiers stuck us all in a pit while their ID program loaded," she continues, "but the group decided if they could do nothing else, they might at least free me, so they climbed on one another to lift me out, and I crawled on my belly to the river. Revolution stopped feeling like a game after that. I found a new gill of the Voyria and starting learning anything anyone would teach me."

"And you've been with them ever since," I say. "So that's what, nine years with the Voyria? Ten? You can't be that much older than me."

"Ten," she says.

"I'm sorry I brought that gel into your life again," I say, but she shakes her head.

"You had no control over that, any more than I did."

"Well, I'm sorry that happened to you," I try.

"Don't be," says Amaris. "It was a long time ago."

"When *I* was nine," I say, "I was junkpicking one day, and I found an intact hypercrystal, about the size of a fist. A bigger kid saw, figured it'd be worth something, and tried to get me to trade for what he had. I told him I didn't want his fragged-up shrapnel, and he stabbed me."

"What?" Amaris's eyes are huge.

"Yeah. Worst part is, he still got the crystal."

"I think the worst part is that you got *stabbed*," she says with a frown.

I shrug. "He was garbage with a knife, so luckily he only left me with this." I tug the neck of my tunic to the side to show her the mark on my clavicle, bumpy and ugly as ever. "That's when I started working on my conning skills. Figured I'd rather lie for a living than depend on a job where the biggest kid gets the best pieces. No such thing as honest work anyway, you know?"

"Cass," Amaris says, squeezing her eyes shut as if she can't bear to think about it, "that's so horrible."

I shrug. "Yeah, well, *it was a long time ago.*"

"Okay," says Amaris. "I do see your point."

"I lied, by the way," I add. "That happened when I was eleven. Thought it'd sell the story better, making us the same age."

"Listen," says Amaris, "about Altair. You're right, I should've warned you. My contact suspected you weren't in league with him, but I had to be sure. For my own safety, and the safety of my crew. But there was plenty of time after that point where I could've—"

"Wait, who was your contact?" I interject. Then I actually think for about two seconds. "Oh, Callidora."

"She's been one of us for years. Mostly, she sends money, but when Altair himself walked into her shop, she knew she'd need to make a full report."

It's hardly the wildest thing I've heard tonight, but still. "So Callidora's really with the Voyria."

"Many are," says Amaris. "It's hard to get an accurate head count among the gills but our sense is on Ouris, we're about one in fifteen people, and plenty more hold sympathies. But I'm getting off track.

"When I tailed you and discovered you seemed to be at the ball only to lift other people's valuables," she continues, "I thought perhaps you had conned Altair as well, manipulated your way into getting an invite for your own ends. I did try to warn you on the dance floor, that the situation was too precarious to be exploited in this way. But the moment I saw the bak knife and realized you'd been framed, I should've let you in on everything. I just—" She sighs.

"You have a hard time trusting people who are only trying to save their own skins," I finish. "For obvious reasons."

"That may be true," she acknowledges. "But I had a responsibility to look past my own ghosts. And anyway, as the night progressed, it became clear to me that you were . . ." Amaris hesitates. "Someone I could rely on, but by then, telling you so late in the proceedings might have destroyed your trust in me, and I reasoned that the mission depended upon your trust, that I would tell you once everything was resolved."

Amaris is quiet for a moment. "Then Hyperion named Altair his heir and it became imperative to get Perseus to safety. He had the motive, he could pass the bio-lock, and given that there were two others who looked passably like him on the station, an airtight alibi would be almost impossible. Once we'd gotten him onto our ship, I went back to find you, but you were gone."

"Right," I say. "I figured I was on decent terms with Altair. He seemed like my best shot at clearing my name, being the next emperor and all, and I wanted to warn him about Thea."

Amaris brings her pointer finger to her mouth and chews on the nail. "You would never have thought that, had I been honest. The Voyria is built on a foundation of trust between its members. I failed you."

She looks so dejected, I feel the last of my anger drain out of me.

"You came through in the end," I say.

"I really thought—" She takes a deep breath. "When I searched the ballroom and couldn't find you, when I checked the bathroom and the library and the vents and you weren't there, I remembered that you were only on the station on Altair's invitation and realized he probably was the one to frame you. And I thought about how the people in his way tend to disappear." She swallows. "Cass, if something had happened to you—"

"I got out of it," I remind her. "You got me out of it, in fact."

"But if he'd killed you, it would've been my fault." She folds her hands and shakes her head, meeting my eyes for a long moment. "And I couldn't—I didn't know how I'd—" A long, shaky exhale. "Well. That's when Perseus intercepted a transmission from the guard that they'd caught a woman matching your description."

I shiver. I can't help it. The narrowness of my escape makes me feel cold all over.

"Do you need a jacket?" she asks me.

I throw her a smile. "I'm fine. Just glad you came." She opens her mouth, no doubt to blame herself again, but luckily I get there first. "No, the end result is that I'm safe, which, again, I wouldn't be if it wasn't for you. You didn't have to come back. I'm not one of you, nobody was under any obligation to help me."

"We have an obligation to everyone under the boot heel of the empire," she says fiercely. "That's what the Voyria is. When I failed you, I failed the mission of the Voyria. If we hadn't gotten there in time—"

"You should've seen those slack-jawed imperial faces when your crew came busting in the room. And the explosion," I add. "I've never been so happy to hear something blow up."

This has the intended effect. She almost smiles. "The crew is quite the bunch, aren't they?"

"I wouldn't look twice at any of them in normal life," I say. "But rescuing me from the heart of the palace station, that took more than just pluck and luck. They know what they're doing."

"Together, they're so much more than the sum of their parts," Amaris agrees. "It gives me hope, seeing what we can become when we all understand what we should aim for." Her face grows somber again. "Cass, if you had come to harm because of me, I don't know how I'd ever—"

"Give it a rest," I tell her. "Honestly. You are light-years too hard on yourself. No harm done. Here we are in the present and I'm fine—" I notice the slight tremor running through Amaris. "Are you shaking?"

"Maybe a little," says Amaris.

"Eat something," I tell her. "I know I passed a kitchen—"

Amaris laughs, a little wildly, and pulls the cloth off the tray she'd brought earlier. It's heaped with cubes of cheese, various sorts of breads, popcorn in a variety of colors, and cut-up fruits I can't identify.

"Apology snacks," she says. "Filo helped."

I beam at her. "See, this is why you're in charge." I take a piece of bread and dab it in a small pot of something bright purple. "Your people flawlessly pulled off their mission to get me back, so just aim your feelings there while we work out what to do about Altair now." I pop the bread in my mouth, chew, and swallow. "Dig in," I say, "it's good."

Amaris smiles weakly. She reaches for a cube of cheese at the same time I do, and for one breath, our fingers brush, electric. Our eyes meet. I think she might blush. She pulls her hand back. Are we having a moment over a plate of cheese, or am I merely wishing we were having a moment over a plate of cheese? This is agony. I want to stay in this room with her forever.

"Seriously," I say, a beat too late, "help me eat all of this."

"You sound like Leyda."

"Like a middle-aged mom?" I say, trying for a laugh.

It doesn't work, but Amaris does seem to perk up a bit, reclaiming her cheese and chewing thoughtfully.

"Leyda is sort of everyone's mom here," she says. "She was even before she was formally elected. Always reminding us to sleep, eat, take breaks."

"It's good that someone's there to do that," I say. I can't imagine how I would've made it to eighteen on Sarn without Dad. "I guess not a lot of people's parents are also in the Voyria."

"Most of us had to leave our families when we got involved," says Amaris.

"Why? So that the empire can't retaliate against them?"

"Sure, or get them to inform on us."

I can't even begin to imagine Dad ever turning me in. "Do parents do that? Rat out their own kids?"

"All the time," she says, voice going ragged. She swallows, breathes in deeply through her nose, and adds, "Hence why people like Leyda are so important to us. The ones who raise you aren't always the ones who birth you."

I turn over her words for a few seconds. Then, like a lockpick clicking its way past a series of tumblers, something drops into place for me. I pull myself to my feet.

"What?" says Amaris.

I square my shoulders, steadying my breath. "I think I know how Altair killed the emperor."

23

Amaris jumps to her feet, presses a button on the wall, and says, "Leyda, if you could please head back to the observation deck." She turns to me. "She should hear this," Amaris explains. "How sure are you?"

"Not sure at all," I say. "I have no evidence. But the pieces all fit together this way, and short of Altair forcing one of Perseus's brothers to commit the murder, it's the only explanation that makes sense."

The door opens and Leyda comes striding into the room. "What's going on?"

Amaris looks at me. I close my eyes briefly, collecting my thoughts. "I have a theory," I say, "as to how Altair got past the bio-lock."

"Go on," says Leyda.

"About twenty-five years ago, Thea gave birth and lost the child, right?"

"Right," Leyda says, "he was stillborn."

"What if she didn't lose the child?" I ask. "What if she *lost the child.*"

"What if the baby was taken from her, you mean?" fills in Amaris.

"Exactly," I say. "The gossip is that Thea never forgave Hyperion after the birth, that she blamed him. Maybe this is why. She tested the DNA and knew that the child was Mynos's, so she sent him away and had him declared a stillbirth. And the baby was placed with King Dorus and Queen Lena of Leithe."

"Thea could've even had the bio-lock installed herself, knowing it would let Altair in," says Amaris thoughtfully.

"I remember thinking at the ball that he didn't seem to resemble the king and queen of Leithe at all, but he's a dead ringer for the empress," I say. "I saw that myself just before you lot came in to rescue me."

Frowning, Leyda produces a glass from her hip pocket. After a few careful gestures and a flick of her fingers, she projects a display to show a series of paparazzi snaps of Thea and Altair, arranged side by side in some sort of facial recognition program. A light-blue grid is overlaid over their features.

"It *is* uncanny," she admits. "Especially when they're annoyed. The area around the jaw, the arch of the nose, and the color of those eyes."

"We need to be very certain we're right before we raise a theory like this," says Amaris.

"Right," says Leyda. "A cover-up of this level would involve not just the emperor's family and the Leithe royal family but also the doctors who delivered the baby."

"That wouldn't be impossible to find out," says Amaris

thoughtfully. "Thea's pregnancy was intergalactic news. I'm sure we could dig up at least one gossip site detailing her medical staff. They would've been the top doctors in the Helian Empire."

"Check to see if they all suddenly retired to a luxury vacation planet," I say. "Or bought top-of-the-line new ships."

"Yes," Leyda says, "And we'll need to obtain Altair's DNA. I'll have one of our people in the palace to get that for us when the lockdown lifts. Failing that, we might have to reach out to a contact on Leithe."

"Hang on," I tell her, fumbling with the necklace I've worn since Altair took me to Callidora's. "See if you can get something from this."

"He gave you a necklace?" says Amaris, eyes narrowed.

"He gave me *his* necklace," I say.

Leyda's eyes widen. "We'll need a sample of your DNA too, Cass, but this is—this is very good."

"We found the doctors," Perseus announces maybe half an hour later. We're all in the cockpit—Perseus, me, Amaris, Leyda, Kleo, Filo, Tarek, Meez the pilot, and someone even woke up Osman. Nobody wanted to be left out.

"Do they each own their own retirement moon?" I ask.

"They're dead," Perseus says with a sigh. "All four doctors who were present at the delivery died within two weeks of the supposed stillbirth. Two ship accidents, one cryotherapy malfunction, and one cleaner-bot combustion that took out a housing pod."

"Well," I say, "that's one way to keep news from getting out."

"Is the DNA analysis complete yet?" asks Leyda.

Tarek holds up the pair of vials plugged into his glass—one containing a scraping from the necklace, the other a hair plucked from my head, so we can eliminate contamination. Perseus's DNA sequence is already displayed on a separate glass.

"Any second," says Tarek. "You know it's actually fascinating what we're doing right now." This leads right into a lengthy explanation of genes and inheritance and the inevitable shared sequences between any clone of Hyperion and any child of Mynos that I absolutely can't follow.

"We would need to solicit a DNA sample from Thea to prove lineage there, of course," Tarek finishes, "but if this is a match, we can at least prove that Perseus, and therefore Hyperion, is genetically Altair's uncle, which will solve the bio-lock question quite conclusively."

"Thanks, Professor College," says Osman with a snicker.

Filo thwaps them lightly on the arm.

"I got something," Kleo says, lifting her glass. She reads, "'Queen Lena of Leithe made quite a stir last week when she emerged with the new royal accessory, a bouncing baby prince. Representatives for the queen confirmed that they had kept the pregnancy away from the public eye out of respect for the royal family's privacy. The official royal announcement, including name and title, are coming soon. In the meantime, we congratulate the queen on the addition to her household, and on how expertly she hid her baby bump.'" Kleo's eyes scan ahead. "There's more in this post but it's all just tips for camouflaging a pregnant belly."

"How did nobody put this together sooner?" asks Osman. "A baby disappears here and reappears there—it's like a bad magic trick. There isn't even a solid misdirection." They wiggle their fingers like a magician. "Not to mention making all those doctors vanish."

"Not like people don't already vanish all the time," points out Leyda. "Especially if they just so happen to disagree with how the empire does things. We've had to smuggle out more than one journo who got a little too close to something the empire doesn't want to get out."

"Some of the minor gossip rags tried to claim it was distasteful for Queen Lena to, ahem, flaunt her baby when Empress Thea had just lost hers," Kleo says. "By flaunt, I assume they mean take him outside and expose him to air."

There's a soft chime from Tarek's glass.

"All sequenced," announces Tarek. "Whoever Altair is, it looks like we managed to scrape a sample from him. Now I'll just import Perseus's data and run it through the compiler—" We stare at the glowing projection on the wall, where a series of letters flash, impossibly fast, resolving into a single number. "Thirty-three percent," Tarek says quietly. "Wow."

"So that's a match, right?" I ask.

"There's a range of how much DNA siblings share," says Tarek, making notes on his glass. "Fifty percent is the average, but it can be anything from 38 percent to 61 percent. A 33-percent overlap places Perseus and Altair within range to be uncle and nephew. They're definitely relatives, and close ones." He sits back in his chair, wide-eyed. "Looks like you were right, Cass."

Osman mutters an awed string of words I've never heard before that are definitely profanity.

"I've often wondered why Altair behaved like the world owed

him something," Perseus says, pinching the bridge of his nose. "This would explain it. He always acted like something monumental had been taken from him, and he was merely taking it back."

"Altair feels entitled to the throne," I say.

"All right," says Leyda, clapping her hands. "People. This is a lot to take in, but our first question is, what's our next step?"

"Do we have any channels we could still use to relay an anonymous tip?" suggests Kleo.

I frown. "Even if we get through to, say, Ambassador Zahur, all we can prove is that Altair is Thea's son. But that doesn't prove he murdered Hyperion."

"Proof, proof, proof," says Osman. "You sound like Amaris."

"Thank you," I tell them. From the corner of my eye, I think I catch Amaris smiling.

"What if Perseus made the case to the Council?" says Kleo. "With compelling enough evidence, the Council would be forced to act, if only to preserve the legitimacy of the Helian government."

"Yeah, let's not delude ourselves," Osman snorts. "There's like two people left on the whole Council who might care at all about the truth. Everyone else worships at the altar of the status quo."

Filo scowls. "But we can try to force their hand, can't we?"

Perseus turns away from the glowing display. "I have no doubt that Altair has taken advantage of my absence to blame me for the Voyrian interruption to tonight's proceedings," he says. "We have to assume that my trusted reputation is a thing of the past."

"Well, we need the Council," says Leyda, massaging her temples. "They're the only ones with the authority to strip Altair of his power. Anything less than that and we'll always have a faction treating Altair as the true emperor."

Amaris sighs. "Which could easily destabilize Helia enough that the Zarinel Federation would seize the chance to attack, completely engulfing our systems in war."

"And of course that's exactly what Altair wanted," Osman says. "Plan B, please. What've we got? Do we storm the palace, extract Altair, and make him fess up?"

"Not so fast. Here's another problem," Meez says. "I can't get close to the station. Even if I turned around and cloaked up, they'll be looking for us now, and I think we can only use the explosion-as-distraction trick once per night."

"I can do it," I hear myself say. "It's dangerous, risky, and maybe stupid, but I know how we can get in." The plan is only just forming at the tip of my tongue, but it's waking me up. It's the rush of adrenaline I get when I'm about to run a particularly tricky con.

"You had us at dangerous, risky, and maybe stupid," says Osman. "Spill."

"You made me think of it, actually," I tell Osman, "talking about misdirection. We need the guards to believe it's their idea to let the Remora dock. Then we give them a big enough distraction to let a few of you slip onto the station, search Altair's room for evidence—he told me himself he still had more CNNP, and I doubt he carries it around in his pocket—and present it to Ambassador Zahur."

"We can make the case to the Khonsanians that dethroning Altair is in their best interest," says Amaris. "They want to prevent a full-scale war, just like we do. And Altair taking power would foil that."

"Ambassador Zahur is credible in the eyes of the Council, even if we aren't. Not to mention, they have the leverage of representing the Khonsanian Collective," says Filo.

"What if we don't find anything in Altair's rooms?" says Tarek. "This whole thing is a gamble."

"There's a good chance Altair will have failed to cover his trail," Perseus says slowly. "Knowing him, he would've counted on someone else taking the fall, and no one even coming close to suspecting him."

"That tracks," says Kleo. "Now we just need a plan for convincing them they want the Remora docking on the station."

"Yeah," says Osman, "what's your magic trick, Cass?"

"Simple," I say. "I'm turning myself in."

24

The cockpit falls into stunned silence, and then everyone starts talking at once.

"Absolutely not," says Amaris, "it's far too dangerous—"

"Are you certain?" Leyda's saying. "Are you absolutely certain?"

"She's got spirit, I'll give her that!" says Osman.

"What are the odds the guards kill her on sight before she can gain us one nanosecond of distraction?" Meez says.

"I have a feeling Ambassador Zahur won't let that happen," says Perseus. "The Khonsanian Collective has rules and regulations for how suspects should be treated, and I believe the ambassador will assert them."

"Good to hear," I say. "But please, you know, work fast."

Perseus says, "They'll insist on keeping the inquiry transparent, which in this case means you'll at least get an audience. Now, as for whether or not that helps you, it depends on you."

"I'm a professional thief," I say, with more confidence than I feel. My stomach is starting to unsettle in a way that has me regretting those snacks. "I trick people all day long, and anyway, all I really have to do is buy enough time for you all to do your jobs."

"No," says Amaris, folding her arms. "I'm the one who got you wrapped up in all of this. We can't possibly ask you to risk everything—risk your life—for us."

"I know," I say, "it's very brave and cool of me."

She pins me with a look. "I'm being serious."

"I can do this," I tell her. "I have to. We can't let Altair take the throne. You said it yourself."

"Can I get some orders here?" says Meez. "Are we turning the ship around? 'Cause I put a lot of distance between them and us. It'll take some doing to get us back there, and we're only getting farther away."

Leyda surveys the crowded cockpit. "Amaris, with me?" she says, and then the two of them file out of the cockpit.

"Try to steer clear of Mynos if you can," Osman tells me. "Don't look him in the eyes for too long. I swear he's one of those Void ghouls. He'll suck years off your life."

"What does that say about me?" asks Perseus, and Osman claps him on the back.

"Dead man walkin'," they say.

"Do you have advice?" I ask Perseus. "You know the royals best."

Perseus grimaces, spreading his hands. His fingers are long, like the emperor's, but his hands look more worn, and he's got an old scar across his palm. "Be careful. The imperial family will do whatever it takes to stay in power. I can tell you from years of experience that succumbing to emotion will not help you. Stay as rational as you can."

"Got it," I say as Leyda and Amaris make their way back into the cockpit.

"Cass," says Leyda calmly, "I want to make it clear here that you have a choice. If you want to return to Sarn, we can deliver you back safely, and with a new identity. You could be there in less than two days."

Only two days and I could see my family. But I know, deep down, that I need to see this through.

"Thank you," I say, swallowing. "Thank you, but I want to stick with the plan."

Leyda studies me, tilting her head to one side. "What made you decide on this course of action?"

I try to catch Amaris's gaze, but she won't look me in the eye. Which is fine. It's fine.

I badly want to crack a joke like I always do, but I get the sense that she'd call bullshit if I tried. It's too bad, because I barely have the words to answer Leyda.

"If Altair killed the emperor, what else would he be willing to do to get what he wants?" I say finally. "He's charismatic, he's popular, and he's willing to do whatever it takes to win. If he truly believes all that dreck about the shining light of the Helian Empire and thinks war is how he'll make it all come true, then where will he stop? And what happens to Sarn? My family?"

I blink hard, thinking about an empire-wide draft, even more mines on Sarn, and nothing but Pink Dream for the rest of my life. No planet is safe, but Sarn will be one of the first to collapse in on itself. For all the time I've spent plotting to leave that dusty little moon, the thought hurts more than expected.

"I'm not a revolutionary," I tell Leyda. "I'm not—noble of spirit, or whatever, and I have a hard time believing we can band together and make a better future, given what the present's like. I can't speak to the future at all, but this is one thing that can be done now." I take a deep breath, fighting to keep my voice steady. "To be honest, I'm in this for selfish reasons. Because if Altair at the helm is bad news, then it's people like my family that'll get hurt. And we're all already hurting. If I can help, if I can do this one thing, then I want to do it."

"Hear, hear!" says Osman.

Leyda and Amaris exchange a long look. "Then we're in agreement," says Leyda. "We're going ahead with the plan. Perseus, you can't be seen with us when the guards sweep the ship. Take the remaining cruiser and get out of here. If all goes well, we'll meet you by the rendezvous point as soon as possible."

Perseus nods grimly. "Best of luck, Cass," he says, slipping out of the cockpit.

A few moments later, a crackly voice announces, "Right-hand cruiser disengaged," and Perseus chimes in on the short-wave. "Perseus to Meez, all clear. As the kids say, let's proceed at warp speed."

Meez whoops and brings up a map of the star system, then traces a line with their finger from our ship to a point behind us. We all brace ourselves as the ship spins and flings itself forward, stars blurring on the edges of the display.

"That speck in the scanners—that's the station," Meez says once our stomachs have had a chance to settle. "We're maybe an hour out."

For a long moment, we're silent. The sudden reality of my decision hits me hard. We sit there, huddled together for several shaky breaths.

Then Filo takes a deep breath and sings:

"*Out in the darkness, the seeds in the soil, out in the darkness where galaxies curl—*"

Osman wasn't kidding. Filo's voice is clear and strong, filling the small space with a thrilling sound that makes me want to dance. Tarek and Kleo join in.

"*They can rail against us in their palaces royal; our seeds will take root and we'll uproot each world!*"

Leyda nudges Osman, and they add their voices to the chorus, belting out, "*For we see, how things could be! For we know, just what we sow!*"

Even Meez is tapping their free hand to the beat as they fly. Surrounded by joyous, raucous singing and this crew, Amaris's crew, the star-streaked black of space before us feels less like a void and more like a beginning, like endless possibilities.

Amaris and I are the only ones who aren't singing. She's nodding along but barely moving her lips. I pick my way across the cockpit to stand beside her, and she finally looks in my direction. I raise my eyebrows. She raises her eyebrows back.

"*Deep in the shadows, we question their order,*" the rest of the group sings. "*Deep in the shadows, we strike at their thrones—*"

"Aren't you going to carry your weight in the group sing-along?" I whisper in her ear.

"*Ideas run free so our land knows no border . . .*"

Amaris shakes her head.

"I can't," she whispers back.

"Of course you can."

"I shouldn't."

"*Think for yourself and you're one of our own!*" everyone else continues. Osman twirls Filo, and surprisingly, Filo goes for it, spinning in a wide circle and almost windmilling into a laughing Kleo.

"You don't like to sing?"

"I like it," she says, "but I'm awful."

"Me too," I tell her, bumping my shoulder against hers. "We can be awful together." And when the chorus starts again, I inhale and belt along with everyone. "*For we see, how things could be! For we know, just what we sow!*" I don't know the next words, so I end up singing just half a beat behind everyone else, my scratchy warble lost in the swooping and soaring voices around me.

"*When stars don't give light we will find other ways,*" sing Filo and the rest. "*When stars don't give light we will fly by our hearts—*"

I glance over at Amaris and wave one hand like a conductor. Finally, she adds her voice to the song:

"*Shine for each other and bask in those rays, remember these days when we are apart!*"

She doesn't manage to hit a single note of it.

See? she mouths. I elbow her gently and gesture for her to keep going.

"*For we see,*" we all sing together, "*how things can be! For we know, just what we sow!*"

Caught up in the moment, I throw an arm around Amaris's shoulders. It could be my imagination, but I think she leans into it just a little bit. Kleo catches my eye and grins, and I feel a flush rise to my cheeks.

"*For we see, how things can be!*" The song is slowing down and there's a collective intake of breath as we reach the final line. *"For we know, just what we sow!"* Everyone holds out the last note as long as they can, and once they've gulped down another breath of air, they start singing it all over again. Amaris falls silent, and now I'm sure she's leaning into me. She watches her crew with a fond smile as their song fills the space, and everything about this warms me right down to my bones.

I'd forgotten how good it can feel to be part of a group. It makes me miss my family on Sarn. I think Dezmer and Mita would like Leyda, and she would appreciate their sarcasm and down-to-earth natures. Babbit would be overjoyed at the chance to play to a voice like Filo's, face lit up and body swaying with the music. Pav would be fretting for all of us, wanting some way to keep us safe. Osman would get a kick out of Jax and their creative profanity. I think Dad would like everyone, even Perseus. Especially Perseus. With Dad's tinkering and Perseus's hacking skills, they could probably even fix up an old ship and fly the lot of us off that dusty old moon.

"All right," says Meez as the final note fades. "That was beautiful. I feel very bonded with you all and so on. Now get out of my cockpit so I can steer us back to our doom."

One by one, we file out of the room. I follow the group out of the cockpit, down a corridor, and to the door of a chamber that I can see is lined with screens.

"Our situation room," says Amaris as the others walk briskly past us inside.

"You have a room that's just for situations?" I offer, but it earns me only the weakest of smiles.

"We need to plan our infiltration," she says. "And while we do that, you should do whatever you can to prepare."

"Not sure how to prepare when I barely know what I'm gonna be doing," I admit. "I can prepare to be scared out of my mind, but I don't see any point in that."

Clearly, that was the wrong thing to say. Amaris's expression closes off. For a moment, I want to be offended that, after all this, she still doesn't believe in me. But I push past that, and pull her toward a small alcove. "You don't think I should be doing this."

"I don't think you should go on the mission, no," says Amaris.

"And you're saying that as the leader of the Voyria?"

"You have no training," she says. "It's not that I think you can't do it, but the task at hand will be much harder and more frightening for you than it would be for a more experienced operative."

"Too bad I'm the one they want," I say, as lightly as I can.

Amaris just looks at me, and I can feel myself start to crumble a little.

"Look," I tell her, "I said I'd do it. I can't let this crew down. There's too much riding on this. And anyway, I don't want to have to see the face Osman makes when they're disappointed."

"It is heartbreaking," she says, a shadow of a smile playing on a corner of her mouth.

"What did Leyda say to convince you?" I ask.

"That I wasn't thinking as a leader of the Voyria," says Amaris. She pauses.

"Then what were you thinking as? An octopus?"

No laugh this time. Not even half a smile.

"I—" Amaris clears her throat. "When I talked to you in the library that first time, I thought you were crass, arrogant, shallow, and dangerously self-absorbed."

"And now you know I'm also shit at singing," I say.

"People can be surprising," she says. "You have surprised me more than once tonight, and I'm very glad for it."

I can't stop the words, and I don't want to. "I like surprising you."

This does earn me a smile, although it's aimed at the floor.

Amaris lifts her head and finally, finally meets my eyes. "In the moment, I don't enjoy being surprised," she says. "But I do cherish my capacity to experience it. I think it speaks to the endless potential every person holds with them."

"You never know what you'll get," I say, shrugging.

"And I love that," Amaris says, so earnestly that it almost hurts to hear. "What you said earlier, that you're selfish because you want what's best for your people? I don't see it that way. Caring for your people is all it takes. The Voyria simply define *our people* a little more broadly. When we expand that circle, when we link hands, we can create something better for ourselves. We can pool together our capacity for surprise, for hope, for something new."

All I can think to say is "I like the sound of that."

"I do, too," she says. "So once this is over and you get back—"

It's my turn to stare at the floor.

Very lightly, she touches my arm. She says quietly, "You don't think you'll return?"

I glance at her hand on my elbow. She pulls it away. I hold out my hand, waggle my fingers, and she takes it. I place her hand back on my arm. She holds on, a little firmer this time, the warm press of her hand radiating through me.

Amaris clears her throat. "You don't think you will?" she says again.

"I don't know." I want to think I'll make it through this. I want to see Dad again. I want so many things, and I can't have any of them dead.

Amaris says nothing for a moment, just closes her eyes and inhales. When she opens them again, she looks directly at me. Her eyes are so beautiful, a deep, warm brown. I've met her gaze so many times tonight, but here, it really strikes me—how gorgeous her eyes are and how badly I want her to look at me again and again and again. For just a moment, every possible deflection or joke flees my mind and all I can do is look back at her.

"I know my team is somewhat . . . odd," she says. "But they're very, very good at what they do. We will find the evidence we're looking for. I know we will. You have the harder job, and I won't pretend there's not an element of luck involved. But if anyone can pull it off, it's you. Think of everything you've done tonight," she tells me, "and trust in yourself."

"Amaris!" Leyda calls from within the situation room. "We need you."

Amaris lets her hand fall from my elbow. "Ask Meez to let you back in the cockpit. You shouldn't have to wait alone, and they're a good listener."

"Right on," I say, slipping my hands in my pockets and turning to go.

"Wait," says Amaris.

I pivot on my heel to face her. "What?"

"You'll come back alive," she says, fixing me with those eyes.

"Is that an order?" I say. I can't help it. Jokes never leave me for long.

"Consider it your fortune told," Amaris says.

We're no longer pretending to be a couple of socialites who are deeply in love, so there is no excuse to pull her close. "I'll do what I can," I promise, and then she disappears into the situation room.

I tap the ceiling, the way I've seen the others do. "Cass to Meez," I say, willing my voice to stay steady. "How would you feel about a little company?"

A crackle of static, and then Meez's voice sounds through the room. "Promise not to touch anything in my cockpit and you're on."

Back in the cockpit, I take a seat in a chair that resembles my favorite perch back home, except it's about a century newer. Meez may be a good listener, but I don't have the opportunity to find out because I find that I don't feel much like talking. I watch the controls and the scanner screens and can't make any sense of it. All I know is that this combination of switches, dials, and screens have been calibrated to send us straight back to the station.

"Sarn, right?" Meez offers after a very long stretch of silence.

"Yeah." Is my voice shaking? I can't tell.

"Any of your friends back on Sarn own a short-wave?"

I blink at this line of questioning. "Dezmer and Mita have one."

"Well hey," says Meez, "if you know their device code, I can patch you through for a few minutes if you want, before the regulators detect you and throw you out. Untraceable. One of my favorite Voyrian tricks."

"What?" I manage. "Yes, please. How can you—I don't actually care how, just yes. Patch me—patch me through."

Meez unfolds a panel from the crowded wall and I haltingly recall the sequence from the many times I've dialed it in for Dezmer or Mita while their hands were full. The speaker emits a series of clicks. Meez signals me to speak.

I clear my throat. "Hello?"

"What the—who said that?" mumbles Dezmer. She sounds like she just woke up. She sounds annoyed and confused, a little tinny from the weak connection. But it's the best sound I've heard since Amaris sang along with me.

I swallow hard. "It's me, it's Cass. Listen, I don't have long. Is everyone all right?"

"Everyone's safe," says Dezmer, "missing you. What's happening? How'd you get ahold of a short-wave? Are *you* okay?"

"I'm, uh." I falter. "Fine. How's Dad?"

"Ask him yourself," Dezmer says. "Give me a tick to wake everyone up." There's a muffled scramble on the other end of the line, and then, just like that, Dad's voice is in my ear.

"Hello?" he says.

On my second try, I get out, "Dad."

"Cassie!" says Dad. "Cassie, what happened?"

"What're you doing at Dezmer and Mita's?"

"Oh, nothing, I've been changing up where I sleep to stay under Theron's radar," says Dad. My stomach plunges, and he says, "I'm good, I'm good, Cassie, I swear. Did you get to Ouris okay? Are you keeping a low profile?"

"Um, no," I say. "Not really. But I'm safe and comfortable, and with good folks." This is true for the moment, anyway. "You'd like them."

There's one person who's always been able to see through my sleight-of-hand. "Cassie," says Dad. "Take care, okay? Look after yourself." He coughs, a terrible hacking that doesn't let up for an awful couple of seconds. "Don't take any unnecessary risks."

"Only the necessary ones," I reply.

"You sound like your mother," he says. Tears are welling in my eyes. I glance at the ceiling of the cockpit, trying to wait them out. "Necessary risks, that's exactly what she would say," he says. "Cassie, I love you so much." He coughs again, and I can hear him thump his sternum, trying to clear his throat. "Stay safe, okay?"

"I'll try," I say, and I can't quite keep the sob out of my voice. I swipe at my face with the back of my hand.

"Mita's sleeping like the dead," says Dezmer, "but if you give me another second—"

"You don't have another second," says Meez, frowning at the dials. "You're about to be booted."

"Give everyone my love," I say.

"Whatever you're up to," says Dad, "just remember we love you, and good l—" His voice recedes into static and then silence.

Meez carefully doesn't look at me as I blot away the last of my tears. Only when my face is dry do they say, "Sounds like you've got good people in your corner."

"Yeah." I take a deep, shuddering breath. "Thank you."

"Don't mention it," says Meez. "Hey, are you a reflect-in-silence kinda person or do you prefer some noise rattling around in your brain?"

"Uh, noise," I say.

"Then have I got the thing for you," Meez tells me, reaching up to flick a series of switches.

The song they cue up might be good. It's hard to tell. I can't make out the lyrics or focus on the melody. I watch Meez nod along to the beat and try to imagine taking comfort in these sounds. The final thud of the drums is still echoing through the cockpit when a crackle of static splits the air, and one of the top screens fills with the image of a scowling security guard.

"Approaching craft, identify yourselves immediately," says a stern voice. I straighten up and look square at the guard.

"My name is Iola Galatas," I say. "I am a member of the Voyria. I have crucial information about the clone Perseus, who I aided in killing Emperor Hyperion. I'm here to turn myself in, but I'll only do so if I can get an audience with Ambassador Zahur."

The guard stares for a moment, then jerks a hand at the screen, silencing himself. He presses a hand to his ear and says something, his mouth moving quickly as he shoots a look back at me, as if I might disappear at any second. Finally, he speaks to us again.

"You will surrender quietly," says the guard. "You will come to us without a fight. Any violence will be met with a barrage of lasers set to sear, aimed directly at your ship. Understood?"

"Understood," I say.

The entire ship shudders and lurches forward, the station dock opening to receive us as we're dragged toward the waiting maw of the palace.

25

Meez stretches up to tap the ceiling. "Meez to all crew. Pressor beams are pulling us in," they announce. "Game faces, people."

"How long?" I ask.

"Not long at all," says Meez grimly, flopping back into their chair. They shake their head. "Pressor beams, should've guessed. I hate dealing with these tyrants."

I swallow. "It's where we're trying to go anyway, isn't it?"

"Yeah," Meez says, "but the feeling of not being able to pilot your own ship, it's—" They throw up their hands in frustration. I remember my own hands, how they wouldn't listen to me with that gel holding them captive.

I picture Amaris as a tiny child, desperately crawling to the river as her friends face their own execution—kids who just wanted a better world, a better life. Probably everyone on this ship has a story like that, everyone in the Voyria maybe. It feels like plunging underwater again, the magnitude of the suffering brought on by the long reach of the empire.

I grip the edge of my seat, my gaze focusing on the growing white dot of the palace ship, how small it still seems for now, lost in the vast expanse of space. Beyond the ship, a curtain of stars spreads outward against a deep and dark blue, flame-like in its brilliance and so beautiful that it almost hurts to look at. I don't think I've ever seen the Void like this, and I think I love it. Strangely, it reminds me of home, of Sarn and its rust-colored dirt and plunging canyons.

For the founders of Helia, dangers lurked in the depths of space. Protection against the unfamiliar and the unknown out-weighed everything and everyone else. But until tonight, I knew nothing of the Voyria and not much of what life could be like, outside the hard scrabble of getting through every day. Maybe the unknown is not so bad, after all.

Back on Sarn, I thought only my crew and my dad really under-stood the shit we've been through. That we were alone in all our pain, and it was up to me to steal a fortune and snatch a better future from the hands of the unfeeling Fates. But we were never alone, even all the way out on Sarn, at the empire's edge.

I think of the flatweed that I used to pull up whenever Dad got a craving for greens. It was bitter, but if you stewed it long enough, it made an edible goop that turned your shit blue. Yank-ing the flatweed out of the ground took all my strength, and when a sprig came out, it would trail clumps of dry dirt and long, tan-gled roots that seemed to go on for ages. There was so much more beneath the surface, all clinging together. An entire network, helping the flatweed survive beneath the harsh Sarn sun.

Things have to change. Things will change, if I have anything to do with it. And I won't be alone.

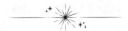

Amaris and the others file into the cockpit just as the station comes into view on the close-up. I was expecting it to look like the transport ship that brought us there, but it does not. It's a long white oval, patterned with what looks like intricate curling gold ferns and dotted here and there with glowing greenhouses and bubble-shaped windows, at once strangely organic and entirely artificial. It's also gigantic. I know it's the pressor beams but as the craft moves powerlessly toward the palace, it feels as if we're being drawn into the station's orbit.

"It's so gaudy," says Kleo with a nervous laugh. "Like someone gilded a shit."

"Are we ready?" says Leyda.

Osman nods. "Good to go."

Someone squeezes my shoulder. Amaris. "Be careful," she says.

"You might as well tell me to be lucky," I reply.

Another squeeze, then her hand drops away. "Be lucky, then."

The ship lurches horribly again, and I can see airlock doors opening, then the airlock itself, and then we are sitting in a cavernous bay with the airlock entrance shut behind us. There's a heavy knocking from the back of the ship.

"Imperial guard, open up!" someone yells, and I feel like I'm drifting in my own pressor beam, pulled inexorably toward the door of the ship. I press the release mechanism and the door slides away to reveal a dozen uniformed guards, railguns trained on me. I step out into the bay with my palms raised. Half the guards surround me while the other half stream into the Remora.

"Oh no, not the ship!" Osman cries. When nobody else is looking, they wink at me.

The last thing I see of the Remora is Amaris standing very straight with a railgun aimed at her. "We'll be fine," she mouths. "Go."

So I go. It's not like I have a choice.

I let the guards lead me out of the bay. I let them lead me down a series of long hallways, and like before, each section of the station we pass through gets fancier and fancier, and unlike before, nothing about this is reassuring. I'm escorted through a door and into a small room where a single figure is waiting for me, wearing an elaborate hand-embroidered sash over his finest military teals: Altair. I must have interrupted some sort of ceremony, maybe even the coronation.

He stands as I enter. For a moment, I'm struck with a weird sense of symmetry: the close quarters, the one-on-one conversation. It all smacks of my meeting with Thea. I'm half waiting for him to order the guards to leave. He doesn't.

Thea was trying to put me at ease, I realize. Altair wants me afraid. So much of a con is showing people what they already want to believe, and like Amaris said, the best lies contain a trace of truth. I really am terrified. I look up at Altair with wide eyes.

"Iola Galatas," he says slowly. "Or, I'm sorry, is it Cassandra Zervas?"

I glance from Altair to my guards and then back to him again. I hunch my shoulders, trying to look small.

"I was promised an audience with Ambassador Zahur," I say in something approaching a squeak.

"Helia keeps its promises," says Altair. "But nobody said we couldn't have a talk first. So, let's talk." He crosses the room, one hand casually resting on his ceremonial sword. "You stand accused of theft, fraud, impersonating a noble, associating with Voyrian insurgents, high treason, and aiding the clone Perseus in his plot to murder Emperor Hyperion, who was the head and heart of Helia, may his name echo outward through the universe forevermore." His lips quirk. "Also, you have been a supreme annoyance to me."

Beside me, one of the guards snorts. Altair doesn't laugh.

"Any one of these crimes would be a problem for you," he continues. He presses his hand to his ear, listening to something, before continuing. "But in light of your many transgressions, I would suggest you choose your next steps carefully."

I stare at the floor. All I can do now is stall for time.

"What do you want me to do?" I say quietly. "I am at the mercy of the crown. I just—" I take a deep, shuddering breath. "I just want this to be over. I want to go home."

Altair is looking at me thoughtfully. "How's this," he says. "Confess to your crimes in front of everyone at the Ascension Ball. You can manage that, can't you?"

"I'll do it," I say quietly. I keep my head down, and let my hands shake, just the tiniest bit. It's not hard, given how exhausted I am.

"And how do I know this isn't another one of your lies?" says Altair.

I let my hands curl in my borrowed sleeves and keep my eyes trained on the floor. I say, almost whispering, "I realize how alone I am. I have no other hope."

"Good," he says. "And remember what I said earlier. It certainly remains true." I nod. Of course I remember his insinuations that he still had doses of the deadly poison left. I'm counting on it.

Altair gestures and the guards each grab me by an arm and drag me out the door and down a hallway, Altair following at a leisurely pace. We pass a series of framed old-fashioned paintings of the previous rulers of Helia, ending in the now very familiar ghostly face of Hyperion.

I can't keep my feet under me, and still the guards drag me toward a set of massive double doors. The doors open, and there we are, standing in the entrance of what has to be the throne room. A throne wrought in gold and silver is placed atop a floating platform at the head of room. Behind the throne stand a semicircle of somber older people who must be the Council. I recognize the stuffy mustachioed Iraklidis and Teresi with her glowing eyes. Mynos and Thea are seated in slightly less grand thrones of their own, off to the side.

The curving walls are covered in gilded ivy, which must've been bred to grow upward in streaks of deep green and gold. All of the ball guests stand together toward the center, looking tired and bedraggled, despite their fabulous clothing. I can tell by the way everyone is staring at me that they have been briefed on my transgressions.

"Citizens of Helia," Altair calls, striding across the throne room. The floating platform descends, and he steps onto it, pivoting to face the crowd as it ascends once more. His voice reverberates around the room, just like Hyperion's did. "The hand of justice has been swift and true. We have apprehended the criminal known to you as Iola Galatas, who colluded with the clone Perseus to strike a blow against the head and heart of Helia. In the interest of transparency, her confession will be taken here, before you. Only in the light of the truth can we move forward as a people."

The guards move from me, standing an arm's length away. Altair gestures to the Council, and Councilor Iraklidis steps forward. He recites my list of crimes and supposed crimes, ending with high treason.

"Cassandra Zervas," says Councilor Iraklidis, "you may speak."

I'd counted on being able to pull Ambassador Zahur aside, but being dragged in front of the entire guest list of the Ascension Ball makes that nearly impossible. Confessing to murder in front of a roomful of socialites, politicians, and royalty is not what I'd had planned.

The things about plans, though, is that you have to know when to throw them away. Sometimes, you just have to roll with the punches.

I can't help it—I grin. I know it makes me look even more like an evil killer, but I can feel the gears in my mind starting to turn faster and faster. I resist the urge to shake the excess energy out of my limbs, the way I always do before starting a day of Good Mook, Bad Mook.

I tell the truth.

"I did not kill the emperor." My words come out all in a rush, and I have to force myself to slow down, to speak loudly and clearly. "Perseus and I were set up to take the fall for the murder committed by Prince Altair of Leithe."

Confused murmurs rise from the gathered crowd. The Councilors look at one another, at least a few of them plainly baffled.

"What—" sputters Councilor Iraklidis. "You know the crimes you are accused of. Speak of them, not this, this absurd tale."

"It's absurd," I say, "but it's not a tale. The emperor was killed by a member of his own family, the royal family. He died in his private bedchambers and—"

"Enough," Councilor Iraklidis says, gesturing sharply. "You arrived in the company of Voyrian rebels. Your guilt is written across you already. What more needs to be said?" He looks up at Prince Altair, who is leaning against the throne the way he leaned against his mother's chair earlier. "Your Imperial Majesty, your generosity knows no bounds, but I believe giving this criminal the chance to speak in public was a mistake."

"You may be right," Altair says with a sigh. "A pity. I was hoping that this confession would provide solace to everyone here. But clearly, I expected too much." He raises a hand and several guards stand at attention. "Take her away."

Just as a guard reaches for me, the doors swing open. Ambassador Zahur enters with two of their aides. They cross the throne room to stand before Altair.

"So kind of you to start without me," Ambassador Zahur says, bowing deeply. "And I apologize for my delay. Your guards continue to be so helpful and so good at getting lost in their own station."

"Don't apologize. We were just wrapping this up," Altair said, lifting a shoulder in a shrug.

"Is that so?" Ambassador Zahur says. They turn and regard me, as if seeing me for the first time in the throne room. "Iola Galatas, was it?"

"No," I say. "Just Cass."

"Rumor has it that you killed the emperor. Is this true?" they ask.

I shake my head. "I didn't do it."

"And what proof do you have to offer?" Ambassador Zahur says mildly, like they're asking me about my favorite soup.

"Go to the cloak room. Check my rucksack. It should contain a change of clothes, a skin of water, a can of Pink Dream, and an invitation to this ball. That invitation's permissions"—I glance up at Altair, who watches me impassively—"were keyed by Prince Altair himself."

The ambassador nods at one of their aides, who slips out of the throne room. I spot Councilor Teresi shooting a startled look at Altair.

"I'm sure you'll find that invitation. The Voyria are known for their skills in systems hacking and forgery," Altair says. He turns to Ambassador Zahur. "You're free to speak with Cassandra Zervas after my security team is done interviewing her."

"I think," Ambassador Zahur says slowly, "I'd like to hear what Cass has to say right now, in front of everybody."

"Suit yourself," Altair says. He finally drops into the seat of the throne and waves a hand. "Far be it from me to question the wisdom of the Khonsanian Collective."

"Go ahead," Ambassador Zahur says to me. "Say your piece."

"I don't know if I have the whole picture, but I think I have at least some of it," I say. I scan the crowd, looking for familiar faces—people I danced with and stole from. Ligeia is there, looking scandalized by what's unfolding. Two servers stand in the back, along with more guards than I care to count. I collect my thoughts and continue: "Empress Thea was recorded the day before the Ascension Ball paying a visit to Drivax, home to very little besides Hasapis-Lykaios, a corporation known for manufacturing dangerous weapons banned here in Helia—"

"I must object to this!" Mynos roars. He rises from his seat, drawing up to his full height. "I will not stand for you to sling accusations at my brother's grieving widow. It is base behavior and—"

"It's all right, Mynos," says Thea, also rising. She's as elegant as ever, and I suspect every eye in the ballroom is drawn to her. "I will explain my visit to Drivax. I can't bear for the people of Helia to think I would betray them in any way." She clasps her hands, gazing out at the ballgoers. "I was picking up an extremely mild poison known to relax the muscles of the face. It was a closely guarded secret of mine. I simply—I wished to look good for my husband, the emperor, on the day of the Ascension Ball."

"You can accuse me all you want," says Altair, descending from his throne. He places a hand on Thea's shoulder. "But do not bring Empress Thea into this. She has suffered enough." He ducks his head, as if the weight of Thea's grief is heavy on him too. He is the picture of a dutiful and kind-hearted royal.

One of the ballgoers steps forward to offer Thea a handkerchief. Thea takes it gratefully and dabs at the corners of her eyes. Altair leans in to say something to Thea, and she gives him a gentle smile.

The more emotional Altair gets, the more sympathetic and genuine he seems, I think. But I don't have Altair's popularity or his charisma. I have to stay calm and stick to the facts. I wonder how many times Perseus has had to make this exact calculation.

"I'm not saying the empress killed the emperor," I say. "But she played a role, perhaps unwittingly."

"And what role is that?" Ambassador Zahur asks.

"Well," I hesitate. I have to start at the beginning, I know that much. "Twenty-five years ago, Empress Thea lost her child at birth. And that same week, Queen Lena introduced her newborn to all of Leithe. But there'd been no indication that Queen Lena had been pregnant."

All eyes are on Queen Lena and King Dorus now. Queen Lena speaks up, her voice trembling with what I suspect is real feeling. "This is true. My dear Altair was adopted. But he's my son all the same. I knew he was from some other royal family who wished to remain anonymous, but why—"

"Why would the empress give her child to us?" King Dorus finishes.

"She'd send her child away if he wasn't the emperor's," I say, before King Dorus or anyone else can cut me off. Shock ripples through the crowd, punctuated by sharp gasps and muttered questions. "If she were having an affair with someone else, like the emperor's brother."

"I—" Thea covers her face. "I would never!"

"You would," I continue, relentless. I can't stop now. "The emperor was so much older than you." I remember how poised and menacing Thea had been when she'd talked to me alone. How she'd described the way she would've killed Hyperion. "And he looked down on you. He didn't see how capable you were. But Mynos loved you, the way Hyperion didn't."

"No," Thea sobs. Mynos wraps an arm around her, drawing her close, but Thea shoves him, putting distance between them. A

275

flash of irritation crosses her perfect, tearstained face. It's a wonder the two kept their relationship under wraps for so long. Mynos couldn't have made it easy.

"Just look at Prince Altair and then look at Mynos and Thea," I say to the ambassador. "And you don't have to just look. Get a DNA analysis of the three of them. If Altair isn't their son, that's easy enough to prove."

I catch Queen Lena and King Dorus looking in confusion at Altair and feel a twinge of guilt. But then I remember that they're mainworld royals, and I don't feel guilty at all. They can wipe their tears with coin from the royal coffers, for all I care.

Altair steps away from his parents. Standing next to them isn't doing him any favors. He turns to me.

"Even if your frankly obscene insinuations are true," Altair says, "the fact of my parentage hardly makes me a murderer."

"It doesn't," I admit. "But it gives you the chance to be one. Only someone related to the emperor or the empress could get past the bio-lock on the emperor's private chambers."

Bakchos, the head of the media, breaks through the crowd in his yellow suit. "Just a moment," he says. "My sources didn't mention anything about a bio-lock. The emperor was found dead in the reflecting pool. Anyone could have done that."

"Not anyone," says Ambassador Zahur. "The autopsy showed that your emperor had been dragged from his private rooms, which were sealed by a bio-lock keyed to the DNA of the Helian emperor and his wife. Only a member of the imperial family could've killed the emperor."

"Only a member of the imperial family could've done it," I repeat.

"A member such as one of the emperor's many clones," Altair says. "Or perhaps his highest-ranking one, who serves on the Council and has political aspirations."

"But he wasn't in the rooms at the time of the murder," I say. "Check the security feeds."

"Convenient that you claim Perseus can produce an alibi given that he is *one of multiple identical clones*," says Altair. He walks up to stand beside me, facing the crowd. "Let me tell you about the woman making these allegations. Cassandra Zervas is a common criminal. She fled the Danae moon of Sarn over fraudulent dealings. Her crimes were flagged by a devoted servant of the crown. That is something that can be verified easily."

He has to be referring to Theron, but why doesn't he just say so? Or at least give more specifics about him. Surely any of Altair's sources would've known it was Theron I bilked, if they know about my face being flagged.

"Who were my so-called fraudulent dealings with?" I ask.

"There are too many to count."

"Prove it. Name one."

"An upstanding citizen to whom you sold a forgery of a fine watch—"

He really is talking around the name. Theron must've given his real name when he filed the report. I remember Jax's predictions, that someone with such a high-class appellation would only end up in Sarn if he'd done something really bad.

I chance it. "Who," I say, "Theron Vouvali?"

Another wave of shock ripples through the crowd, and the murmuring rapidly swells into a roar. Theron must've really put his foot in it, whatever he did.

"Why are you covering for Theron?" I ask Altair. "Why were you even in contact with him?"

"I wasn't in contact with him," Altair says. "I read the magistrate's crime report—"

"And purposely left out his name just now in the telling?" I ask. "Why?"

In the din of the crowd, I hear someone say, "—was accused of trying to poison the major general no less than a year ago—"

"He sells watches on Sarn now," I say. "Which, come to think of it, is probably a front. Why would an upstanding Helian citizen and candidate for the throne associate with someone like Theron Vouvali?"

"What about the stab wound?" demands Bakchos. He's clearly appointed himself the voice of the ballgoers. "Explain that."

"Altair dragged the body to the reflecting pool and stabbed him with one half of a set of bak daggers because he intended to frame me, a Sarnian, for the murder," I say. "That's why he invited me to the ball in the first place, as my invitation will clearly show. And with his ties to the military and the Asipis corporation, obtaining the means for murder wasn't too difficult for him."

"Well, you've certainly spun an intriguing story for us," says Altair. "Though I happen to notice *you still have no proof*."

"But I do," says Ambassador Zahur.

26

The ball guests turn to gape at Ambassador Zahur, who walks forward to address the Council, nodding to each of them in turn.

"On an anonymous tip, I had two of my assistants search Prince Altair's rooms," says Ambassador Zahur. "And there we found a small green case bearing the Hasapis-Lykaios insignia and containing a nanotech injector, as Zervas described."

Ambassador Zahur holds up a hand for silence. "This being unusual enough to bear further investigation," they say, "the handle was swabbed for DNA, and the sequences we found there were identical to the sequences found in a sample retrieved from a tongue exfoliator in the en suite bathroom."

"I am disappointed in you, Zahur," says Altair. "Aides can easily be bribed or intimidated. Perhaps they were doing it for the money, or their families were being threatened—"

Ambassador Zahur coughs. "Fear not, my aides' families are safe, and I pay my aides handsomely to put up with me. The genetic information on the injector and the exfoliator shared striking overlap with that of Perseus Castellanos. Enough to place the owner of these items on our late emperor's family tree. Although further tests would be needed to prove this conclusively, it is true that the shared DNA is entirely consistent with Ms. Zervas's admittedly far-fetched story of Prince Altair's provenance.

"I also took the liberty of telling one of my aides to check the station's cloak room," adds Ambassador Zahur, "and my people tell me that a large rucksack was found containing an invitation exactly as our suspect described it. Down to the permissions granted by Prince Altair himself."

The throne room door swings open a third time. I'm expecting someone from Ambassador Zahur's staff, but it's the crew of the Remora, looking no worse for wear. Relief floods my system, along with a spark of joy when I glimpse Amaris among them.

The ballgoers are buzzing with speculation now.

"Who the Void are they?" says the aloof blue-haired woman whose bracelets I stole many hours ago.

Osman waves to the crowd. Kleo mutters something to Leyda, who nods.

I catch Amaris's eye. She scrunches her nose, just the tiniest bit, then faces Altair. Altair, though, is staring at a serious-faced man clad in black, standing in the back.

"Hello," Perseus says to Altair, striding forward. "I suppose I should say hello, nephew."

"Perseus," says Altair, face contorting in a sneer. "I must admit, I never would've imagined you'd have the creativity to pull off something like this. You've always been so . . . unoriginal."

This earns Altair a distinctly unimpressed look. "Ah, yes. Clone jokes. May they keep you laughing when you've been exiled."

"You—" Altair snarls, and then, in a practiced motion, slides something small and silver from the hilt of his ceremonial sword and plunges it into Perseus's neck. Perseus collapses, his eyes rolling back in his head. A pair of guards rush forward to pull Altair back.

"Perseus!" I race over to him, but the rest of the Voyria beat me to it. They surround him, warding off the guards and the ballgoers.

"He's dead!" I hear Ligeia shriek. Perseus suddenly sits up, clutches his head briefly, then stumbles to his feet, ripping out the silver device Altair jabbed him with. Kleo presses something into his hand, which turns out to be a thumb-sized blue bandage. He applies it to his neck wound, wincing.

"How—" I don't understand how Perseus is here, if he got into that cruiser. Then I realize the obvious. This is Theseus or Orpheus, dressed in Perseus's clothes. Looking closer, I can see that this clone lacks the pronounced shadows under the eyes, and has a bit of a tan besides.

"Potassium chloride," says Theseus-or-Orpheus, mistaking my confusion. "A touch old-fashioned. All clones are practically raised on poisons, so we can taste food for His Excellency when he doesn't feel like trusting the scanners. Doesn't affect us. Still, not my favorite feeling."

"Did you have to faint like that?" Osman says acidly. "Just about gave us a heart attack."

"What can I say." Theseus-or-Orpheus laughs. "I have a flair for the dramatic."

It's near impossible to hear anyone talk now. The throne room is in chaos. There's sobbing, shouting, and the telltale hushed tones of gossip being shared. A brisk clap punctuates the air.

"I think we've seen enough," says Councilor Teresi. She brushes a few stray white hairs from her eyes and turns to the guards. "Please take Prince Altair to a secure holding room. And as the matter of the injector may implicate both Empress Thea and His Late Imperial Highness's brother, please take them away for questioning."

The guards holding Altair exchange dubious looks.

"Quickly now," Councilor Teresi snaps. "Before I lose my patience with everyone in—"

In a whirl of limbs, Altair wrenches free and charges at Theseus-or-Orpheus. Amaris throws herself forward, sliding along the polished floor in one smooth movement. She kicks Altair's feet out from under him, snatches his sword, and levels it at his prone body. The edge of it pricks at his neck, drawing a trickle of blood. Another pair of guards race to Altair's side and pull him away, each grabbing one arm.

"Every so often, the law applies no matter who your parents are," says Amaris, smoothing her clothes back into place. If I didn't already love her, I would now.

The ballroom has lapsed into stunned silence. The guards start to march Altair away. As they approach the double doors, Altair knocks both of the guards to the ground.

"Andino!" he shouts, and Enforcer Andino tosses Altair a railgun. Altair snatches it out of the air and aims it at Councilor Teresi.

"So," Altair says almost conversationally, like he's commenting on the weather, "it seems like we can't come to an agreement, which is a shame. If I were to take the throne, I would have returned Helia to its former glory." Altair's voice has a slight edge to it now. "We could have claimed what's ours and shed the light of Helia on the deepest depths of the universe. But it seems none of you are interested in that." Altair sighs, as if the whole empire has disappointed him. "Well, I think it's about time I took my leave. Someone get me a ship, now."

"Think this through," says Ambassador Zahur, approaching slowly. "If you're innocent as you say, there's no reason to run. And there's certainly no need for bloodshed—"

Altair lifts his railgun, shifting his aim from Councilor Teresi's heart to her head. "Unlock my ship from this station, or I'll blow a hole straight through the Councilor." He jerks his head toward Enforcer Andino, who raises his own weapon at a different member of the Council. "And then I'll take my pick of the next one."

"Do as he says. Unlock the ships!" one of the Councilors orders, an older woman with a mole high on one cheek. She turns to one of the other guards. "Now, Enforcer!"

"Councilor Makris, I—I don't have the clearance," says the enforcer in question. "They won't listen to me."

"As we cannot rely on previous leadership, you are hereby promoted to captain of the guard!" barks Councilor Makris. "Now do it!"

The enforcer nods, swallows, and presses a hand to her ear and reels off a few commands.

"Ships are unlocked," she announces.

Railgun still aimed at Councilor Teresi, Altair begins to back out of the room.

"C'mon," he tells Andino, who raises one hand in the air.

About a third of the guards jump to attention, leveling their rail-guns at the crowd as they bolt across the room to stand by Altair's side.

Thea starts toward Altair, pulling Mynos along with her.

"Empress Thea and Emperor Regent Mynos," Councilor Teresi says, "you are ordered to comply with Ambassador Zahur's investigation."

"I think not," Thea says. She hitches up her skirts and strides to Altair's side. "Let's go."

"Gladly," says Altair, and then he leads Thea, Mynos, and the assembled guards out of the throne room.

Nobody says anything for a long moment.

"Captain," says Leyda, breaking the silence, "I'd suggest putting a tracer on the first departing ship. We need to move fast."

"We don't—it's unclear procedurally who has the authority when it comes to activating the station's defense system," stammers Councilor Iraklidis.

The new captain of the guard puts a hand to her ear and gives the orders, looking around the room as if daring someone to stop her.

Nobody does.

"We need to decide who's in charge here," says Councilor Makris, "and we need to do it very quickly."

"There is no protocol for this particular chain of events," says Councilor Iraklidis.

"Well, we have to come up with something!" snaps Councilor Teresi. "Once news reaches the Zarinel Federation that we're running about headless, with a murdered emperor and an empty throne, we will be engulfed in a fresh wave of combat. The Zarinel ships will reach our borders by the next orbit."

"But we cannot afford to act rashly," another councilor protests. "Let's think this through, form a committee, perhaps—"

"If I may," says Leyda. All eyes go to her. She straightens, and somehow despite her short stature, with the light catching on her streaky hair she seems like the tallest person in the room. "Might I suggest, as emergency interim leader, the next available person in the line of succession who has not committed a criminal act today."

"Perseus," Councilor Teresi says.

"Perseus," Leyda agrees.

The Councilors stare at one another. "We must adjourn to make our ruling in private," says Councilor Iraklidis.

"As representative of the Voyria, I request to be included in your talks," Leyda adds. Theseus-or-Orpheus nods gravely.

"On whose authority?" Councilor Makris says, bristling.

"At this moment," says Leyda, "other than the Khonsanian Collective, the Voyria is the largest, most organized, and most functional governing body represented on this station. Our members are present on every major and minor planet, and our leaders are chosen democratically. We are as legitimate an organization as any, and partnering with us will prevent a full-fledged intergalatic rebellion, something which you all have the clearance to know remains a real threat."

"And if we refuse to work with you?" says Councilor Iraklidis.

"Then you may not like what your people do without either a voice in your government or a united empire to keep them underfoot."

"Is that a threat?" says Councilor Makris.

"I think," Councilor Teresi says slowly, "she meant it more as an acknowledgment of the reality in which we find ourselves."

"Take it as you will," says Leyda. "You have one day to decide what to do. Once the news of your headless empire reaches its supposed subjects, the rest is up to them."

"I would never dream to tell the Helians how to run their government," Ambassador Zahur puts in, "but this does seem the wisest course of action."

"It would be dramatically unprecedented," says one of the councilors.

"Everything about this situation is unprecedented," Theseus-or-Orpheus says. "But we must move forward, and at this juncture, it is in our best interest to allow the Voyria a seat at the table."

"Agreed," Councilor Teresi says decisively. "Now let us adjourn and take this to the Council room, before anyone else here attempts to commit murder."

To my great surprise, the Council mutters their assent and files out of the throne room.

"Well," I say. All of the adrenaline that's been powering me through the encounter leaves me at once. My knees fold and I sit down in the middle of the throne room. I'm in a little bubble all my own as guards and politicians and socialites move past, hurrying to who knows where.

Amaris hesitates, then joins me.

I incline my head at the doorway through which the Council disappeared. "Theseus or Orpheus?" I whisper.

"Orpheus," Amaris mouths.

"Lucky that he's also got a head for politics."

"He doesn't," whispers Amaris. "We had to coach him on what to say. But he was willing to help us to help his brother."

"Do you really think Altair couldn't tell it wasn't him?"

Amaris hums. "I think Altair has a hard time understanding motives that have absolutely nothing to do with power. He underestimates the power of family—of all kinds. That's his weakness."

"One of them," I say. "That trick where you took his sword, that was—"

"But I let my guard down," Amaris says, shaking her head. "Altair got away, after everything he's done."

"You did your best," I tell her. "And it was so—you looked—it was really—"

"Oh hey, party on the floor," says Osman, kneeling to join us and mercifully bringing my stammering to an end. "Hey kid," they tell me, "you did good."

"You really did," says Amaris. "We heard most of it through Ambassador Zahur's aide's earpiece. You held your own against Altair. You were—it was impressive."

"Well, a certain someone wished me luck," I say. "I think that helped."

Osman glances between us. "You know," they say, standing once more, "I have a sudden and desperate curiosity about what's happening on the other side of the room. See you around, Cass."

I can't help laughing a little as Osman beats a retreat. Then Amaris meets my eyes, smiling, and all I want is to curl up in the feeling that smile sparks in me.

"Cassandra Zervas?" says a familiar voice, and I look up to see Ambassador Zahur.

I scramble to my feet. "Ambassador."

"You do realize that you are still accused of attempting to steal over a million drocks' worth of assorted precious jewels," they say.

I take a deep breath and nod.

"However," Ambassador Zahur continues, "every person who volunteered testimony that you stole the jewels has left the station with a man who stands credibly accused of considerably worse crimes, including treason and murder." They purse their lips. "This scenario was not covered in my law classes."

"I bet not," I manage.

"As such, I believe you will find there is nobody left to offer any solid evidence against you," they say. "I would, for the record, suggest doing what you can to stay out of similar trouble in the future."

I nod. "Of course," I say. "I will be engaging in zero trickery, thievery, or tomfoolery. You won't get a single shenanigan out of me."

"Good," says Ambassador Zahur.

One of their many aides taps them on the shoulder. "Ambassador, the Council wishes to speak with you."

"Ah," Ambassador Zahur sighs. "Here we go," and then they're gone.

27

We have to wait some time for the Council's ruling. We wait long enough that I manage to convince Amaris to tell me the rest of that story she started when she braided my hair, about the epic showdown between General Vitalis and Flavia Felice.

We've just gotten to the part where Flavia Felice's spy in General Vitalis's army has triple-crossed his pirate boss when the Council, led by Perseus—the real Perseus, now that he's had time to return and make the switch-out—as well as Ambassador Zahur and Councilor Teresi, trails back into the throne room and up onto the floating dais. The speaker feed goes live, magnifying Councilor Teresi's voice.

"Is this live?" she says. Her voice is scratchy but brisk, and magnified twice over by the speakers. Whoever's left in the throne room turns to face her.

"These are unprecedented times," Councilor Teresi begins, "and as such, they call for unprecedented solutions."

Well, that could mean anything.

"We find ourselves at present without a head of state," she continues, "and without the guidance of our beloved emperor. The Council has elected to appoint Perseus Castellanos, First Clone of Emperor Hyperion Castellanos, as our new emperor regent."

Murmurs rush through the throne room, followed by tentative applause. Around me, I can see people lifting their glasses, shock written across their faces as they process the news. On the edges of the throne room, a few of the servants look pretty happy about the proclamation, Hess among them.

On the dais, Perseus kneels, and Teresi lays an obviously improvised sash around his shoulders.

"By the authority of the Council of the Helian Empire, we appoint you the head and heart of Helia," she intones. "Arise, Emperor Regent Perseus Castellanos."

Everyone applauds, with varying degrees of feeling. Osman whoops, pumping their fist. The guests standing closest to Osman take several nervous steps away.

"Thank you," says Perseus. "My first act as emperor is to establish a triumvirate, consisting of myself, Leyda Pallas of the Voyria, and Councilor Medeia Teresi, facilitated by Ambassador Akila Zahur."

The clapping ceases. The guests are staring, astonished.

"My next act as emperor," Perseus continues, "is to formally dissolve the role of emperor."

He pauses. "The triumvirate is now the highest authority in the land. Together, we will govern until such time as a system of elected leaders may be chosen, to be voted on by any adult on any planet or territory within the Helian Empire."

"The first act of the triumvirate," says Leyda, "is to set a date, thirty-six hours hence, at which point formal peace talks will begin between the Helians and the people of the Zarinel Federation."

The murmurs of the crowd are swelling to a roar.

"The Helian Empire has become unfortunately overextended, militarily and diplomatically," Leyda continues, raising her voice. "The war has placed a disastrous degree of pressure on the common people of our system, taking lives, draining resources, and unraveling the fabric of this universe that holds us together. We must focus on serving the people of Helia, not swelling our coffers as our cities crumble, our planets collapse, and our people suffer."

"We anticipate dramatic savings in our military budget," says Perseus, "and our current plan is to direct a major portion of those funds to outerworld support, which has been neglected and even outright harmed during this period of rampant expansion. From planets like Danae and Haddan, to moons like Nephele and Sarn."

Amaris nudges me gently in the side, and I almost tip over. Hearing Sarn is what makes this real to me. I'm already dreaming of a better life there, of the changes that are possible with more funds and more freedom.

"Again, peace talks begin in thirty-six hours," says Leyda coolly, looking around the room. "And this station docks on Ouris in ninety minutes. I suggest you get your affairs in order, and quickly."

Osman wanders over to us and raises their eyebrows. I shake my head, disbelieving. Perseus follows.

"Thank you," Perseus says to me. He bends in the slightest bow. "I'm not sure I said that yet."

"Thank *you*," I reply. "What you said about funds—what are the odds that actually happens?"

"The triumvirate is in agreement, so I'd say it's highly likely," he says. "Further down the line, our goal is to make arrangements for all the planets in Helia to elect their own representatives and govern themselves on a local level, with the Khonsanian system as a model."

I nod and make a mental note to ask Amaris what exactly that means at a later date.

Meanwhile, the stunned, crestfallen nobles and would-be nobles watch as the orchestra strikes up the Helian anthem. Some talk furiously among each other. Others swarm the newly formed triumvirate, pressing them with questions, indistinct in the tumult. Still others stare numbly into the middle distance. A few clasp their hands on their hearts and start singing:

> *From world to world, with endless grace,*
> *Helia, Helia!*
> *From star to star, across all space,*
> *Helia, Helia!*
> *May our reach yet expand as our visions are grand,*
> *For we serve at the empire's mighty command,*
> *Helia, our home!*

"Maybe get a new song while you're at it," says Osman under their breath. "Even Filo couldn't make this dreck sound good."

"What now?" I ask.

"I'm not certain," Amaris replies as Kleo hurries over.

"Leyda will want to speak with you as soon as she can sneak off," says Kleo, breathless.

"Right," says Amaris, standing and scrubbing a hand down

her face. "We have a lot of work ahead of us, but—"

"The work comes tomorrow," Kleo says. "Tonight, we enjoy this. Now, go rescue Leyda from the crush of buffoons."

Amaris nods. "Will you be all right if I leave you here?" she asks me, oddly formal.

"Yeah," I say.

"She'll be in the best hands there are," says Osman. "Go."

I watch Amaris walk briskly to where Leyda is still being mobbed by disgruntled socialites, the new captain of the guard standing by her side.

"I was meaning to speak with you," Kleo tells me. "Iola Galatas, your false name?"

"What about it?"

"You'll want to choose your aliases with a little more care, should you decide to do this kind of thing again," she says.

"What do you mean?"

"The *Iola* was a registered cargo ship some sixteen years ago," says Kleo. "Piloted by a woman whose family name was Galatas."

"My mom, I know that," I say. "I mean, not the ship name, the family name. But how did you—?"

"Tarek looked it up for me," she says. "Knew it sounded familiar. That's probably why Altair chose to target you. Your connection to, well . . ."

"To what?"

Kleo's eyes go wide. "You mean you don't know?"

"Enlighten me," I say slowly.

"Your mother ran supplies for us," says Kleo. "At least seven times. Including once when she diverted a surplus rations shipment to a rebellion on Cadmus. A bunch of students had barricaded themselves in the planetary governor's headquarters. We couldn't manage to get them food and supplies, but she did. Her ship went down shortly after the handover."

Suddenly all I can hear is the roar of my heartbeat in my ears. I take deep, steadying breaths. "You knew her?" I manage.

"Not well," says Kleo. "I just heard stories. I wish I'd gotten the chance to meet her."

I nod, swallowing hard. I remember Dad's comments, about soldiers searching her ship, and for the first time, I think I might have a sense of what they were looking for.

"I don't know if you ever managed to get ahold of this, but in case you haven't . . ." Kleo says, pulling out a glass and summoning a file. "Final transmission. It's mostly corrupted. Tarek did what he could, but you know how it is."

Kleo gestures, and a recording plays. It's blurry and badly lit, but the woman recording the transmission has a certain familiar quality to her voice. She sounds like—well, like me.

"Status update: instruments all reading well," she says. "We're fueled up and headed out." She smiles, glancing back at what must be the control panel. "Looking forward to going home again." Her transmission dissolves into static.

I blink several times in quick succession. "Do you mind if I, uh—"

"Watch it again?" says Kleo, her voice gentler than I've ever heard it. "Go ahead."

I lose count of the number of times I watch the video, and then someone is tapping me on the shoulder. I look up, swiping at my eyes, and standing before me is Amaris.

"Did you hear?" she says.

"Probably not," I admit.

"Now that we've got our connection back, the triumvirate is preparing some some sort of press conference, going out on every feed."

That sounds deadly boring to me. "Are you needed for that?"

"No," says Amaris. She grins, an unusually mischievous look on her face. "Want to get out of here?"

We wind up back in the main ballroom, picking over the remnants of the magnificent spread.

"The Council is in an odd spot where you're concerned, you know," Amaris tells me between bites of melon. "Years ago, they passed a resolution guaranteeing a five-hundred-thousand-drock bounty to anyone turning in a person found to have made a proven assassination attempt on a head of state. They didn't specify a time frame on that reward, so technically, your exposure of Altair guarantees you the money, even if it was too late for Hyperion's purposes."

The bounty seems too good to be true. I don't want to believe it.

"The trouble is," she continues, "the Council is aware that you probably stole a fortune's worth of jewels. But nobody is willing or able to levy any proof against you, so they can hardly prosecute you. My sense is that they feel that publicly giving you a large monetary prize would send the wrong message."

"I'd take it in credits," I offer.

"Which brings me to my next point," she continues. "I've talked to Leyda about Ligeia and Gennadios's spider-silk operation. Specifically about the worker abuse. It turns out there are laws against forcing one's employees to work in conditions that permanently harm their well-being. The laws were rarely enforced by Hyperion and the Council, but they're on record, technically. And the penalties can be quite steep."

"Do you think they'll actually get in trouble for it?"

"I think the Council is about to seize all their property," she replies.

"They can do that?"

"The triumvirate is looking for high-profile cases of abuse of power—to set an example."

"That's good," I say. "That's something."

Amaris hums. "In the process of acquiring said property, some smaller pieces might happen to go missing."

She reaches into her pocket and pulls out the emerald earrings I'd lifted off Ligeia so many hours before. They glitter by the light of the chandeliers. I stare at them, and then at her. I catch myself thinking that Amaris outshines them by far, especially with the small smile tugging at one side of her mouth.

"Cass," she says, "how much do you think you could get for these?"

"You're joking."

"They're worth considerably less than the bounty, but I figure it's better than nothing," says Amaris. "Use it to help your dad. And Babbit, and the rest of them." Very gently, she reaches out and takes my hand. She drops the cool stones into my palm and folds my fingers around them.

My heart is racing now as she holds my gaze, as steady and constant as the orbit of moons. Her fingers are warm and calloused, and still wrapped around mine, as if she doesn't want to let go. Or maybe I'm imagining it because I don't want to let go. I want this, whatever this is, for as long as I can have it.

A holo of the new captain of the guard blinks onto the east wall. "Station docking in Amphor in fifteen," she says, and then she blinks out again.

Amaris lets her hands drop back to her sides. I pocket the earrings. Those will be earning me a profit soon.

"So," I say, and thankfully my voice comes out light and even, "where are you off to after this? Some other daring Voyrian adventure?"

"I have no idea," says Amaris.

I grin. "That's a new one. Seems like you always know what to do."

She bites her lip. "The Voyria is entering the world of politics. I think the days of daring escapades and underground rebellion are behind us. My skill set isn't relevant here."

"I don't know," I say, "some of those politicians could benefit from being flipped over your shoulder."

"We need leaders like Leyda, who can navigate between worlds in a single step."

"You've been moving between worlds most of the night," I remind her. "Dalia Galatas, remember her? The love of Iola Galatas's life?"

But Amaris shakes her head. "It won't be the same. I'm not cut out for hours of stuffy meetings, and I'm not even sure I'm right for these sorts of missions." She picks up a small fruit made of lots of little fleshy pods and fiddles with the stem. "I almost lost my head any number of times."

"You didn't," I tell her. "You were incredible."

"You, too," says Amaris, with so much sincerity I have to look away. "I'm on vacation," she admits with a sigh. "Leyda says if I don't take a week off from my work, she'll dump me somewhere on the beaches of Dyonia and leave me there." She frowns. "I don't even like the ocean," she says, sounding lost.

An idea occurs to me. It may be a colossally stupid idea, but once it's in my head, it sticks.

"Well," I say, as casually as I can, "how do you feel about lots and lots of dry sand?"

Amaris looks up at me.

"You could see the Big Split," I tell her. "We could even go to the Oasis resort and see Babbit, maybe play pranks on the tourists. It's not much, but you're welcome to come along if that's your idea of a good time."

She drops the fruit, the individual pods splitting apart and bouncing all over the floor.

"Are you certain?" she asks as we both crouch down to sweep them up.

"Of course," I say on my knees. Suddenly, I want to see how Dad and Dezmer and Mita and all the rest would react to Amaris more than I want to see anything else. I can picture Mita pressing cup after cup of tea into Amaris's hands, Dad asking questions about the history she's studied, Dezmer eagerly absorbing all of her Voyrian gossip. Reading between the lines, it sounds like Amaris isn't close with her family anymore, and I realize how badly I want to lend her mine. "We'd love to have you."

Amaris scoops up the last of the pods and we stand. "I'm told I can be stiff and awkward and too intense," she says, hunting for some place to deposit our fistfuls of smashed fruit. Ever the good citizen and somehow also an entire revolutionary. I like her so much.

"That's perfect. I can be crass, arrogant, and shallow." I hand her an empty goblet from a forgotten tray.

Amaris snorts. "Cass," she says, "I mean it, I'm not—fun." We dump the whatever-it-was into the cup and step back. Now that my hands are free again, I am very aware of them, and of how easy it would be to reach across and take Amaris's in them again.

"Who told you that? Sheltered little rich babies at university?" I press. "What do they know?"

"You have a point," she says.

I pick up a pastry the size of my palm, split it down the middle, and hand half to her. "Besides, when I wasn't terrified or certain I was about to die, I had a pretty good time with you."

"And when was that?" asks Amaris.

I take a bite of the pastry and chew thoughtfully. "This right now I'm enjoying. The hair-braiding and the story was lovely. Dancing, I had a good time there until you started being ominous. That time you brought me snacks, I was a fan of that. And it was fun to pretend we—" *It was fun to pretend we were a married couple rapturously in love* feels like saying too much. My cheeks warm. "I learned an interesting fact about deep-sea life," I finish, a second too late.

"This could be a disaster," she says.

"Trust me," I tell her. "Don't worry about everyone else. Just come with me."

Amaris throws a piece of pastry at me. I catch it and offer it back to her, like I'm presenting her with a precious jewel.

She laughs. "Okay," she says. "Never mind the risks. Let's give this a shot."

When we land on Ouris and the doors finally open, there is a stampede of absurdly well-dressed people fighting to get off the station. Perseus, Orpheus (back in his own clothes again), and the members of the Voyria hang back, watching as the guards struggle to herd the guests into a single-file line.

"Keep in touch," Kleo tells me. "I'll send you that footage as soon as I've got a place to send it to, yeah?" She hugs me, squeezing tightly. Not for the first time, I think of Dad and his easy affection. Maybe my mom was like that, too. I nod, blinking hard. Leyda wraps Amaris in a fierce hug.

"I don't think we need to give you the take-good-care-of-her-or-you'll-pay speech, do we?" Osman says to me. They smile, tattoos bunching on their cheeks. "You know what we're capable of, right?"

"I do," I say. "And it's just a little trip, it's not like—"

"Sure it's not," says Osman agreeably. "Sure it's not. Hey Meez, wait up!"

Amaris knows the way to the nearest station in Amphor. "It's not far," she says. "Just beyond the fourth office district."

We make our way on foot, walking in companionable silence. I can tell it's late, but the sky is stained an orangey pink, reflected all around us on the buildings' shiny angled sides. It feels almost dreamlike, as if we're walking through an unending sunrise.

"Light pollution," she explains as we arrive at the station, a towering structure made of polished stone and glass, with a long row of docks at the side and a flight schedule projected into the sky. Apparently, we're just in time.

"Never heard of that," I admit.

"The cost of all the streetlights and glowing buildings and things," she says. "It's never completely dark on Ouris. The light of the Helian Empire never goes out, you know how it goes. It's a problem on Haddan, too."

"That's one thing Sarn's got," I tell her. "Half the year, the sky is black. You can stand outside and see all the stars from your back door."

"I've never actually seen them like that." She pauses, considering. "I suppose there's still a lot out there to see."

I spot the ship before she does—a pinpoint of green in the hazy sky.

"What do you say we put our names on the manifest as Iola and Dalia Galatas, for old time's sake," I say.

"How about we travel as ourselves," she says, "and see where that takes us."

I take her hand. She smiles and swings our joined hands between us. As the ship approaches in a *whoosh* of air, Amaris pecks me on the cheek, quick and sweet as a piece of stolen candy.

"Okay," I say, "let's give this a shot."

ACKNOWLEDGMENTS

First of all, I need to say a tremendous thank-you to my parents, Robb and Mary, who helped shape me as a person—both very literally and, in a thousand ways, metaphorically. In the earliest days of this manuscript, I would read them whatever I'd written that day, and their feedback kept me going. Sorry that I never took your advice to pad out the story with a scene where the characters adopt an adorable puppy, Mom. (Maybe next book.)

An enormous thank-you as well to my super-talented and insightful editor, Jessica Yang, for taking a chance on me, for brainstorming with me, and for coaxing the story along to its final form. If you enjoyed this book, please know that part of what you enjoyed were Jessica Yang's creativity and her tireless, smart improvements.

A big thank-you also to the rest of the team at Quirk, including Alex Arnold, Elissa Flanigan, Jane Morley, Kassie Andreadis, Nicole De Jackmo, Kelsey Hoffman, Christina Tatulli, and Sylvia Sochacki. And another thank-you to everyone else at Quirk whose hard work allowed this book to happen. My gratitude also to Christina Chung, for the amazing cover illustration!

My brother Casey was the perfect sounding board for ideas (and had some killer ideas of his own), and my sister-in-law Lauren, cousin Colleen, and cousin-in-law Taylor also provided key emotional support. My friend Kim has many years of experience as my resident space expert, and it was her idea to locate the heart of the Khonsanian Collective in a radiation field.

When I first started telling sci-fi stories in earnest, my initial project was a scripted podcast called *The Strange Case of Starship Iris*. It has been warmly received, and this gave me the confidence to do things like try to write a space mystery novel. Thank you to everyone who has consumed the show, to everyone who helped make it a reality, and especially to my friends who shepherded the first two seasons along with their living room performances and their perceptive comments: Manisha, Emily, Emily, Lily, Emma, Heather, Sunanda, Tamara, Rae, Ella, Kim, and Eleanor. Reading this list, I am struck by how fortunate I am to know so many wonderful people, and also by how many of their names start with *E*.

The first people to look at any part of this story were my mom, Sunanda, and Genevra, who generously agreed to read the first pages of the book (the bit with the spiders) on a tight turnaround and whose input really helped.

More indirectly, I want to thank Maki Namekawa for her piano cover of Philip Glass's *Mishima* soundtrack. Any time I want to psychically beam myself back to the experience of writing this book, I can just put on her album *Philip Glass: Mishima*, which I listened to on an endless loop for basically the whole time I was working on the first draft. The music feels both majestic and jittery, in a way that really helped me get into the right mindset. My editing music was mostly the soundtrack to *Kin*, by Mogwai, so an indirect thanks to them as well.

Finally, my paternal grandma died several years ago but she was one of my first supporters and would've been over the moon that I published a novel. My profound gratitude to Phyllis Best, currently and forever residing in the brightest star of Orion's Belt.